The Eternal Keeper

Books by R. J. F.

Tales of the Multiverse
Book 1: Monster versus Mortal
Book 2: Sarah
Book 3: Scar
Book 4: Planet of Shadows
Book 5: The Mysterious Four

Darphopia
Darphopia: The Godless Land
Darphopia: The Godless Land Collector's Edition
Darphopia: The Second God War
Darphopia: The Second God War Collector's Edition

Standalone Books
The Eternal Keeper: The Story of How I Fell in Love with a Shapeshifter

R. J. F. Shorts
The Seducter (e-book only)
The Council of Cats (e-book only)

Gamebooks
Pencilventure: The Ancient Forest Temple

The Eternal Keeper

The Story of How I Fell in Love with a Shapeshifter

R. J. F.

For the ones who paved the road upon which we walk,
for the ones who maintain and improve that road, and for
the ones who are born with the right to walk that road
freely.

To all those who came before, all those who are here now,
and all those who will come in the future.

That which is true cannot be suppressed for ever, just as
that which is false cannot imprison us for ever.

And to have the wisdom to know the difference between
the two, that is true freedom.

Preface

hat is love? Do you know? Do any of us really know? It's so many different things, isn't it? It's the bond we have with our best friends, our mothers, our fathers, our grandparents; cousins, partners, family dogs, that actor you fancy on telly … We call all those things *love*. But they're different, aren't they? It's as if the concept of love in its entirety is just too big a thing to share with a single person … But what if it wasn't?

This is the story of how I met Flynn, the person whom I came to love in every possible way, all at once. Impossible, right? Every form of love shared with just one person. Well, what if I told you that Flynn never stays the same for long? What if I told you that, for better or worse, Flynn is ever-changing?

What if I told you Flynn is a shapeshifter?

4 May

The most remarkable things always tend to happen on the most unremarkable days. It was a rainy Thursday morning in Thivleton—a small town in the south of England. I was walking down to my local café, shivering in my pink raincoat because it was nippy and the country hadn't figured out that winter had ended two months ago.

I entered the quaint shop, smelling coffee beans and seeing an unexpectedly large queue. I was used to there being one, maybe two, people ahead of me; today there were five. I queued up and took out my phone, rereading the text message Kate had sent me a few minutes ago:

Hey, kitten. Do anything new today?

I shook my head and grinned while moving up in the queue. It sounded innocent, but this was Kate's way of referencing my mundane life. I tend to do the same things all the time—read, work, watch a bit of telly, have a takeaway sometimes, and more or less stay in my little flat. If I do go out to do anything "special," it's usually one of my pre-planned excursions or because Kate's dragged me out. She wants me to live more loudly, enjoy my twenties and be reckless. Especially because she knows I didn't get much of an opportunity to explore myself when I was younger.

I messaged back:

Might try something new from the café.

She responded:

**Sticking to the border of your comfort zone.
Nice one.**

I smirked and typed:

Fuck off.

She sent me a middle-finger emoji followed by a smiley face before texting:

**So what's 'something new from the café'?
Gonna put some cream in your coffee?**

I glanced at my dark skin. She was not talking about coffee.

That's nasty, Kate.

Hey, baby girl, I don't judge.

Kate's been teasing me like this since secondary school because it makes me blush and she loves that. The more lewd she is, the redder I get. It only bothers me superficially.

"What can I get you today, love?" said the plump barista when I reached the front of the queue.

I stared at the handwritten menu, which was posted on the wall on a little blackboard, and desperately tried to find something that was not my usual French Vanilla coffee with two sugars. Just when I was about to give up, a voice in my head (which greatly resembled Kate's teasing little squeak) told me to just pick anything.

"Uh, surprise me," I said.

I swear the barista kissed her teeth at me.

I moved to the side to let the next person order and went back to texting Kate:

> **Think I pissed off the barista. Told her to surprise me. Pray for me.**

Good girl!

> **Watch her spit in my drink.**

Don't be pouty, kitten.

I texted her a frowny face.

Seriously, Ange, I'm proud of you. It's good to see you getting out of the rut … even if it's not getting cream in your coffee.

> **Shut up!**

Love you, too!

The barista came back with some too-posh-for-my-blood drink. It had whipped cream, chocolate and caramel drizzle, fancy edible decorations, and it was probably the most expensive thing they had.

"£5.50, love." Yep. Upsold, just like that.

"Cheers," I grumbled, paying and walking off with my waste of money. Then I immediately banged straight into someone.

"Oh, shit, sorry," I gasped.

I dropped my drink, but the man I'd bumped into had caught it and was already handing it back to me. "Nearly," he said with a soft smile.

I was lost in his brown eyes for a second before embarrassment forced me to collect myself. "Good reflexes," I said, brushing back my hair and trying to seem like I had my shit together.

I didn't say anything for a bit, so the guy asked, "You all right?"

"Yeah … yeah, no, I'm good. Brilliant. Um …" I took back my stupid drink (which had been shaken up and now looked way less fancy). "Cheers," I squeaked and flitted off to a table.

The seat creaked a bit when I sat. I was just silent for a moment, waiting to not feel so embarrassed. When the silence didn't cure me, I decided to sip my drink instead and pretend I wasn't completely mortified. The drink was sweet, too sweet, and there was definitely a hint of cinnamon. I convinced myself I was okay with that.

I went back to texting Kate:

> **How'd Bridget's stream go last night?**

You didn't watch?

> **I was working. I've got a big manuscript to get through.**

Mmm, I'll let you off just this once, kitten. We did a hot-pepper challenge.

> **Yeah? How'd you two do? Could you handle it?**

Are you mad? I didn't do it. Bridget was on her

own for that shit. I just gave her water. She was fucking dying, though.

You know water does shit all to spicy food, right?

Bridget's rules; not mine. Her chat didn't let her hear the end of it.

I smiled.

That sounds fun. I'm sorry I missed it.

Yeah? That's all right, baby girl. You know how to make it up to me.

Fuck off, Kate.

"Uh …" I looked up from my phone. It was the bloke I'd bumped into. Crap. "Sorry, I don't want to bother you. I just noticed you sitting here alone and was wondering if you wouldn't mind a bit of company?"

I stared at him silently. He was tall, had dark skin, a chiselled bone structure but soft features, and he was holding a drink that looked much better than what I had. His hair was short and well-groomed, and he was clean-shaven. After I had taken him in, my gaze fell back to his brown eyes.

"Or if you want to just keep to yourself, that's fine," he continued.

"Uh, no, no, don't be silly. Sit." I motioned to the seat across from me.

He smiled softly and sat down. "I'm Flynn."

"Angelina. But everyone calls me *Ange*."

He sipped his drink. "That's a nice name."

"Thanks … Uh, listen, I'm sorry for bumping into you just now. I don't know why I'm so clumsy."

"Don't worry about it. It happens."

I sipped my drink, slowly getting used to the obnoxiously sweet taste.

"So, do you come here often?"

I looked at him suspiciously. "Do I come here often?"

He chuckled. "No, I didn't mean it like that. This is my first time here."

"Oh, okay. You just move house?"

"No, I just keep to myself mostly. If I'm honest, I've been in a bit of a rut. I'm trying to get out and do some new things. You know what I mean?"

"Oh, my god, yes," I said a little too loudly. I got a few side eyes from the other people in the café. "Sorry, I didn't mean to say that so loudly. It's just, I fully get what you mean. My friend keeps banging on at me about getting out of my rut and trying new things."

"Sounds like a good friend."

I grinned. "She's a bit of a lovable prick."

He smiled and sipped his drink. "So, what're you drinking?"

"Uh …" I swished my drink around a bit in my cup. "I'm not too sure. I was trying to get something new instead of my usual."

"Do you like it?"

"Not even a little."

"Well, you tried, right?"

I smiled and suffered another sip of my drink. "What're you drinking?"

"Hot chocolate."

"Mmm, that sounds so much better."

"Why don't you get one? I can get you one if you want?"

"No, it's fine. I need to suffer the consequences." I sipped my drink again.

He laughed. "You're funny. I'm glad I bumped into you."

"You mean you're glad *I* bumped into *you*."

"Right."

I looked at his eyes again; their green tint made me feel better about how we met … Hang on.

"Everything all right?" he asked.

I just kept staring. "You've got green eyes."

"Yeah." He was probably waiting for me to explain what was so significant about that.

"Sorry, I don't mean to stare. I just … I could have sworn your eyes were brown."

He looked down quickly. "Yeah, yeah, no, that's just the light. They look different depending on the light … Um, listen, I have to go. It was nice meeting you."

He picked up his hot chocolate and stood.

"Uh, hang on," I said. "What'd you say your name was again?"

"Flynn."

"Flynn. Listen, Flynn, I usually go to the park on Fridays and take a walk, get some fresh air, exercise, and that. I'll be there around noon tomorrow if you want to join me. It's Oak Corn Park, the one with the little pond." He didn't say anything. He seemed a bit uncomfortable. He was biting his lip, and he wasn't looking at me. "You know what, forget I said anything. You have a nice day."

"What? Sorry, no, that sounds good. I'm not doing much tomorrow; I'd love to see you again."

"Yeah?"

"Yeah. Tell you what," he handed me his phone, "let's exchange numbers, and we can sort out the details tomorrow."

I handed him my phone, and I put my number in his phone. Then I gave it back to him, and he gave me mine with his number in it.

"Okay," I said. "Guess I'll see you tomorrow."

"Guess so." He touched his forehead quickly. "Sorry, I really have to go. Nice to meet you, Ange."

"You too."

He walked out rather quickly. I wondered why he had to go. If we hadn't made plans, I'd think he just really wanted to get away from me.

I reluctantly sipped my drink again. The drink may have been a bust, but at least I met a cute guy. Should I tell Kate? She'll probably make another coffee-and-cream joke. I'll tell her later, once I've had more time to get to know him. Quite something, though, for getting out of a rut—

crap drink and a cute guy. Not bad, Ange.

I forced down the rest of my drink and trekked back home in the rain. I didn't live too far away; my flat was pretty close to most things I needed. Saves money on transport to just be able to walk everywhere.

I entered my building and took the lift up to my floor. Then I stepped out and walked to my flat.

"Hello, Angelina."

I turned away from my door to see the woman who lived across from me. "All right, Mandip. How are you?"

"Can't complain, my love, can't complain."

Mandip's been my neighbour for as long as I've lived here. She's a few decades older than me, so I see her as kind of a cool aunt.

"You just get back from doing the messages?" I said, pointing to the bags in her hands. She looked at me, confused, and I had to correct myself. "Sorry, that's my mum speaking. I mean did you just get back from the shops."

"Ah, yes. You lost me for a bit there, love." She chuckled. "Yeah, I've just got back. Had to restock. What about you? Just get back from the café?"

"Am I that predictable?" I smiled shyly.

"Oh, my love, you are very predictable. But there's nothing wrong with that, is there?"

"My friend Kate seems to think so."

"Well, that's what friends are for, innit? We all need people to push us out of our comfort zone."

"Push? Kate likes to rocket me out of my comfort zone."

Mandip smiled, and her flawless skin stretched into place without a single wrinkle. "Sounds like a good friend."

"She has her moments." I shrugged.

"Anyway, my love," she flicked her key out of a pocket on her coat. "Some of this stuff is going to melt, so I'll chat with you later."

"Right. Laters."

She winked at me and entered her flat.

I turned the key and opened my door. When I flicked on the lights, I was met with the little hole I lived in. It wasn't messy per se, just cosy. I hung my raincoat on the hook by the door and went to the kitchen to make myself a sandwich. Then I took that sandwich over to my little table in the living room by the window and took a bite. I had my diary open on the table as well, and I wrote in it everything that'd happened today. Keeping this little diary—the same one you're reading—is new for me. I figure it will be nice to look back on in the future, either to prove to myself that life gets better the longer you live it, or to prove that at one point my life wasn't all that bad. I expect it'll be the former; I hope it will. In a lot of ways, my life now is already better than it was before.

I took a bite of my sandwich and looked out the window, out at Thivleton. There weren't many cars, and there were only a few tall buildings. It's a quiet little place. I've lived here my whole life, raised mostly by my mother. But she moved back to Scotland three years ago, so now it's just me here, me and Kate, who I met back in primary school. She's like my sister—I love her and hate her all at the same time.

My eyes locked on to a house in the distance. It was hard to miss; it's one of the largest and oldest houses in Thivleton. It wasn't a mansion or anything, but it was quite the display of wealth. If anyone actually lived there, that is. It was old, thatched roof and all, probably older than the town that surrounded it. But it doesn't really seem lived in, so most people debate whether or not anyone actually lives there. For all anyone knows, it could just be a property that someone overseas is paying to keep maintained.

I finished my sandwich, put my plate in the sink to wash later, and got my laptop and sat on the sofa. I opened up the manuscript I had to translate and got to work on the next chapter's first sentence: *Elle le regarde avec frayeur ; incroyablement, il a changé.*

5 May

It was quarter past twelve on Friday afternoon. I texted Flynn, and he said he was on his way to the park. I felt a bit anxious waiting for him; I really don't do this sort of thing often.

It was sunnier today than it was yesterday, so I could wear lighter, cuter clothing. Nothing too extravagant—just a plain yellow top, some loose trousers, and a cute little backpack to carry my diary, wallet, and stuff. (I was trying to look casual.) I did my hair, too, cleaned it up and made it fall nicely on my shoulders—again, casual.

I was sat at a park bench, watching people enjoy the grassy area and sit around the pond.

I checked the time on my phone. Twenty past. I pulled my diary and a pen out of my backpack and started scribbling in the day's exploits so far.

"Sorry I'm late."

I looked up from my diary and into his brown eyes. They looked a little different from before, and a lot different from when they looked green. I guess he was right about them looking different depending on the light.

"Hey." I smiled at him. "You're not late. We agreed *around* noon, didn't we?" I was being generous; he was late. "I'm just glad you came."

"Were you afraid I wouldn't?"

"Well, you left so suddenly yesterday."

He scratched the back of his head. "Yeah, sorry about that. I had a stomachache."

"Yeah? You all right?"

"Yeah. Must've eaten the wrong thing. Mind if I sit with you?"

"Actually, I thought we could walk around a bit. I mean, I do usually come here for exercise."

"All right, cool. Lead the way."

I got up and put my diary back in my backpack.

"What is that?" he asked, referring to the book.

"Oh, nothing. Just a little diary I like to keep."

"Aw, that's nice."

"Do you journal?"

"You know, I probably should, but nah, I just respect those who do." He gave me a little grin that made it seem like what he said was an inside joke of some sort. But he didn't say anything more, and I didn't ask him to explain.

We started walking. I took a quick stock of what he was wearing—a red flannel shirt and jeans. He went casual, too, or at least was doing better than I was at seeming casual.

I was slightly taller than average for a woman, but Flynn was still taller than me. I liked that. It felt good walking next to him.

"So, Flynn, tell me about yourself."

"What do you want to know?"

I shrugged. "Dunno. What do you do for a living?"

"Uh …" He looked down.

"What? Is it embarrassing?"

"Well …"

"I won't judge."

He smiled. "Tell you what, you tell me what you do first, then I'll say."

"Okay." I adjusted my backpack. "I'm an editor/translator."

"That's cool. What do you edit/translate?"

"Mostly manuscripts. Sometimes articles."

"And what languages do you translate?"

"French to English."

"That's brilliant. I'm rubbish at French."

"Yeah, it's a rough language. It can be pretty stupid sometimes."

"Have you got French family?"

"No, my family are Japanese."

He looked at me. "Really? I wouldn't have guessed you were Asian."

"Yeah, I don't really look it, do I? I'm mixed race—Asian on my mum's side and black on my dad's side. But I guess I look mostly black, except for my hair—it's naturally wavy—and a little bit in my nose, I think."

He scrutinised my face. "Oh, yeah, I see it. So, you didn't want to translate Japanese, then?"

I shook my head. "Too complicated. My grandparents moved from Japan to Scotland when they were young, and they learned to speak English perfectly, so very little Japanese actually got passed down, you know? No head starts for me."

"Sure. I mean, learning French well enough to translate it sounds complicated, too."

"It's not that bad. I learned it when I was seventeen."

"You're joking. In school?"

"No, mostly self-taught. Took a few trips to France as well when I was younger."

"Well, that's impressive."

I smiled. "All right, your turn. What do you do?"

He hesitated.

"Come on, I promise I won't judge. My mum wasn't too happy at first with my work being online. And my best friend is a sex worker, and her girlfriend is a live streamer. I'm very used to unorthodox careers; I won't judge."

"Okay, well, how about no career?" he said sheepishly.

"Like, you're unemployed? Okay, that's fine. They tell us when we're young that we need a job, but having a job is a privilege, not a right, and they're hard to get. It's definitely not equal for everyone."

"Sure, but I mean more like … I'm unemployed because I'm quite … well-off."

"Like, you're rich?"

"Well, not *rich* rich, but I've got money, yeah." Suddenly what he was wearing seemed way more casual than before. "I mean, I've worked before, odd jobs and that, but I don't *need* to work."

"Why would you be embarrassed about that?"

"Because people act weird when they know you have money, especially if you inherited it. My parents died a while ago and passed all their wealth down to me. They had a lot of investments, too, so I've got a lot of passive income streams. I've never really had to work."

I appreciated him trusting me with that. "Well, I promise I won't act weird now I know."

He smiled.

"And sorry about your parents, by the way."

"That's fine. I didn't have the best relationship with them."

"I get that. I don't have a good relationship with my dad."

"So you get it. It's a bit complicated when your parents do everything for you, but they're also not very nice people."

"Not exactly. My dad left when I was fifteen, and he did shit all for me. I'm much better off without him. But I do get what you mean."

We walked near the pond and took a seat at a neighbouring park bench.

"So, tell me some things you do for fun," Flynn said.

"Okay, um … I like to read," I offered.

"Yeah? What sorts of stuff do you read?"

"Well, I do a lot of romance and slice-of-life stuff for work, so I like to read the complete opposite in my own time: fantasy, sci-fi, thrillers … Do you read?"

"Not as much as you," he laughed. "I think I've read a few books here and there, but I don't really have the attention span for that."

"You can get audiobooks."

"Yeah, I should try that someday. I've read quite a few graphic novels, though, and comic books and manga."

"Never read one of those," I admitted.

"Oh, you should. Done well, that medium can really make a story come to life."

I chuckled, and he smiled at me.

"What?" I wondered.

"I like your giggle."

"Uh, that was a chuckle."

"If you say so."

"It was."

"Okay."

I smacked his shoulder lightly. "Tell you what, I'll get around to reading a graphic novel, and you get around to listening to an audiobook."

"Deal."

"So, what about you, then? What does Flynn do for fun?"

"Um … honestly, not much."

"Oh, come on. Is that a secret, too?"

He grinned and shrugged. "I dunno. I guess I paint."

"Shut up. No you don't. Can I see? Do you have pictures?"

"I mean, it's just a hobby; I'm not that good," he warned me as he took out his phone. "Uh … here's one that's not too bad."

He showed me a picture of a painting of a tree by a river stream. It was beautiful and used lots of warm colours that gave it a very cosy feel.

"What are you on about? This is excellent. How long have you been painting?"

He shrugged. "Years."

"It shows."

The day went on, and we eventually left the park and walked the streets of Thivleton together. We chatted nonstop all day. We stopped for a Chinese takeaway when we got hungry. (He paid, and as promised, I wasn't weird about his being rich.) Flynn was really nice and easy to talk to. I felt comfortable with him, and today was really great.

Flynn looked up at the darkening sky. "I guess it's

getting late."

"Guess so," I sighed.

"Would you want to come back to mine?"

"Um …" I looked around. There were a few people about, probably heading home from work or something. Here's the moment I've been dreading. "I have to tell you something first."

"Okay." He looked at me attentively.

Easiest way is to just say it. "I'm trans."

I waited for his reaction. "Okay," was all he said.

"Like, I'm transgender, male to female."

"Yeah, I know what you mean," he chuckled.

"And … you're good with that?"

"Yeah."

"Okay, then … Sorry, I was just expecting you to react differently."

"How so?"

"I dunno. Stuff like that's usually a big deal to people. At best I thought you'd be shocked, and at worst I thought you'd be disgusted."

He smiled. "Well, I don't think I could ever bring myself to be disgusted by you, but if you want, I can try to be shocked."

I laughed. "No, that's all right. You just caught me off guard a little. I was braced for something different."

"Well, hey, I promise I won't act weird now I know."

I reflected his smile.

"Besides, that's not the most interesting thing you've

told me about yourself today."

"It's not?" I was genuinely shocked about that.

"No. That honour goes to teaching yourself French at seventeen. That's amazing."

"*Merci bien. Je suis heureuse de t'avoir impressionné.*"

He grinned at me stupidly. "I don't know what the fuck you just said, but it sounded like butter."

I giggled. (Yep, that time it definitely was a giggle.) "All right, let's go back to yours."

"Yeah?"

"Yeah, let's go."

LATER

"Ho-ly shit!" I gasped.

"Here we are."

We were standing in front of the massive, old house. *The* massive old house. The one with the thatched roof. The one everyone talks about.

"You do not live here," I said.

"Yeah, I do."

"But this is the house, *the* house, the one everyone debates whether anyone actually lives in it."

"They do? Blimey, I have to get out more."

The house was beautiful; it had that old-English-cottage vibe. It was one storey, had a thatched roof and stone walls, and the garden could have had fairies in it and I wouldn't have questioned it. There were loads of gorgeous flowers and vines that crept up the house walls.

I turned to Flynn enthusiastically. "Can I have a tour?"

He smiled. "Follow me."

The door opened with a satisfying creak, and he led me inside. He switched on the light, and I was a little disappointed to discover that the history of this house's interior had been almost entirely wiped away by renovations. But the disappointment was fleeting. Even though it looked very modern inside, it was still a nice place.

While we removed our shoes at the entryway, I pressed my hand against the stone wall. It was cold, and if you looked closely, you could even see little fossilised creatures in it. The walls were probably the only things left untouched in the house.

Flynn led me to the front room first. There was a fireplace, a nice sofa, a little coffee table, and a decent television. It had a very cosy vibe. (Not cosy like my flat; proper cosy.) There were also tall wooden bookshelves filled with neatly shelved books.

"I thought you said you didn't read much," I wondered.

"I don't, but books make for good decoration."

"So, they just sit here unread, collecting dust? That's horrible. That's, like, book abuse."

He laughed loudly. "That's a good one. It's not abuse; I'm just showcasing them. Makes the home feel artsy. I usually get books with covers I think will look nice on the shelves."

I glared at him. "Mate, that's disgraceful."

He grinned.

"No, it's not funny; that's horrid handling of these books."

He threw his hands up. "No, you're right. Absolutely atrocious. I have no excuse." He was still grinning.

"What about your graphic novels?"

"Oh, I read those off my phone mostly. It's easier."

I stared blankly at his beautiful bookshelves. "I feel like you've just taken me to the zoo, and all the animals are sad and miserable."

He laughed again. "Come on. I'll show you the rest of the house."

He showed me the kitchen next. It wasn't anything special, just what you'd expect from a kitchen. There were double doors with large glass windows leading out to the garden, though.

"Do you want a drink or anything?" Flynn offered.

"No thanks. Maybe later." Somehow my subconscious had already decided I was going to be here later. And judging from Flynn's slight grin, he caught that, too. Well, why not, right? Let's just have some fun, enjoy ourselves. Man, Kate has well gotten into my inner monologue.

We continued the tour. He showed me the bathroom and the loo, which were separate. He showed me two bedrooms, one with the door cracked open and one with the door firmly shut. Then something caught my eye.

"What is this?"

I ran ahead of him and picked up a beautiful dress that was just hanging nonchalantly on a doorknob. I held it up. It was midnight blue and sparkly like the night sky.

"This is beautiful. Is this yours? Are you GNC?" Judging by the confusion on his face, I guessed he wasn't. "Gender nonconforming," I explained.

"Oh." He nodded, understanding. "No, I'm … that's, uh … I don't wear it." It sounded like he gave me three different parts of three different answers.

"You sure? I bet this would look great on you. You've got the figure for it."

"You think?" he questioned dubiously.

"You don't have to be embarrassed. I mean, look who you're talking to."

He plucked the dress out of my hands. "If I say it's mine, will you shut up about it?"

"Maybe."

He smiled, opened the door, and chucked the dress inside. "Maybe we keep this room out of the tour, yeah?" He shut the door, and we moved on.

I noticed a lot of paintings around the house, giving the place even more character. "Did you paint this?" I asked when we passed one depicting a bright, sunny sky.

"No. Got that from an auction."

"Oh."

"But I did paint this one."

He guided me over to another painting that put the last one to shame. It depicted a naked man and woman sitting in a grassy meadow on a sunny day. The shape came mostly from the lighting and the values; the contours were quite blurred. They almost merged into each other. It was hard to tell where the man ended and where the woman began, or where the sky met the ground.

"You painted this?" I whispered, captivated by the composition.

"Yeah. It's one of my better ones, I think. That's why I hung it up."

"I love how you light your paintings. It just … it really makes you … feel something." I was looking at him now, right into his brown eyes, and yeah, I was definitely feeling something.

6 May

Shit.

Fucking shit.

I did it. I slept with him, and it was great. But now it's morning, I'm waking up naked in his bed, and he's not here. There's another bathroom attached to the bedroom, and I'm pretty sure he's in there being sick. And I know it's stupid, but the first thing I thought was that he was so disgusted after he slept with me that he had to rush to the toilet to be sick. But that's not true; I know it isn't. That's ridiculous. Absurd. I mean, that's just the British media poisoning my mind, making me believe my own body is inherently disgusting. It's not true. I mean, he did say he had a stomachache before at the café, didn't he? Maybe he hasn't gotten over it. Please let that be it.

I slunk out of the bed, plucked my bra and pants off the floor, and quickly slipped into them. I felt exposed and vulnerable enough as it was; I didn't want to be fully naked on top of that.

I could hear him being sick again. It sounded violent, like he was in pain. I desperately tried to listen to the voice in my head telling me that it was utterly absurd to think that the guy I shagged was so disgusted with me that he ran to the toilet the following morning to boak.

"Flynn?" I called, plucking up the courage to speak. "You all right?"

There was a crash, like something had fallen over, then a reply: "Uh … yeah." He cleared his throat. "I'm fine."

He sounded strange—feverish and hoarse, but there was something else. I couldn't quite place it, but his voice sounded different somehow.

"Do you need any help? Can I get you something?" I called.

His response was immediate. "No! No, I'm fine. Don't come in here." There was a silence, and then he said, "Uh, listen, Ange, I think it's best if maybe you—" His sentence was interrupted by his being sick, but I knew what he was going to say.

"Yeah," I said. "Yeah, I'll, uh, I'll just go." I picked up the rest of my clothes and quickly put them on. I didn't say anything else; I just got out of there as quickly as I could. I was mortified.

After five minutes, I was out walking in the brisk morning air, walking far away from the beautiful old house. In thirty minutes, I was back to my part of town. I stopped for a coffee (a French vanilla with two sugars. I was not rolling the fucking dice on that today), and when I reached my flat, the first thing I did was plop myself down on the sofa and sip my drink like it was a dummy comforting a baby.

I stared off into space for a bit, wondering how something that started out so great could end the way it did. I mean, even if we assume he had a stomach bug—which was clearly the most logical thing to think—why did he want me to leave so suddenly?

I shut my eyes tight and groaned. What did it even matter? I was so embarrassed. Why do I let Kate talk me into things like this? My rut is fine. It's comfortable. I don't need to break out of my routine; my life's great … Yesterday was nice, though … while it lasted.

I decided to text Kate and catch her up on everything, and her response came quickly:

Got a shoot tomorrow. Meet up at the chippy before I go, and you will tell me EVERYTHING!

7 May

I met Kate at the local chippy we always meet up at when

we need to have a girl talk and are also craving chips. We hugged, ordered some chips, and then sat at a table by a window.

"All right, baby girl, details," said Kate, tying her blonde hair up so it didn't accidentally brush her chips whenever she turned.

"All right, so, I met him at the café, and—"

"What's he look like?"

"Uh, dark skin, soft features. Anyway—"

"Oh, you've got to do better than that, babes."

"What do you care? You don't even like men."

She grinned. "But you do. I want to know how he made you feel. Paint me a picture."

I rolled my eyes. "I dunno. He was fit, I guess. He was nice, well groomed …"

"Is he a bloke or a dog?"

"Shut up, Kate."

"Make me, kitten." She winked and moved a single chip in and out of her mouth in a suggestive way that made me blush.

"Anyway," I continued, "I met him at the park on Friday, and we chatted, and, you know, we were really getting on."

"Did you tell him you're trans?"

"Yeah. Public space, lot of witnesses in case he didn't take it well."

"And how did he take it?"

"Really good, actually. Didn't really faze him. Then we went back to his"—Kate stifled a giggle—"and you'll never guess where he lives."

"Where?"

"*The* house." I stared at her with raised eyebrows until she got what I meant. Then she almost choked on her chips.

"No fucking way," she said. "*The* house? So he's fucking minted. Oh, my god, what was it like inside?"

"Nice. It's been renovated to look quite modern, but it's a nice place. So, anyway, he was showing me around the house, and one thing led to another, and we …"

"You didn't sleep with him."

I nodded sheepishly.

"Oh, my god, good girl!" She smacked my hand before trying to suppress her grin. "You in him or him in you?"

"Kate!"

"Or no one in no one? Was it a petting and stroking situation?"

"Ew, no, Kate, I'm not telling you that."

"I was promised details."

"That doesn't mean I'm gonna tell you who was inside who. No."

"Wow, baby girl, you're being so bratty."

"No. I'm not telling you shit," I laughed.

She leant back in her chair and chewed on a chip with her arms crossed. "Fine."

We ate our chips in silence, Kate's gaze slowly wearing me down. Then I whispered, "Him in me."

She almost squealed. "Oh, good girl!"

I rolled my eyes. "Obviously it was him in me; you

know me, Kate, I could never penetrate."

"Because you're submissive and very breedable."

I kicked her shin under the table and grinned. "Fuck you."

"I bet you want to."

I kicked her again.

"Okay, okay, I'll relax." She barely ate one more chip before she said, "You know, on the list of things that trans women have over cis women, biological strap-on is pretty high up there."

"It's all right." I shrugged.

"Sounds so much more convenient."

"Only if you like to penetrate."

"I do, I really do."

I smiled at her. "You know, even if I wanted to, I don't even know if I can do that anymore. Oestrogen changes a lot; it's a lot softer than it used to be."

Kate shrugged. "Still better than menstruating."

"Sure, but at least you can get pregnant."

"That's only good if you want a kid, otherwise it's pretty annoying."

"Want to switch genitals?" I smirked.

She put out her hand, and we shook on it.

"Would be nice, though," I continued, "getting pregnant, giving birth, breastfeeding—"

"You can breastfeed," she interrupted while taking another chip.

I stared at her. "No I can't."

"Yeah, you can. You've got boobs, don't you?"

"Kate, how can I breastfeed if I can't get pregnant?"

She shrugged. "I dunno. You get it medically induced or something. Ask my mum; she breastfed me."

Kate's mum was also trans. She's been like a second mother to me. She was the first person I came out to, and she really helped me when I was starting my transition: helping me find a knowledgeable doctor; assuring me my PMS-like mood swings, bloating, and cravings weren't in my head; explaining why my penis leaks discharge like a fucking faucet.

"Did you really not know that?" asked Kate.

"Well, they don't exactly teach sex-ed about trans people in school."

Kate shrugged. "I guess I forget what isn't common knowledge about trans people. I've known that my whole life. Sorry. If I'd known you didn't know, I would have rocked your world sooner." She winked, and then she added, "Oh, you know what else? You can pee standing up."

"I don't, though."

"But you could; that's pretty sick."

"I guess. It's harder now, though."

"How come?"

I considered. "You know, I'm not sure. Maybe I'm out of practice, because I don't stand very often at all. Or maybe it has something to do with things being smaller down there and my hips tilting inwards now, so the angles are all different." I shrugged. "I mean, I can still do it, but it's not as convenient as it would be for a guy, you know?"

"Well, in that case, I take it back about switching genitals. I'll stick with my fanny."

"What, my genitals aren't good enough for you anymore?"

She popped another chip into her mouth. "Doesn't benefit my needs, does it?"

I laughed. "Sorry *you* brought it up."

"Anyway," she continued, "we're getting sidetracked."

"Whose fault was that?"

"Shut up. You were shagging the cute guy you met. Continue."

"Right. Okay, so, I woke up in his bed the next morning, and he was in the toilet being sick."

"Why? Was he all right?"

"He didn't say. But I was bloody mortified. All I could think was that he must have been so disgusted by me."

"What? Ange, don't be stupid. You really think he would fuck you and then delay his disgust until the morning after?"

"Yeah, I guess it sounds stupid when you put it like that."

"Babes, trust me, all he was thinking was how fucking breedable you looked."

I kicked her shins again, and she laughed.

"I know you're right," I sighed. "But I can't figure out what happened, then. He essentially just kicked me out. I thought we were really vibing. I haven't heard from him since."

"You texted him?" she enquired.

"Just once, just to see if he was all right."

She put her hand out. "Show me."

I gave Kate my phone and showed her the text I sent Flynn, which read:

Hey, just checking in to see if you're feeling all right. You sounded pretty sick yesterday morning.

Kate nodded and handed back my phone. "Guess you'll just have to wait and see. If he wants to see you again, he'll let you know."

"What if I want to see him again?" I grumbled.

"Wow, that good, huh?"

"Shut up." I grinned.

"It'll be fine, Ange. Don't worry about it. If he wants you, which he does, he'll come get you. He probably just felt embarrassed because he was sick and he didn't want you to see him like that."

"I guess," I sighed.

I ate a few more chips and changed the subject. "How's work? You said you had a shoot?"

"Yeah. Heading up to Manchester to meet up with Nigel."

"Should you be eating so many chips, then? Won't that bloat you for the shoot?"

"It's tomorrow. Long drive to Manchester, and I plan on sleeping in a nice hotel bed when I get there. Have to stop off at Queer Corpus as well." That was a clothing shop that specialises in gender-affirming items: gaffs, wigs, binders, and lots of different clothes.

"Why you stopping there?" I wondered.

"Need a collar for the shoot." Queer Corpus also had an adult section in the back.

"I thought you already had a collar."

"Not one with a bell on it. Should be a fun shoot, actually. I'm quite flexible, so Nigel wants to try some new stuff with me."

Kate was out of chips now, so she let her hair back down and crossed her arms on the table. "I'm also narrating an erotica."

"Hey, I'm doing a romance; we're matching."

We fist-bumped, which we did every time this happened. Our jobs were pretty different, but every now and then, she would work on an erotica audiobook and I would work on a steamy romance novel, and it was the most similar our jobs ever got.

"Should be a nice change of pace for you," I said. "More words and less moans."

"Oh, no, baby girl, there'll be plenty of moaning. The moans are my brand. That, and the drunken-monkey face."

I made the mistake of looking at her, confused. She rolled her eyes back, started rocking in her seat, and moaned like she was having the world's best orgasm. "Oh, Ange, oh yes, yes …"

I could feel myself turning red as we started to attract

curious eyes. "Oh, my god, Kate, stop. Stop! I get it!"

She laughed. "Oh, kitten, look how red you are. That's so adorable!"

I rolled my eyes. "I keep forgetting not to set you off in public."

She blew me a kiss.

"Anyway, babes." She stood up. "I've gotta shoot. You need a lift anywhere before I go?"

"No, I'm fine. I like the walk."

"Yeah, I know you do. Who needs a car with thighs like yours?" She bent down to hug me and kissed my cheek repeatedly.

"All right, Kate, get off," I laughed. "Love you, too."

"Bye, baby girl. Text me any updates."

8 May

It was Monday, the weekend was over, and I still hadn't heard from him. I didn't know why it was bothering me so much—clearly, he doesn't want to see me again; move on. Maybe it's a closure thing. It was very sudden and jarring. I just had to focus on something else. He's probably not going to text me back. Time to continue on with my life.

I was in my flat, sitting with my legs up on the sofa and working on my laptop. I had on some watchable rubbish out of Essex on the telly as background noise. I translated a few pages, and then I had to look up a forum for translators for suggestions on translating something a bit difficult to convey in English. While I was reading the responses, I came across someone translating a historical fiction novel that took place mostly in an old English cottage, and my thoughts instantly went back to Flynn. I managed to pull myself back from that, though, and continued translating.

All this stuff with Flynn was starting to feel like a big mistake, and thinking about him was the forbidden pathway I dared not follow. But I couldn't help feeling like I'd missed something, like maybe I shouldn't avoid thinking about him because, if I did for just a little longer, I might just put something together. But I couldn't. I mustn't. I had a nice time with him, and now it's done. Moving on.

I continued translating for about an hour. Then I got hungry and made some lunch. After eating, I went back to translating. Then I got up and changed my oestrogen patch, since I'd forgotten to do it this morning. Then back to translating. Then I did a bit of exercise with my little weights. And then I read for a bit. I had to put the book down when I read something that reminded me of Flynn. I was beginning to get annoyed at how much I was thinking about him. It was an intrusive thought I couldn't escape.

Then there was a knock at my door.

I opened it, and there was Mandip, smiling at me.

"Hello, my love," she said. "Fancy some company? I'm having a cuppa, if you want to join me."

That's what I needed, some social interaction. "Yeah, sure. I'd love to."

I followed Mandip back to her flat, and she sat me down at her little coffee table and put the kettle on. I noticed she was walking with a cane.

"You all right?" I asked her.

"Oh, yeah, just dislocated my knee this morning."

Mandip has Ehlers-Danlos Syndrome. It's a genetic disorder which essentially boils down to she's too flexible for her own good and her body has trouble keeping itself together. It also means she's in pain a lot.

"Should you be up, then?" I asked. "I can make the tea. You should sit down."

"No, that's all right, my love. If I sit for too long, I'll get stiff. I've got on a knee brace; I'll be fine."

"All right. Let me know if you need me for anything."

"Well, I need you to tell me what sort of tea you'd like."

"Um … do you have mint?"

"I do." She got the teabags out of the cupboard. "So, how are you, Angelina? I feel like we haven't caught up in a while."

"I'm good."

"Do anything exciting recently?"

"Not really." I did do something exciting, but I'm trying not to think about it.

Mandip poured the hot water into two cups and started steeping the teabags. "You sound a bit distracted, my love."

"Do I? Sorry."

"Don't be sorry." She brought the tea over, placed it on the table and sat down slowly.

"You all right?"

"Yes, just being careful not to mess up my dodgy knee again. So what's on your mind?"

I used a spoon to press the teabag to the side of my cup. "I'm actually trying to get it off my mind."

"Something worrying you?" she asked, stirring her own tea.

"Not exactly."

She smiled. "You don't want to talk about it, do you?"

"Not really," I admitted.

"That's all right, my love." She sipped her tea. "Henry's moved house, by the way." That was Mandip's son.

"Yeah? Did he decide to stay in Thivleton?"

"Yes, just found a bigger place. He and Loli were a bit crowded where they were."

"Yeah, I bet." I sipped my tea as well.

"In fact, that reminds me. Henry will be painting the new place, and he sent me some colour options and asked for my opinion." She showed me a picture on her phone of what I assumed was a room in Henry's new place. Then she showed me a few colour options: red, brown, cream … "Which do you think?"

"Mmm, I like brown."

"That's hazel, dear."

Then a forbidden thought tore through my attempts at suppression: Flynn's eyes. When I saw him at the park, his eyes were brown, but I thought they looked different than they did at the café. They weren't brown at all; they were hazel. That makes sense. That must be why they looked green at the café as well. That makes perfect sense! So why can't I move on from this? What am I missing? Saturday morning wasn't the first time he wanted to get away from me. He left pretty quickly at the café, too. But he texted me back after that; now he won't even tell me if he's okay … What if he's not okay?

"Angelina, are you all right there?"

"Huh? Yeah, yeah, sorry, I just … Never mind. Yeah, I think hazel. He should paint it hazel."

She smiled. "I think so, too."

LATER

It was evening, and I had taken a shower and changed into some comfy pyjamas. Now I was doing the washing-up and watching Bridget's live stream. Someone in her chat asked where Kate was.

"Yeah, just me today, chat," she explained. "Kate's in Manchester for work."

Bridget was very boyish. She liked to dress in guys' clothes, she didn't shave her legs or underarms, and she generally looked quite masculine, which got her misgendered a lot in public until she spoke and unleashed her feminine drawl. She often leant into this for her streams and full-on cross-dressed, using cosmetics to create the illusion of facial hair.

Someone in the chat donated money to have their comment read out loud by text-to-speech: **You mean Kate has a job outside of streaming? I hope you pay her for all the time she spends on stream, then.**

Bridget smirked. "Yeah, I pay her with sex and food."

The chat exploded with comments scrolling too fast for me to read, but Bridget could read pretty quickly. "Oh, relax, chat," she said. "I'm joking."

She made a popping sound with her mouth. "Oh, chat, that reminds me. I've got a story for you. So, for anyone new here, I have Tourette's. So if you see me making popping sounds, or snorting, or saying something random, it's cool; I'm just malfunctioning.

"Anyway. So, a thing that can happen with Tourette's is getting stuck in a specific tic—that's what the random sounds and movements are called. Sometimes it's like a loop, where you get stuck doing the same tic over and over and over, and sometimes it's your muscles tightening and freezing in whatever position they were in. So me and Kate were at the shopping centre the other day, and we were queueing up (or lining up for any Americans watching). I was having a particularly bad tic day, which sucks because people stare at you, and it can be kind of embarrassing. But Kate's pretty good at making me feel better about it. Anyway, anyway. I have this one tic that is basically flipping someone off, I mean, well, it is flipping someone off. And—ah, I see some of chat's already seen where this is going—I did the tic, got stuck like that, and just had my finger up the whole time, flipping people off. I mean, can you imagine how mortified I was, chat? There were children present."

She read the chat for a bit and responded to some questions. "*'What kind of store was it?'* Clothing shop ... *'Do the tics hurt?'* Uh, yeah, sometimes. You gotta think, it's like exercise, chat. If you lift weights for a bit, your muscles will get tired eventually. If you keep lifting—Pop your trainers on!—sorry. If you keep lifting, even after you get tired, your muscles will start to hurt. Tics are like not being able to stop exercising, even if it hurts. I mean, my finger was defo killing me ... Oh, you have Tourette's, too, Cottonswab64? I see you. Actually, let's run a poll on that. One of the mods, do a poll for how many people in chat have Tourette's. And while we're waiting on the results, anyone with Tourette's, put your worst/most annoying tic in chat."

I'd finished the washing-up now and was sitting on the sofa, trying to wind down before heading to bed. Bridget's streams usually went on quite a ways into the night. A lot of her audience were Americans, so she often tried to work around those time zones.

"*'Yelling "fuck".' 'Gagging.' 'Punching the wall' ...*" she read out the chat's worst Tourette's tics. "*'Responding to people'*—oh, man, I feel that one. It's crazy; it's like Tourette's has a mind of its own. I swear my tics could hold a whole fucking conversation with someone just with responding-tics alone. But it would make me say some weird shit, I'm sure. And that shit messes with your sense of agency, too. Like, someone could say something to me, and my Tourette's could come up with some weird-ass response that sounds plausible enough for the other person to think, 'Boy, I guess she meant that. She thinks I'm a twat.' And then I have to say, 'No, no, that was a tic. You're good. I don't think you're a twat.' It's mental."

She read another comment while making another popping sound with her mouth. "No, see, that's not true. That's a myth. My tics don't reveal what I'm actually thinking; they're just random shit. Think of it like yawning, chat—it just comes out sometimes, it's hard to control, it can happen more often if you're tired, and seeing other people do it can make you want to do it, too. But if you're talking to someone, and they yawn really big and loud, it doesn't necessarily mean they're bored with the conversation. Same way if someone tics something rude, doesn't mean they were actually thinking that."

I was feeling more relaxed now than I was during the day. That's why I liked Bridget's streams, not just because she's my friend, but because she's good at helping people wind down. She's quite laid-back. I almost wasn't thinking about Flynn anymore. Almost.

The results of Bridget's poll came in. "Shit," she said. "Thirty-two per cent of you have Tourette's as well. I guess a lot more of you watch for the Tourette's rep than I thought."

I watched the stream for another half hour before

switching everything off and going to bed. But not before checking my phone to see if I had missed any text messages …

9 May

I was sat on the sofa in the afternoon, reading, when there was a knock at the door. I marked my page, put my book down, and went to answer it. The woman at the door had short, spikey hair, was a touch shorter than me, and looked at me with her patented mixture of love and condemnation.

"Mum?" I gasped.

She smiled. "Well, don't act so bloody surprised. You do remember what I look like, don't you?"

She let herself in, and I closed the door and stared at her, bewildered. "Mum, what are you doing here?"

"I was in the neighbourhood."

"What do you mean *you were in the neighbourhood*? You live in West Dunbartonshire."

"I thought I'd take a wee road trip and see some of my English friends."

"You drove here?" I gasped again. "That's some bloody road trip. What is that, a nine-hour drive?"

She waved her hand, staring around my flat. "Ah, it was nae bother, Adrian. I've been down here for a wee while, flitting about from place to place. It's just a wee holiday."

There it was. Guaranteed to happen at least once any

time I talked to my mother. The one word that snapped me straight back to how depressed I used to be as a child. I knew she didn't mean to say it; it just slips out when she's not thinking. She has the luxury of not thinking about it. I sighed. "Mum, that's not my name."

"Eh? Oh, oh, yes, of course. Sorry. Angelina. Though, I'll never understand why you changed it. Adrian was a perfectly fine, gender-neutral name."

"It's not about that, Mum. That's not my name. End of."

"All right, all right. Dinnae fash." She walked over to me and put her hands on my shoulders. "It's good to see you, Angelina."

I smiled reluctantly. "You, too, Mum. Do you want a cuppa?"

"Oh, no, don't bother yourself; I'll do it." She made her way over to the kettle.

I didn't bother fighting her on it; she had a tendency to walk into other people's homes and treat it like her own home. I just let her crack on with whatever and went back to the sofa.

"Are you having a cup of tea, Angelina?"

"Sure, I'll have some of my tea that I bought with my money that my mother has taken upon herself to offer me as if she was the one who bought it."

"Well, you came out of me, so in a roundabout way, everything you do belongs to me."

"Not how that works, but whatever."

"Bloody hell, Angelina. This flat's a bloody pigsty."

"For God's sake, Mum, please don't start cleaning my flat; it's fine."

"Oh, I'm just straightening up." She was already moving all my stuff around.

"*Mou!*" I moaned. That was one of the few bits of Japanese that had survived the generations of my family. It's basically just a sound you make to express that you're annoyed.

"Don't you *mou* me, child, it's a bloody mess in here."

I rolled my eyes and just let her get on. I checked my phone and was attacked by the fact that I had my messages to Flynn open. I still haven't heard from him, and I'm still obviously having trouble moving on from that.

"What is this, a cookbook?" Mum said. "You don't cook."

"I can't take up a hobby?"

She grumbled and put the book away someplace I'd have trouble finding later.

She brought over the tea and handed me my cup. "Budge up, dear."

I moved my legs off the sofa and made room for her to sit. She relaxed into her seat after taking a long, deep sip of tea.

"You knackered?" I asked.

"Aye, came down here fae London, seeing a few friends."

"You gonna be staying here? Do I need to set up a bed?"

"No, no, no, I've got a hotel. I'll just go back there. This is a holiday for me; I can't be staying with my child, now, can I?" She grinned and sipped her tea.

That was the other thing I had to put up with. *Child.* She never says "daughter." She calls my brother "son" all the time, but I'm just "child" or "bairn" or something else gender-neutral. It's not exactly disrespect, but it's not affirmation either; it's this weird middle ground. It's the bare minimum, which I guess I have to be happy with because I'm honestly not even guaranteed that. But aside from that stuff, she's been a good mother to me, and I do love her. She's just annoying to have around sometimes.

She sighed. "It's nice to be back in England. Your dad and I used to holiday here all the time."

"I don't want to talk about dad," I snapped.

"No, I'm not. I'm just reminiscing." Sure. That's how it starts. "We used to go round to so many different places. That's how we decided to raise you and Andrew here. And he used to—"

"I said I don't want to talk about dad." I didn't say it with much force; I didn't have the energy when it came to this subject.

"All right, fine." She sipped her tea.

"Like, I don't know why you even want to talk about him; he left us. He decided having a trans daughter was so fucking bad that he left. You were so distraught about it, you moved back to Scotland. You couldn't even live in this fucking country anymore."

She sipped her tea again and said quietly, "I thought you didn't want to talk about it."

I groaned, and that was the end of that.

"Aside from all that, Angelina, how have you been?"

"Fine." I sipped my tea finally. It was lukewarm now.

"Just fine?"

"Yep."

"Well, what about Kate? I stopped by there as well, but her girlfriend said she was away for work?"

"Yeah, she's in Manchester. She should be coming back today." I checked my phone reflexively and was attacked again by Flynn's name and my unanswered text.

"What's wrong, Angelina?"

"Nothing."

"Tell that to your face," she mumbled.

"Oh, my god, Mum. I'm fine." I got up and went to the kitchen, pretending to be busy with something.

"Is it because I spoke about your father?"

"No! Not everything's about him. I said I'm fine!"

"Oh, no, no, no, you're not doing that shite with me, Adrian."

"That's not my name," I sighed.

She stood up and looked at me. "Angelina, what's the matter? Why are you so irritable? It's not those oestrogen patches, is it?"

I squinted at her. "Are you being funny?"

She just sipped her tea and shrugged.

I sighed. I wasn't sure my mother was the person I wanted to talk to about this, but what the hell? "I met this bloke the other day. We went out, and I spent the night at his. Woke up in the morning, and he was boaking in the toilet. Then he kicked me out. I didn't even see him; he just told me I should go, from the bathroom. It's not the first time as well. Before, I met him in a café, and he left pretty suddenly then, too. But this time, he's not responding to my text. I haven't heard from him since. And I can't stop thinking about it. I mean, he clearly doesn't want to see me again, and I just need to forget it and move on, but it's nagging in my head. I'm missing something. I know I am. We were having a good time together; none of this makes sense. I keep analysing our interactions, and there were loads of weird things. He showed me around his house, but I got the sense there were things he didn't want me to see. When he spoke about himself, he spoke vaguely sometimes. Like, he said his parents died 'a while ago'. He couldn't have been any older than me; how long ago can 'a while ago' be? And I know none of that sounds particularly sus, but I'm telling you; something's not right here. I must be missing something. And I can't stop thinking about it."

Mum just sipped her tea and said, "Sounds like you like him."

I took a breath. "Yeah, I did," I admitted.

"Well, Angelina, I don't know about all that other shite, but isn't liking him reason enough to pursue him? You said you were at his house before. Go back there and get an explanation out of him."

"I can't do that."

"Why not? You're no gonnae let him just fob you off,

are you? It barely even constitutes as fobbing you off as he couldnae be bothered to fabricate a proper excuse. Now, I don't know about the rest of it, but if you like him, and you feel there's something more there, then you go and bloody well sort it. Just because you're a woman now, doesn't mean you have to be dainty and doesn't mean you have to put up with a man's shite. Follow your gut, Angelina. Go after him, and at the very least, get the closure you bloody well deserve. This won't resolve itself unless you take charge of the things you want in your life." She sipped her tea again and added, "That's what I would do, at any rate."

I smiled at her. As annoying as my mum could be, this was why I loved her.

10 May

It was early Wednesday morning, and I was on my way back to that beautiful old house. I just couldn't get over this, and I had to sort it. Even if he says, "Fuck you, you crazy bitch. I never want to see you again," at least that'll be the end of it. But I'm trusting my gut here. I'm trusting that there is something else going on. No matter what, this ends now, and then I can stop bloody thinking about it.

When I got to the house, my heart started racing, but I ignored it. I was propelled mostly by what my mother had said more than anything. I walked up to the door, held up my fist to knock, and … froze. I just froze. My fist was up, but I couldn't knock. What was I doing? Why was I here? This is mental. This is absolutely mental. I mean, what the fuck is my plan here? Knock on the door, he opens it, and I say what? "Hey, Flynn, sorry to bother you. Just wanted to know why you ghosted me. Also, I get the feeling you're hiding something, and I feel entitled to know what it is."

This was stupid. I walked away from the door and toward the side of the road, where I sat on the kerb with my head in my hands. After five minutes of limbo, trying to decide if I should knock on the door or go back home, I pulled out my phone and texted Kate. I updated her on the Flynn stuff, let her know my mum was in Thivleton and there was a good chance she might stop by and see her, and asked her how her shoot went. I read her response, not fully paying attention, and then I heard someone speak.

"Can I help you?"

I looked up. A middle-aged woman was standing over me. She wore a long, flowy purple dress and a wide-brimmed purple hat. She looked at me, confused.

"Sorry," I said. "I was just…" I looked back at the house and sighed, then I looked back to my phone.

I noticed the woman staring at the house, too. "Were you looking for the man who lives here?"

I stared up at her. "Do you know him?"

She eyed the house again. "I see him around."

I looked down.

The woman took a seat on the kerb next to me. "How do you know him?"

"Went out with him once," I said nonchalantly.

"I understand he doesn't get out much." The woman's responses were very hesitant, like she was putting a lot of thought into what she was saying. "I'm surprised he's taken the time to go out with anyone."

"Yeah, he said. We were both in a rut. He said he was trying to get out more."

"Yes, I … I expect he did."

I looked at her. "Are you sure you don't know him?"

"Well, I have spoken to him on occasion. I come round here quite often."

"To see him?"

"No. No, just passing through. I go to play the lottery just down the road." She was avoiding my gaze. "Why did you come to see him, if you don't mind my asking?"

I sighed. "I don't really know. He sort of ghosted me. I had a really nice time with him, and something's just not sitting right with me." I looked back at the house and sighed. "Sorry, I don't mean to bug you with this." I stood up. "I just need to move on. That's not his issue; it's mine. It was nice to meet you."

"Yes, you too," she said slowly. She must have thought I was well mad. I should never have come here.

I walked back home and went on with my day. I finished up the manuscript I was translating, read for a bit, got into a new programme which I binged all throughout the evening, and just when I was about to go to bed … I got a text:

Sorry I haven't texted you back. If you don't hate me, meet me at that café we met in at ten tomorrow morning.

11 May

10:00 a.m. Thursday morning. I'm sat at a table in the café with a coffee.

I've been here since half eight. This was not my first coffee. My foot was tapping, my thumbs were twiddling, and I didn't see Flynn anywhere. He said ten, and it was ten. Any minute now. I wasn't even sure what I was expecting. I wasn't sure what I wanted to happen here. I just wanted to see him, talk to him. I didn't know what I wanted to say, or even what I wanted him to say, but I had to talk to him. Maybe then, whatever happens, I could stop thinking about this.

Someone walked into the café. It wasn't Flynn, but it was someone I recognised. That woman from yesterday with the wide-brimmed purple hat. She spotted me and came over to my table.

"Hello again," she said.

"Hey. What're you doing here?"

She bit her lip and sat across from me. "I came to talk to you."

"About Flynn? Did he speak to you?"

"No, I …" She took a breath, looked around the shop,

and then leant in and whispered, "I'm Flynn."

I stared at the woman blankly, the middle-aged, shorter-than-me white woman who looked nothing like the man I met before. "What do you mean you're Flynn?"

She continued to whisper. "I'm Flynn. I'm the man you met in this café last Thursday."

I laughed to myself. "No you're not."

"Yes, I am."

I scrutinised her: crooked nose, a few minor wrinkles, blue eyes. "No, you're not. You can't be."

She sighed. "Look, Ange, I know this is difficult to grasp—"

"How do you know my name?"

"You told me, here, last Thursday, when we exchanged numbers."

I was shaking my head uncontrollably.

"Hang on," she said with her index finger up. She pulled out her phone and typed something. Then my phone went off. "Check your phone."

I was almost afraid to look, but I pulled out my phone and checked my messages. There was a text from Flynn that simply read:

This isn't a trick, Ange. I really am Flynn.

She showed me her phone as well so I could compare it with mine and be sure she actually did send that message from her phone to mine under Flynn's name.

"What did you do to Flynn?" I still didn't believe it.

"I am Flynn," she answered calmly.

"No, you … you stole his phone. You … This is some sort of trick the two of you are doing to, what, get something from me? Kidnap me?"

"No, no, Ange, listen to me. We met here last Thursday. You had some expensive drink you didn't care for because you were trying to break out of your rut. You bumped into me with it when you were leaving the queue. I came up to you and asked if I could sit with you. We talked. We exchanged numbers. Then we met again at Oak Corn Park the next day, because you always take a walk in the park on Fridays. We spent the whole day talking, and then you came back to mine. You spent the night, but I was … feeling sick in the morning and asked you to leave."

I stared blankly at the woman, and she stared back at me, awaiting my response. "Why would he tell you all that? What do you want from me?"

"What? No, I … He is me, Ange." She whispered again. "If I weren't Flynn, how would I know you have a birthmark on your stomach shaped a little like a cat's paw?"

"How—?"

"I saw it when you took off your shirt."

I stared at the woman and considered this. I think—I mean, it's possible—that maybe she's telling the truth. Or at least she thinks she is. But how can this woman be Flynn? I mean, that's not just dressing in women's clothes; it's not cross-dressing or drag. Flynn wasn't white, Flynn was taller, his voice was deeper, his intonations were different, his fingers weren't as long, he was younger, he didn't have boobs, his posture was different …

"I don't understand," I admitted very seriously. I waited to hear this woman's explanation.

She took a breath. "Ange …" She bit her lip, hesitating. "I have a condition—an illness."

"What sort of illness?"

"I don't know if it has a name. As far as I know, I'm the only person who has it. But it means I … change."

"Change how?" I sounded deadly serious. This wasn't funny in the slightest.

She gestured to herself. "Everything. Skin, hair, eyes, sex, age; absolutely everything. You said before that you thought my eyes were brown, but then they looked green. You weren't seeing things. That's how it starts, small things—eyes, body hair … My eyes were changing when we met, and I could feel it coming, I was going to fully change soon. That's why I left so suddenly. But I didn't change, just my eyes. So I put in some coloured contacts and went to see you at the park. I wanted to see you. I thought I had more time; I thought … I don't know what I thought. But I didn't mean to make you think that anything that happened had to do with you. I did want to see you, I do want to see you, and I'm sorry if I made you feel …" She didn't finish. She looked like she was deciding what to say next.

"So when Flynn … or you … were being sick in the toilet—"

"I was changing, yes. And I didn't want you to see, so I had to get you to leave."

"But why did you change? Why not get rid of me and then do it?"

"I don't do it on purpose. I can't control it, and I can't hold it back."

I took a breath. I was out of it since the comment about my birthmark. I didn't know what to think. I felt so confused and exposed and awkward all at the same time. If Flynn was having me on, he was doing a bang-up job; I would never live this embarrassment down. "Okay, if this is real, *if* it's real, why would you even talk to me? Why did you get involved with me if you weren't planning on telling me this sooner? I mean, I told you my thing before we went back to yours; you didn't think to tell me about this 'condition?'"

"I know. I should have, and I'm sorry. I just … I'm lonely," she admitted with a sigh. "I don't really have anyone. I don't have any family, any friends. I don't even really have acquaintances. I get to know someone, and then I change, and they don't recognise me anymore. I can't build a relationship with anyone longer than a few days. And I can't tell anyone because who would believe me? I've been living the same life, alone, for God knows how long. And I thought I'd feel better if I tried something new. So I came to this café for the first time, and I saw you, and I wasn't thinking. I just wanted to pretend for a second that I was just like everyone else. I wanted to know someone. I wanted to spend time with someone. And I didn't think about what I would do when I changed; I didn't want to think about it. But then I did change, at the worst fucking time, too. You were still in my bed, asleep. I didn't want to wake you; I didn't want you to see. But it was selfish because I probably made you feel like I didn't like you, that I didn't have a good time, and I'm sorry, I'm so sorry if I made you feel that way."

I sat silently, thinking, considering. "Why are you telling me this? If you didn't want me to know then, why are you telling me now? I wouldn't even be able to recognise you. You could've just continued ghosting me. Why didn't you?"

She rubbed her temples before answering. "Because … I like you, Ange, and I want to get to know you. I want you to get to know me, the real me."

She stood up suddenly and held her forehead with her hand.

"Where the fuck are you going?" I whispered harshly.

"I'm sorry. I have to leave. It's going to happen again. Soon."

"The change?"

She nodded. "You … you said you go to the park on Fridays, yes? I'll meet you there where we met before, at noon, and you can ask me anything, anything you want."

I just stared up at her suspiciously.

"I promise; I'll be there … if you want me to be. I won't ghost you again, and I'll tell you anything you want to know. But I think … I'll probably look different tomorrow."

"Different how?"

"I don't know." She held her head again. It looked like she had a headache. "I really have to go, Ange. I hope I can see you tomorrow. I'll let you know who I am; you won't recognise me."

Then she left before I could say anything else, and I just sat alone at the table with my now-cold coffee.

What was that? What just happened? Do I believe that? Do I believe that Flynn changes like some … some sort of shapeshifter? Whatever I was expecting out of seeing Flynn today, it wasn't that. I mean, I don't believe that, do I? It's mental. It's insane.

I kept questioning whether I believed any of this rubbish on my way home and for the rest of the day. But when I checked my phone next, the text Flynn sent me at the café popped up:

This isn't a trick, Ange. I really am Flynn.

And I knew then, I had to know more.

12 May

I was sat at a park bench in Oak Corn Park at noon. I had texted Flynn, and he confirmed he was coming. I waited quietly, writing in my diary. Even though I'd had a night's sleep to turn things over in my mind, I still didn't know what to think. Did I believe? Did I not? Was there anything that Flynn could say that would make me understand? Did I want to understand?

"Hey, Ange," came a high-pitched voice.

I looked up from my diary and saw nothing but the top of a fluffy afro. Then I looked down at the small, dark-skinned girl looking up at me.

"It's Flynn," she said.

"No you're not," I refuted.

"Yes I am," she asserted calmly.

"No. You're not."

She sighed. "Ange, we went through this yesterday."

"No. No, you're not him. You're a little girl; you can't be more than ten years old. There is no way you are the man I met a week ago."

The girl sighed again and climbed up onto the bench to sit next to me. "I told you I'd answer your questions, and I meant it. Ask whatever you need to, and I promise I'll tell you the truth."

She wasn't looking at me; she was watching the other people enjoying the park. But I was looking right at her, desperate to find proof—proof she was him or proof she wasn't, I didn't know which I wanted more, but either was better than confusion, uncertainty, fear.

I asked my first question: "How old are you, really?"

She answered immediately. "I don't know."

"No. No, no. None of that. You said you'd give me answers."

"I don't know," she asserted. "My condition affects my

memory—short term's fine but long term is … dodgy. The memories get mixed up, and they change whenever I change. I don't know when or where I was born." I just stared at her, but she must have read the concern on my face because she said, "I am an adult, if that's what you're worried about. I definitely remember the noughties, so I'm at least over twenty."

I shook my head. "No, no, you know what, you're having me on. Who are you, really? 'Cause you're not him. You can't be him."

"Oh, for fuck's sake, Ange, we went through this yesterday. Do I need to text you again? Do you want me to recount everything we've done? Do you want me to tell you about your birthmark again? Or do you need me to tell you from the mouth of a ten-year-old girl the exact details of us having sex?"

"Okay, okay, shush!" I looked around. Luckily, I didn't think anyone heard that.

"I'm sorry," she sighed. "I'm just stressed, and I'm sure all this must be stressing you out, too. I really want you to understand, but you have to meet me halfway, Ange. I realise this is strange—impossible—but it's the truth. This illness is part of me; it's who I am. Please."

I stared into the eyes of this little girl and listened to her words, and I was brought back to eight years ago when I was pleading with my family to understand who I really was. I thought about my mum, who didn't understand how her son could really be her daughter, but she tried so hard to understand because she loved who I am more than she feared what I am. And I thought of my dad, whose love for me was conditional, revocable. Because if I am who I am, then I am no child of his, my mother is no wife of his, and our family are a shame from which he must escape.

This little girl—Flynn—she was looking into my eyes, begging me to accept who she was. The question was: Did I care about who she was more than I feared what she was?

"I believe you," I said. "I believe you're Flynn, and I want to understand."

"Really?"

I nodded.

She took a deep breath and wiped away the moisture from her eyes. "Okay. Ask me whatever you need."

"How did you get like this? Were you born this way? Did you catch it from someone?"

"I don't know. Can't remember. I don't think it's contagious, though; no one's ever caught it from me."

"How often does it happen, these changes?"

"Every few days. Longest time between changes was five days, I think. But it's usually every two or three days."

"And who are you changing into? I mean, who is this girl? Who was the woman from yesterday?"

"No one. I've never met anyone who looks like me, like any of me. Every person I am is a unique, new person."

"Is it just people? Do you ever turn into animals, objects?"

She shook her head. "Just people. Different ages,

different sexes, different ethnicities."

"And you don't remember how you started? You don't know what sex you were born as, what ethnicity you were born as?"

"No clue."

I tried to imagine that. "That must be hard, to have no idea who you are."

She looked at me and smiled. "Sometimes."

"Well, what about your gender? How should I think of you? As a guy? As non-binary?"

She shrugged. "I don't really care. I've been a lot of different people, and I've been seen in a lot of different ways. I'm just me. However you want to think of me is fine by me."

I nodded, mulling this over. Then I asked, "What does it feel like when you change?"

"Painful. Violent. Some times are worse than others, but it always feels like I'm dying."

"Is there a medication you can take? Painkillers?"

She laughed darkly but stopped when she realised that was a serious question. "Painkillers make the pain worse. It's like I can feel my body actively rejecting them."

I felt for her. It was a pain she couldn't escape, a burden she had to shoulder. And at that moment, I wanted to help her bear that burden.

"Do the people you turn into ever repeat?" I asked.

"Sometimes. Very rarely. And just pieces, not the whole body. When I change, it's not one body for another, it's parts of me changing individually to create a new person. Most of the time, those parts match up well enough, but sometimes they don't."

"What do you mean?"

"Like, sometimes I look young but sound old. Sometimes the skin on my body is a different colour than the skin on my face. Sometimes I'm a woman with a beard or a man with boobs, and it becomes so much harder to blend in. When you don't look the way people expect, it can be difficult to exist as part of society."

"I get that." I could see she was starting to relax, and I was, too. This didn't feel as stressful anymore. I was just getting to know Flynn, the real Flynn.

"Have you ever tried to cure it?" I wondered. "Go to a doctor or something?"

"Who would believe me?"

I smiled at her. "I do."

She looked at me hopefully, but it faded. "Not everyone's as good as you, Ange."

"Maybe. But I'm sure there are more people than you think who might understand."

"But what if they don't? What if I'm a freak of nature? What if they fear me? Look at all of human history; look at what people have tried to do to the people they don't understand. I'm one person, Ange, not a community, just one person. The second someone decides that I'm not entitled to human rights, that I'm a deviant, an abomination, what do you think they'll do to me? And what could I do to stop them?"

"So you live in secret."

"Yep. I just blend in and carry on."

I felt like I really understood her. My experiences as a trans woman and Flynn's experiences as a shapeshifter were somehow similar. The more she spoke, the more I saw myself in her.

"One last question," I said. "Why are you trusting me with this? You keep this a secret from everyone else for your own safety, but you're telling me. Why?"

She played with her hair, pulling down a few strands from the mass of her afro and revealing their true length before letting them spring back to her scalp. "I guess … because I haven't really been living. My whole life, I've been surviving. When I went out with you at first, I just wanted to break the mould. I never intended to tell you about my condition. But then I got to know you a little, and I wanted to know you more. And I thought—I hoped—that you could be the person who understood. But I got scared. I didn't know how to tell you, and I was afraid that I'd left a bad impression on you, that you wouldn't want anything to do with me. I'm still scared. I've never let anyone in like this; I've never trusted anyone with this before."

"Well, I promise you can trust me, Flynn."

Unexpectedly, I opened my arms, and equally unexpected, she instantly hugged me. And as I rested my chin atop her fluffy hair, I was excited for the future … and at the same time, terrified.

Interlude

nd so I had met Flynn, and nothing could have prepared me for how my life would change. I fancied the man he was when we met, but I felt for the girl who confided in me in the park. I had to learn that I couldn't love every version of them in the same way.

That's another thing: The more Flynn changed, the harder it was to see them as that bloke I met in the café. I often ended up referring to them by whatever pronoun I felt matched the moment, and I don't really think of them as a man anymore, nor a woman, nor a girl or a boy. They're just Flynn, the strangest person I've ever met.

Over time, my love for them developed, and it was hard for me to manage. To love a shapeshifter was to love adaptively—to be whomever they needed and to love and accept whomever they were able to be for you. I wasn't perfect, and this relationship took a lot of my time and focus.

I made mistakes …

1 June

Flynn and I had been spending a lot of time together. It had been almost three weeks since they told me about their condition. And because they didn't work and my work was flexible in terms of when and where I could do it, we had a lot of time to be with each other and grow closer. Sometimes it felt like our relationship was developing so quickly, like I'd known Flynn for years, and not just one month. But every time they changed, it also felt like I was meeting someone new, and the relationship was only just beginning.

Today was Thursday, and Flynn said he wanted to show me something. He led me through his beautiful house, and today he resembled an East Asian man in his late twenties, with black hair down to his shoulders and a patch of brown skin on his neck from the last body he inhabited. He said the colour would probably lighten up to match the rest of him eventually.

Flynn never let me stay with them when they changed. They didn't want me to see, and I respected that. They said it was because it was violent and grotesque and not something I would want to see. But I believed it was because it was vulnerable and personal, and they didn't trust me with that quite yet. I understood, but I was curious.

We arrived at the room he was leading me to, a room I hadn't been in before.

"Isn't this where you had that dress hanging on the doorknob the first time I came here?" I remembered.

"Yep," he said with his androgynous voice. He had been a woman before this most recent change, and his voice hadn't finished adjusting yet. It had been gradually deepening all day.

He opened the door and stepped inside. I followed and was greeted by a massive room filled with clothes. It wasn't messy; everything was neat and organised, and there was lots of space to walk around and look at everything here. But what struck me was that this was like a clothing boutique; there were so many: T-shirts, cardigans, jumpers, button-ups, tank tops, dresses; skirts, jeans, dungarees; sun hats, caps, beanies; sports bras, bralettes, camisoles; boxers, briefs, thongs, boy shorts, hipster pants, period pants; high heels, wedges, trainers, sandals; long coats, raincoats, blazers; ankle socks, woolly socks, thigh highs; belts, scarfs, handbags, backpacks … Basically, if a human being could wear it, he had it. Sometimes the same thing in multiple colours, and often the same thing in multiple sizes.

"This is my walk-in wardrobe," he said, "filled with everything I've collected over the years."

"Wow," I breathed, taking it all in.

"In here I have loads of different clothes to suit loads of different bodies. Different sizes, different colours, different styles. And here," he walked over to a long mirror, "here's where I check the fit. Make sure the clothes suit the body I'm in."

I walked around the spacious room, eyeing everything I could. "I wish I had this many clothes. Look at this jacket; it's gorgeous."

"Put it on," he said.

"Really?"

He walked over, and I slipped my hands into the sleeves as he put the jacket on me. I looked at myself in the mirror. The jacket was white and cropped, with a puffy collar and sparkly sleeves.

"Looks great on you," said Flynn.

I posed and turned around, checking the fit from different angles. "It's a little big, though."

"That's all right. I've got a smaller one." He went off and fished around for a smaller version of the jacket, which he found quite easily. Then he took the jacket off me and put the new one on.

"Oh, it's beautiful," I said.

"You can borrow it if you want."

I looked at Flynn as he was nonchalantly putting back the other jacket. "Really?"

"Yeah. You look good in it; you should wear it." He approached. "In fact, you can borrow whatever you like from here. Anything you want to wear, anything that would make you feel good, it's yours. You don't even have to ask."

I smiled, and that forced a smile out of him.

"Come on," he said. "I want to show you one more thing."

He led me to another room in the house—his other

bedroom. He opened the door and invited me in. The bed with a single mattress and no covers was the only indication that this room was a bedroom.

"What is this?" I asked.

"This is my disability room," he explained. His voice had gotten a little deeper now.

He pointed around at the different things present. "Wheelchairs, walking canes, mobility canes, crutches, braces, splints, glasses of various prescriptions, hearing aids of various prescriptions, orthotics …"

"Why do you need all this stuff?"

"I'm not always able-bodied when I change. Sometimes my legs are paralysed, sometimes I'm visually impaired, or my joints hurt, or I can't balance right … This is a collection of things I might need. Like the clothes, I've collected them over the years. I get eye tests and hearing tests all the time to collect different prescriptions."

"You need different prescriptions?"

He looked at me, and there seemed to be a sad acceptance in his expression. "Every change gives me different eyes. When I change from a man to a woman, even the colours I can see change."

"That happened to me, too, when I started taking hormones," I said. "Well, supposedly. It's hard for me to tell the difference since the changes from oestrogen are so gradual."

"Well, there's definitely a difference. When I change, it's nearly instant. With female eyes, I can distinguish between colours more easily, and with male ones, I notice movement more easily. It makes things look a little weird until I get used to it."

He walked over to the other end of the room and continued. "And these are gender-affirming stuff: gaffs, binders, packers, breast forms, make-up and shaving supplies ..."

I examined all of it. They were arranged nicely in a little closet. There were even drawers filled with different types of condoms and menstrual products.

I felt the fabric of one of the gaffs. "Oh, I remember these days. Early in my transition, I felt so uncomfortable with what I had going on downstairs. I used to wear gaffs all the time."

"Yeah, they're good at flattening things out, but they hurt your balls after a while."

"Exactly!" I agreed. "I mean, you can stick them up your tubes, but you have to get used to that feeling."

"Tubes?"

"Your inguinal canals. Sorry, I call them *tubes*. It's a cuter name."

He looked at me, confused.

"You can stick your balls up your inguinal canals to put them back into your abdomen," I explained. "That gets them out of the way. Takes practice, though."

He looked stunned. "This is the first I've ever heard of this."

"Really? So you know about packers and binders and

stuff, but you never learned how to tuck properly?"

He just smiled and shrugged, and I gave him a chuckle.

"There's that giggle again."

"Chuckle," I corrected.

"If you say so."

I stuck my tongue out at him.

He came over to examine one of his gaffs. "Are you still uncomfortable with what you've got?" he asked.

"No. Not anymore. Oestrogen changed a lot about how it works, so I feel more comfortable with it now."

"Good." He smiled.

"The balls had to go, though," I added. "Got an orchidectomy as soon as I could afford it."

That made him laugh. Then he said, "Hang on, you had to pay for that? I thought that sort of thing would have been covered."

"Nope. I'm afraid I didn't quite meet the million and one requirements necessary to receive coverage for that," I said in a mock authoritative voice while rolling my eyes, and he smiled.

"Do you mind if I ask you how you figured out that you were trans?" he said.

"No, that's fine." I brushed my hair back behind my ear. "It was my friend Kate. Well, she's more like my sister, really. Her mum's trans, and she told me that one day back when we were in school—it just came up in conversation—but that changed everything for me. Up till then, I knew that if I could go back in time to when I was born and somehow change things so I would be born a girl and not a boy, then I would do that without question. No hesitation. But that's impossible. I was a boy, and I just had to find a way to live with that. That's what I thought. Then I found out about Kate's mum; I found out that being transgender was a thing, that I didn't have to be stuck in a boy's body. There was something I could do about it.

"Margaret—that's Kate's mum—she was the first person I told. I was at her house, hanging out with Kate. And then Kate went to the toilet, and while she was in there, I found Margaret and just told her everything. It all just spilt out of me. I was crying. I didn't realise then how much I was holding in. It was like I had my eyes open for the first time, and once I saw how my life could be, I couldn't ignore how my life was. I couldn't go back to convincing myself that I wasn't a girl and that my life was fine. It wasn't, and I knew that now."

"Wow. It's lucky you had her."

"Yeah. Her and Kate; they're my family. I lived with them for a bit, and that's when Margaret became like a mother to me, and Kate like a sister."

Flynn shook his head. "I can't even imagine that. To have your entire perception of yourself just flipped on its head. To realise something that big about yourself. How old were you?"

"Fifteen."

"Wow."

"Yeah, it was rough. It wasn't just dealing with how I

felt about myself, it was also the kids who used to bully me, and my dad kicked me out then as well."

"What?"

"Yeah. He kicked me out the second he found out I wanted to transition. That's why I had to live with Kate and Margaret."

Flynn's mouth was wide open. "That's horrible."

"As I said: It was rough."

I wanted to ask him about his illness, about how he figured out he was a shapeshifter. But I already knew what his answer would be. *I can't remember.* That was one of the biggest differences between Flynn and me—I could never forget the events that got me to where I am today, but Flynn could never remember. His past was a mystery.

I looked at him, then at the gaff he was now holding. "Do you get dysphoria?" I asked.

"What, like, about my gender?"

I nodded.

"Not really, no. I mean, not the way you do, I'd imagine."

"Then why do you have all this stuff, all these gaffs and binders?"

"Makes it easier to blend in," he sighed. "It's hard to exist in society as a man with boobs or a woman with a bulge."

"Yeah, you're telling me," I agreed.

"All this stuff just makes it easier."

I looked at him. "Well, you don't have to worry about any of that stuff with me."

He took my hand. "Neither do you."

3 June

I knocked on the door early Saturday morning, and a large, smiling woman answered it.

"Hey, Margaret," I greeted.

"Oh, Angelina, it's lovely to see you." She gave me a big cosy hug and then invited me in.

It had been a while since I'd seen Kate's mum, so I was due for a visit. She ushered me into the front room and sat me down on the sofa.

"How have you been, Angelina?" she asked after she had gone into the kitchen and returned with a tin of freshly baked biscuits for us to snack on. She placed the tin on the coffee table before sitting down in her chair.

I took one and said, "I've been good. Work's going well; I just got in a new manuscript to edit. Also had an appointment yesterday about HRT and transition and stuff."

"And how was that? Everything good with your hormone levels?"

"Yeah," I sighed. "Had to prep myself for all the weird questions, you know? How are my boobs developing? How is my penis functioning? How's my sex drive? Am I happy with my sex life?"

She smiled knowingly while taking a bite out of a biscuit. "Yes, that's how it goes. They're just doing their job."

"I know. Their job is so invasive, though."

"Perhaps there are better ways it could be done, but they're looking out for you, making sure you're healthy. That's much better than what women like us had back in the day."

I loved seeing Margaret because she was a trans woman who was older than me. She'd been through it all before, and she's helped me in my life in more ways than I could count. She was proof I had a future, that being trans wasn't a death sentence, that it was possible to be trans and live a full and long life. But I was also aware that the only reason she could be that for me was because she was a survivor: conversion therapy, homelessness; she had to hide the fact that she was trans for fear of what would be done to her if anyone knew. She'd lost a lot of friends and family in her life—people who turned their backs on her because of who she was, and people she cared about who weren't lucky enough to have survived the things she's survived. My visits with Margaret were always bittersweet. I loved her, but the stories of her past, as interested as I was to hear them, were hard to stomach.

I bit into another biscuit. "I also met someone."

"Did you?" She leant in enthusiastically.

"Yeah, they're … he's a nice bloke I met in a café." I decided that whenever I would talk about Flynn to other people, I would speak of them as if they have always been and will always be that bloke I met at the café. I didn't feel it was my place to share the details of Flynn's condition, and since I told Kate about them before I ever knew about their changes, I decided just to stick to that original description.

"Oh, that's lovely, Angelina. And is he treating you right?"

"Yeah, he's lovely. He even took the whole transgender thing really well."

"Oh, I'm so happy for you. You know, when I met Kate's father, there was quite a learning curve for him to understand all that. I'd already had the surgery by that time, and not letting on that I was a transsexual was what was best for my safety. I waited until, oh, a year into our dating to tell him. Probably not all that advisable, but in those days, especially, we had to be careful who we trusted with that information. That's how I lost …" She must have read the expression on my face. I'd heard the stories of violence she and her old friends had received from their partners before, and she chose to skip retelling it.

"I've always thought that was unfair, though," I said. "Should someone who's bisexual have to disclose their sexuality on a first date? Do people disclose how high a libido they have on the first date? Why is it expected that we have to disclose as soon as possible that we're trans?"

"Well …"

"Yeah, I know," I sighed. "I just think it's a bit shit. I mean, I'm not being deceitful if I don't feel like giving you my medical history upfront, and it's not your right to know unless we're gonna sleep together. And even then, if you've had bottom surgery, it's really not anyone's business but your own. I just wish that was information that could come up later on when I know and trust who I'm with, and when I do choose to say it, it wouldn't be such a big deal."

Margaret smiled at me. "We're not there yet, hon. Long way to go until we're considered a normal part of society. But that day will come, Angelina, trust me. I've seen things getting better over the years. Before you know it, being a transsexual will be like saying you're left-handed."

I grinned sourly. "You mean one of these days being a woman with a penis will be a non-issue? Shock horror. When's that gonna happen?"

She gave a short chuckle. "For now, at least you've found someone who's with it. Even Kate's father didn't know what to make of me at first. But he loved me, so he tried, he learned, and … speak of the devil."

A man came rushing down the stairs wearing a black, white, and red football shirt. "All right, my love," he said, poking his head into the front room. "I'm off to see the game with the lads. Oh. Angelina. Didn't see you there."

"All right, Dave," I greeted.

"Sorry I can't stay; running late as is. Must love you and leave you." And then he was gone, out the door at a speed rivalling professional sprinters.

Margaret rolled her eyes and grinned at me. "Football."

"Oi, don't knock it," I said. "That's a national British pastime."

"So are tea and crumpets, but I hate them, too." She chuckled.

"Honestly, and you call yourself English." I joined in her chuckle.

"So," she said, recovering from what had become a good laugh, "this bloke, do you love him, or is it too soon to say?"

I considered. "You know what, maybe it is a bit soon, but yeah, I think I do. I mean, I've got a good feeling."

"Well, remember, love is a promise just as much as it is a feeling. Be good to him and accept nothing but goodness from him."

I smiled. "Of course."

"Oh, you'll do all right, Angelina. You're a lovely, strong, charming woman, and you deserve everything good in your life and more."

This made my mind flick toward a potential future, just for a second, but it reminded me of something Kate had said to me. "I wanted to ask you," I said. "I was talking to Kate the other day, and she was saying that you breastfed her when she was a baby?"

"I did." Margaret took another biscuit.

"How? I mean, I didn't think that was possible."

She smiled at me. "Anyone can breastfeed. Even men. We're all mammals, and even if it's harder for some than it is for others, we can all do it. It's just that certain people wish to vilify certain other people for doing what is natural. If you're not the right race, gender, sexuality, then your milk is poisonous, and you're demonic for producing it. But yes, we can all do it."

"How did you do it?"

"Oh, well, I once thought like you, that you had to be pregnant to breastfeed. But I was talking to one of my friends from the women's shelter one day, and she told me that she was adopting and that her doctor was helping her induce lactation so she could breastfeed her adoptive baby. That was the first I'd heard of breastfeeding without pregnancy, and I wanted to see if I could do it. So I made an appointment and expressed this desire with the doctor. I said I was adopting, and I wanted to breastfeed my child. It wasn't entirely a lie, as Kate was adopted, but it was the nineties; I couldn't tell anyone I was a transsexual if I wanted to get fair treatment from a doctor, especially when it came to this. Though, I don't recommend doing that nowadays. You should definitely be truthful with your doctor. I was given medication to help induce lactation, and they could very well have reacted badly to the hormones I was already taking. Luckily nothing too bad happened.

"This all began a little over a month before Kate was born. I had to use a breast pump as well and massage my breasts, build up my milk supply. But in the end, yes, I was able to breastfeed Kate."

I imagined my possible future self breastfeeding a child. It was something I'd never imagined before because it felt unattainable and therefore pointless. But now I knew it was possible. "That's amazing."

She smiled. "That's what I thought. Some of my happiest memories are of little baby Kate latched onto my boob, nourishing my daughter in a way I never dreamed possible when I was young."

I smiled at her.

"Oh, Angelina, you know I love you and Kate so much. When I see the two of you, I think, 'That's why I'm here.' We all had to struggle so much back in my day, and many of the people I loved and cherished didn't make it, but I survived. And I often wondered why—why I had to live through all that; why I'm here when they couldn't be. But when I see you, and when I see Kate, when I see the two of you thriving, I know: That's why I survived."

4 June

I ran into Mandip on my way into my flat. "All right, Mandip."

"Hello, my love. I haven't seen you around in some time."

"Yeah, yeah. I've been spending a lot of time with my boyfriend."

"What? How is this the first I'm hearing of this? Who is he? What's his name?"

"Uh, Flynn. Met him a month ago at the café. Sorry, I meant to tell you."

"Oh, no, you don't need to apologise, my love. Can I ask how it's going?"

"Really good. Flynn's great."

"Well, good. I'm happy for you. Anyway, my love, I'm

off. Going to see Henry."

"All right. Say hi to him for me."

"Will do, my love."

She left, and I entered my flat. It looked a little strange—familiar yet unfamiliar. I'd been sleeping at Flynn's a lot. They don't ever come here because my flat isn't equipped to deal with their changes. It's better to be at Flynn's, where there are disability aids and different clothes and no one around to wonder why a woman entered my flat today, but a child came out the next day.

Now I'd been away from it for a little bit, my cosy place was seeming a bit more like clutter. (Maybe Mum was right.) I got a call from Kate while I was straightening up a little.

"Hey, Kate."

"Hello, baby girl. How have you been?"

"Ah, you know."

"How's Flynn?"

"How's Bridget?" I deflected, knowing she was only asking about Flynn to get more intimate details out of me.

"Bridget is excellent, very sexually satisfied. How's Flynn?"

Well, that backfired.

"Come on, baby girl, I'm waiting."

I smiled. "Yes, Kate, if you must keep tabs on my sex life, things are going very well."

"Hmm. Acceptable for now. But next time, I'm expecting more details, kitten."

I laughed. "Anyway. What're you up to?"

"Getting groceries. On my own today, so thought I'd give you a ring."

"Bridget didn't go with you?"

"No, she had a pretty bad tic attack yesterday, and now she's tired and in a bit of pain."

"Oh, that's too bad."

"Yeah. She hit me and called me a fucking degenerate whore about a hundred times, so I think she's feeling really bad about that, to be honest."

"Well, those are just tics, right? That's not her fault."

"But it was still her who did it, even if she didn't mean it. It's those tics that really get to her. Fucks with your sense of agency, as she would say."

"And what about you? Does any of that get to you?"

"Not at all," she laughed. "I mean, Bridget lovingly calls me her bitch wife on stream all the time. I find it kind of funny. The hitting tic did hurt, though. I am a little bruised, and I know she feels bad about that."

"Well, let her know I'm thinking of her." I retrieved a backpack from my wardrobe (larger than my usual one) and put my laptop inside.

"Will do. So what are you up to, babes?"

"Getting some things from my flat to take to Flynn's."

"Really?" There was surprise in her voice.

"Yeah, really."

"What sort of stuff?"

"Uh, my laptop, some clothes, the book I'm reading,

some teas he doesn't have …"

"Wow, so things are going really well. You've moved in and all."

"What?" I laughed. "I haven't moved in."

"Kind of sounds like you have."

"I think I'd know if I'd moved in, Kate."

"Well, let's see. Do you spend a lot of your time there?"

"Yeah, but just to spend time with Flynn."

"Do you sleep there?"

"Obvi."

"Does he leave you there alone?"

"Sometimes, I guess, if he has an appointment or something and I don't feel like going with him."

"Babes, sounds like you've moved in."

"Kate, how could I have moved in? I still pay rent for this flat. I don't even have a key to his place."

"Yet you're collecting things to bring over there, including your laptop to, what, not work there? You sleep there, you spend a lot of your time there, you're planning on doing your work there, and he even leaves you there alone. Baby girl, you're living in his house."

"If you say so, Kate." I rolled my eyes.

"I know so, kitten.

"You know, I feel like we haven't caught up in a bit. We should plan something."

"Yeah, we should."

"What're you doing next Saturday? You could come by mine."

"Uh, yeah, sure. Sounds good."

"Then I'll see you then. And I expect you to be a good girl and give me details."

"Not gonna happen, Kate."

"We'll see. Anyway, babes, I've gotta shoot. Talk soon."

"Right. Laters."

6 June

Flynn and I were sitting in her front room. We sat on either side of the sofa, our legs intertwined in the middle. We were doing different things—she was watching the telly and I was reading—but I enjoyed this, us existing in the same space.

Today, Flynn was a young woman with brown skin and short hair, and she had a round face with eyes that smiled almost as wide as her mouth. I noticed something as well, as I gained more experience with Flynn's changes: Their appearance wasn't the only thing that changed. Often their personality changed, too. Not enough to not be Flynn anymore; it was more like highlighting different facets of the same person. The woman sat across from me was happy and giddy; she always looked like she was enjoying life. She had lots of energy and was currently expelling it by tapping her foot on my thigh.

"Flynn, you're kicking me."

She giggled. "Sorry."

I love Flynn no matter who they are, but if I'm honest,

I do sometimes miss some of the people they've been. And, of course, I then immediately feel guilty for missing them. It's not Flynn's fault they're always changing.

"Flynn, you're kicking me again."

She just grinned at me and continued tapping her foot on my thigh.

I put my book down and grinned. "You're doing it on purpose, aren't you, you little minx?" I nudged her with my foot, and we got into a bit of a kicking fight.

I found that I had to change, too; I had to match Flynn's personality. They couldn't always be that man I first met at the café, the one who would love me passionately and care for me carefully. Sometimes, Flynn was playful, and so I had to be playful, too. Sometimes, Flynn was sombre, and so I had to be calm and kind. Sometimes, Flynn was young, and I had to be like a mother; and sometimes Flynn was old, and they were like a parent to me. It was strange, and the juxtaposition and frequency of the changes sometimes gave me whiplash. But I was becoming used to it, and changing how I treated them was starting to feel natural.

We had been play-fighting for a few minutes until we ended up in each other's arms. Flynn smiled and kissed me excitedly. But I froze. This wasn't the first time we'd kissed, far from it, but it was the first time she'd kissed me as a woman.

She read my expression and backed off. "Sorry, I wasn't thinking."

"No, it's okay. I just wasn't expecting …"

She twiddled her thumbs. "Sometimes I forget how much I change. I didn't think that … I mean, maybe you're not okay being kissed by a woman." She looked at me. "Are you?"

I looked back at her. Somehow, it still seemed like she was smiling even though her expression was concerned.

"I don't know," I admitted. "I mean, I like men, and I've never really questioned that."

"Right. Of course." She nodded.

"But … I dunno. It feels different with you. I wouldn't date a woman, I don't think," I kissed her, "but I love you, Flynn, even as a woman."

She grinned brightly and placed her hands on my thighs. "I love you, too."

She pushed me back onto the sofa and climbed on top of me like a cat stalking a mouse. Her enthusiasm made me giggle, and I tugged on her shirt and pulled her to me. As we kissed, I could feel her practically vibrating with excited energy. I ran my fingers up her back because I knew this version of Flynn liked to feel things. She craved touch like a puppy dog, and I had to be very giving in the way I loved her. Sometimes that was hard. I like to feel protected by the one I love; I like to feel like I belong to them. But Flynn can't always give me that. It's up to me to change how I show up for them, and that's an adjustment. But I can choose to show up differently for Flynn. I can choose to be what they need. Flynn doesn't have a choice. They are who they are.

But we're not always out of sync. Sometimes Flynn is exactly who I need them to be. And when that happens, it's wonderful; we fit together like pieces of a puzzle. And you'd think that all this relationship was was me waiting for us to sync up, but even though I preferred when we were in sync, and I often missed those times when they were gone, being out of sync wasn't all that bad. There was a satisfaction I felt when I could be what they needed. Even if I was assuming a role I wasn't used to, I was making Flynn happy, and that made me happy. Love is rarely selfish; it's a selfless contract of negotiation. And every day, I was more and more pleased that I had decided to enter into that contract with Flynn.

She nestled her face into my neck as I continued to draw circles into her back with my fingers beneath her shirt. She breathed in sync with me, relaxed by the calmness of my breaths and the steadiness of my heart.

I looked over at the telly to see a bunch of blokes ripping duct tape off each other's hairy chests.

"Hey, Flynn?"

"Yeah?"

"What the fuck is on telly?"

She grinned. "I dunno; I wasn't really watching it."

She lifted her head and put her hand on my cheek, turning me to face her. And then she kissed me, and the telly no longer mattered.

10 June

I was taking a cab to Kate's house in the early morning. It had been a while since we'd got to spend some time together, so I was happy we were getting to do it now. It was also a good distraction. Flynn was changing right now, and as usual, they didn't want me there for it. Too violent. Too personal. But I still worried, and it was made worse by the fact that I didn't know much about what it was like. I couldn't help; they wouldn't let me. So seeing Kate was the distraction I needed today.

When I arrived, I paid the cabbie, got out, walked up to the house, and knocked on the door. It was Bridget who answered in all her frat-boy-meets-rock-star glory.

"'Sup, Ange," she said, sticking her hands in the pockets of her tracksuit bottoms and whipping her hair back to flick her fringe away from her face.

"Hey, Bridget," I greeted as she let me in.

"Kate's in the kitchen."

"Oh, okay." She whipped her hair back again, and I realised she wasn't doing it on purpose. It was a tic. "How have you been?"

"Fucking knackered, at the moment. Streaming all night. Going to bed now."

I nodded as we walked into the kitchen.

"Hey, kitten," said Kate when she saw me. She rushed over to hug me and kissed my cheek.

"Right," said Bridget, whipping her hair back again. "I'm going to bed. You two have fun."

Kate kissed Bridget. "'Night, babe."

"Oh, also," Bridget added before making it to the stairs, "could you have some nosh ready for me when I wake up?"

"Sure," Kate said. "What do you fancy?"

"Preferably something edible. 'Night." Then she went upstairs.

"What's 'something edible'?" I asked Kate.

"That's Bridget speak for 'Bitch, I'm too fucking tired to answer questions. Figure it out.'"

I laughed.

"I'll probably get her a cheeseburger later."

"Speaking of food," I said, "have you got any chocolate?"

Kate looked at me suspiciously. "That time of month again?"

"God, I hope so. Otherwise, this chocolate craving is gonna make me put on some serious weight."

Kate smiled and threw me a chocolate bar from the fridge.

"Cheers, Kate." I took a bite immediately. "You know, it's so hard to keep track of a cycle when you don't bleed. Especially since my symptoms are so mild most of the time, I don't even notice it. Then it just hits me one month."

"Count yourself lucky," said Kate. "I feel my cramps every fucking month. I don't crave chocolate as much as you, though. Maybe I should donate my stash."

I stuffed more chocolate into my mouth. "I'd be so grateful."

She smiled and threw me another chocolate bar from

the fridge. "Go take a seat in the front room. I'll go get the wine."

When Kate says 'wine,' she means cranberry juice. I don't drink, and it was too early for her to start drinking, but she always liked to create the illusion that she was drinking even when she wasn't. She would probably switch her cranberry juice to regular red wine later on, though.

I sat in the front room and started on the second bar of chocolate while I was waiting for her to bring the drinks. In the meantime, I texted Flynn to see how they were doing. I was still worrying about the change.

"Okay," said Kate as she came in with two wine glasses. "So, funny thing happened the other day. I was up the shops, queueing up, and I notice this bloke staring at me. So, I'm like, 'Can I help you?' and he says that he recognises me."

"Oh, you just love that," I joked, taking my drink from her as she sat down. "Where did he know you from?"

"Well, that's what I was wondering. Didn't ask because, you know, don't ask questions you don't want answers to. But I was fucking analysing his face, trying to figure out if he had the face of a man who ... Hey, baby girl, you listening?"

"Hmm? Yeah, sorry." I was responding to Flynn. They were updating me on how the change was going. This helped me feel a little more at ease; I couldn't be there with Flynn, but they'd let me know they were okay. Apparently, they'd just finished being sick, and now they were sitting down and trying to stop their head spinning.

I put my phone down. "Sorry, Kate, I'm listening. Continue."

"All right, well, I'm watching his face, trying to figure out if he had the face of a man who'd seen me on Bridget's streams or if he'd seen me naked."

"What would be the difference between those faces?" I chuckled.

"All in the eyes, babes. They get really wide when they're thinking, 'Fuck, I've seen that girl's fanny.'"

I laughed. "What if they haven't, though? What if they recognise you from your less-revealing pictures?"

She shrugged. "Then it's admittedly more difficult to tell. I hate being recognised, though."

"Well, you're around, Kate. You're gonna be recognised."

She stuck her tongue out at me, but she did so through her V-shaped fingers and moved her tongue around to make me redden a bit. But I wasn't really looking. Flynn had texted again. They had to search their collection of glasses for the right prescription.

"Texting Flynn?" Kate grinned at me.

"Yeah, sorry. Guess I'm a little distracted."

"That's all right, kitten. Just focus on me, and I'll tell you what to do."

I grinned. "Man, you're quick."

"But I can go slow, too, if you want, baby."

There it was. Rosy-red cheeks. I made it way too easy for

her.

Kate took a sip of her cranberry juice. "Since we're on the topic of Flynn, I believe I was promised details."

"Sure. Or you could do one."

"I could do you."

"Shut up!" I laughed.

I finished my chocolate and texted Flynn for another update.

"So what have you been up to, babes?" said Kate.

"Not much. Visited your mum."

"Yeah? How was she?"

"Good. Haven't seen her in a bit, so it was good to visit."

"Yeah, I've got to meet up with her at some point, too. Kinda stupid that we rarely ever see her together, innit?"

"Yeah, why don't we?"

"Dunno. Guess we're shit daughters."

Kate and Margaret often included me as being one of Margaret's daughters. Not just because of how close I was with Kate and how much Margaret helped me with my transition, but also because Margaret took me in when my dad kicked me out, and I lived with her, Dave, and Kate for three months before my mum could convince my dad to let me come home. For all intents and purposes, I was her daughter during those months. All these years later, I still remember it so clearly—how it felt like my whole world was crashing down around me, but also how it felt like my life was finally beginning. I remember when I was in Margaret's house, hiding behind a wall with Kate. We were spying on the grownups' conversation. My mum had come by to speak to Margaret about me.

"Thank you for taking care of him," Mum had said to Margaret.

"My pleasure. She's a lovely girl." At this point, Mum refused to use female pronouns to refer to me, and Margaret refused to use male ones, so this was how the conversation had to go.

Mum had sighed when she said, "I don't know. I don't know what I'm doing anymore. I don't know what the right thing is to do. But, clearly, whatever I'm doing now is the wrong thing."

"Don't be too hard on yourself, Miko. It's a lot to come to terms with. It's a transition for everyone, not just her."

I remember seeing Mum look at her—suspiciously, I thought then, but in hindsight, maybe it was more dubiously. "I've been fighting with Michael for three bloody months," Mum had said. "I'm tired. I'm sick of all this shite. I haven't seen Andrew in for ever. He's sick of his parents arguing, I'm sure. Always out with his mates, or his girlfriend, or working extra shifts … I feel like my children are avoiding me like the bloody plague."

Margaret hadn't said anything, and I assumed then that she had given her a reassuring look that I couldn't see from behind the wall.

"I don't know anything about this transsexual shite or whatever it is," Mum had said. "But I want my kids back, both of them. I don't want them to resent me over this. I don't want to argue with Michael anymore, and I don't want to feel … I don't know."

"Miko, are you asking for my help?" Margaret had said. "Is that why you're here? I can help you understand all of this; I've been through it myself."

I remember Mum hesitating at the offer. "I'm really grateful that you've opened your home to Adrian. And he and Kate really do get on. I'm sure that's made it easier on him … And you seem … competent enough. You seem like you have your life together."

"I pretend to, like the rest of us."

"Right. So, I wonder if … I hope, maybe, in the end, Adrian might …"

"Maybe Angelina will turn out just fine?"

Mum had given that dubious look again. "Maybe."

Mum took me home that day, and the following three days were full of near-constant arguing between her and my dad. And then, on the third day, Dad left, and we never saw him again.

My mum and Margaret aren't that close, but she's always been grateful to Margaret for how much she's done for me.

"Oh! That's what I was going to say." Kate took out her phone, and I refocused on the present. "I wanna show you some of my new pictures. Not sure if I want to release them."

"Sure. Show me."

I checked my phone as she was pulling up the pictures. Flynn was doing better; the change was almost complete.

"You looking, Ange?"

"Yeah, yeah. Show me."

"Right, so here's one version." She showed me a picture of her naked and on her knees, covered in a thick, red liquid. There was also someone standing over her, but I could only see their legs.

"Who's this?" I asked, pointing at the legs.

"That's Nigel."

"Really? Wow, he's got nice legs."

"Yeah, he does."

"This is a nice picture as well."

"Oh, thanks, babes. New camera. So, we've got this one, and here's one with white liquid instead of red. There's one with me lying down." The differences between all the pictures were very subtle—different colours, different angles, different positions. Kate was an artist in that sense—she obsessed over the most minute details. But her pictures were always beautiful—equally erotic and artistic.

"It was fucking hard to get a good picture while covered in that shit," she said. "Don't really think I pulled it off for most of them, but which do you think looks the least ugly?"

"None of them are ugly, Kate."

"Thanks, babes. But this one is defo ugly, I mean, come on."

I looked at the picture; her eyes were a bit wonky. "Yeah, sure. Looks like some of it got in your eyes."

"Babes, you don't know the half of it."

"What is it you're covered in, anyway?"

"Water, food colouring, and thickener. We used different thickeners for different pictures."

I nodded and looked through the pictures. "Um … I like this one."

"Yeah?"

"Yeah …" I was checking in with Flynn again. They were okay, just recovering.

It wasn't just worry that kept me constantly checking in; it was also interest. I mean, Flynn is a shapeshifter, a real-life shapeshifter. I felt like the girlfriend of a comic book hero, like I was protecting a secret identity while also trying to figure out how these powers worked. I couldn't say I wasn't curious. How did Flynn get like this? Were there any patterns to who they'd change into? It became like a puzzle that I was constantly working on in the back of my mind.

"Ange, I feel like I'm only getting half of you here." I looked at Kate. Her arms were crossed.

I put away my phone. "Sorry, sorry. You're right."

She kissed my cheek. "Want to watch a film?"

"Sure."

26 June

It was Monday morning, and I was making Flynn breakfast at his house. Today, he was a small boy with blond hair and a bit of a stocky build. He was too short to reach any of the cooking appliances. Usually, he would just order in in these situations, but I volunteered to cook instead.

I handed Flynn some eggs and a bowl. "Can you crack those for me while I do the bacon?"

"Sure," he said in his short, high voice.

I got out some bread after I put the bacon in the pan.

"What are we making, anyway?" Flynn asked.

"French toast, I hope. Never actually done it before."

"Neither have I, so you're on your own."

"That's why I'm making bacon as well. I've done that plenty of times; it can be a palate cleanser if need be."

I was very used to Flynn's place by now. I knew where everything was. I helped myself to food and drink, clothes, and the books in his bookshelf that he never read anyway. I was starting to think that maybe there was some merit to Kate saying I'd moved in here. I mean, I work here, I sleep here, and the only reason I ever really go back to my flat is when Flynn changes. That's not a bad thing, though. I love Flynn, and I love spending time with him.

"Did you crack the eggs yet?" I asked while turning the bacon.

"Sort of. I think I may have gotten a shell in it."

"What? Seriously?"

"It's not my fault. Takes a second to build up my dexterity. My hands are all stubby now."

"Hmm, I dunno. Sounds like an excuse to me."

"You try going from tall man's piano hands to little boy's baby-fat fingers. It's like fucking reverse growing pains."

I went over to him, leant down and kissed his forehead, and then took the bowl he'd cracked the eggs into and used a fork to fish out the shell.

When Flynn was like this—a child—our relationship was closer to that of a parent and child, or maybe like I was his older sister. There was such a strange uniqueness to our relationship, and at this point, I was pretty good at dealing with the constant and sudden role changes. But I wondered how Flynn felt about it.

When we had finished cooking, and we were sitting at the table to eat, I continued thinking about it.

"For your first go, this is pretty good, Ange," said Flynn after he bit into the French toast.

"Thanks … Can I ask you something?"

"Yeah. What is it?"

I hesitated a bit, figuring out how to say it. "We had sex yesterday." Maybe I should have work-shopped that for a bit longer.

"Yeah, we did," Flynn said simply.

"And today, you're a child."

"I am."

"I guess what I'm wondering is … we don't sleep together when you're like this, because you're a child, but you're also not, really. Do you ever find that jarring?"

"Not really. That's kind of my whole life, Ange."

"Right, sure. But you and I take on different roles based around your changes, yet your mind is an adult mind still, no matter how you look."

"Right," he confirmed.

"So do those roles ever blend together for you? D'you know what I mean? Like, do you ever, for instance, want sex when you're like this?"

He considered for a moment. "Not really. Sure, I do always have the same adult mind, but my changes aren't just aesthetic. This is the body of a prepubescent boy; I couldn't be sexually attracted to you if I tried, Ange. Not that you're not really pretty."

I smiled involuntarily. "No, I get it. I just wondered."

"It is hard when I'm a teenager, though. Then I have a too-strong sex drive, and it doesn't mesh well with my adult mind. And I also don't want to make you uncomfortable; I'd still be in a child's body. I dunno, I kind of just go with the flow. That's just my life. I don't always get to be in the body I want."

"What do you mean?"

"Well, if we're talking about sex, I much prefer to have a penis when I'm doing it, but sometimes I have a vagina. And beyond just sex, sometimes I want to go for a run, but I don't have a good running body. Sometimes I want a different hairdo, but I don't have the right sort of hair for it. Sometimes I fancy a specific food, but the tongue I have doesn't like the taste."

"Wow. I didn't realise the changes went that deep."

"I mean, it's not the end of the world. Like I said, I just go with it. Just because I'd prefer something else, doesn't mean I hate how I am."

I had a question I was almost afraid to ask. "Do your feelings towards me ever change?"

He looked at me with his round, innocent eyes. "I'm always in love with you, Ange. The way I express my love may change, but no matter what body I'm in, my love for you doesn't change."

Perhaps I shouldn't have been, but I was honestly surprised that changing roles was as difficult for Flynn as it was for me, probably more so. The closer I got to him, the more his illness became my illness. I wasn't afraid of that. Actually, it felt empowering. To be part of each other's lives so deeply that we shared a similar struggle, and perhaps lessened the burden of that struggle for one another.

I took a bite of French toast. Flynn was right; I did well.

"You're defo the most interesting person I've ever dated," I said.

"Yeah? Who am I being compared to?"

"Well, everyone, really; you're the most interesting person I've ever met. But in terms of the people I've dated, just two. The first guy, I kind of liked, but he didn't really see me as a woman. He was bi, and he saw me as a guy with a splash of femininity. It was a best-of-both-worlds thing for him, I guess. Plus, if he was ever mad at me, he would start calling me a man, as if his referring to me as a woman was a privilege he could revoke if I upset him. True colours, innit?" I smiled ruefully, and Flynn shook his head like he was annoyed on my behalf.

"And the other guy I dated was a bit of a chaser," I continued.

"What's that?"

"What, a chaser? It's someone who's a little *too* into trans people. Like, they fetishize trans people."

"Oh, I see."

"Yeah. I was just an experiment for him. He didn't really care about who I was as much as he did *what* I was."

Flynn nodded thoughtfully.

"How about you?" I asked, taking another bite of French toast.

"What, like, who have I dated?"

"Yeah."

He smiled to himself. "I like to think I've had a very interesting and storied love life, but honestly, I don't remember."

"You don't remember who you've gone out with?"

He shrugged his stocky shoulders. "It's the illness. Maybe I've gone out with loads of people; maybe I've gone out with no one. I honestly have no clue."

I suppose I should have seen that answer coming.

"But wouldn't the people you've gone out with know they went out with you?" I questioned. "Wouldn't you have told them about your illness?"

"Not necessarily. I mean, I wasn't planning on telling you about it originally."

"What changed your mind? Why did you decide to tell me in the end? I mean, I know you said about wanting someone to know the real you, but what actually made you do it?"

"Seeing you sitting on the kerb outside. Just the fact that you came back. You weren't done with me. And when I saw you, when I talked to you as a different version of me … I don't know. I just got the sense that I could trust you."

"So I'm probably the first, then. You couldn't have gone out with anyone else longer than a few days unless you told them about your illness."

"Maybe. Or maybe whoever I went out with before agreed to keep my condition a secret, and now I've forgotten I ever went out with them."

I stared at him for a long moment. "As I said: You're the most interesting person I've ever met."

1 July

It was Saturday afternoon, and Flynn was out donating blood. They do that often. I find it quite admirable. Every change brings with it the possibility of a new blood type, so Flynn's like a universal blood donor in that way. Of course, you need credentials to donate blood, and with Flynn's ever-changing body, I wondered how that worked. I mean, before I had my ID changed, it was quite the hassle to convince anyone that it was my ID and that I hadn't stolen it off some bloke who looked suspiciously like he could have been my brother. I could only imagine how hard it was for Flynn. How do things like public health and birth registry work for a shapeshifter? When I brought that up to them, that's when I learned that they know a guy who makes fake IDs and that, for any face Flynn has. Apparently, he's even able to change government records. Flynn was his best client; he was under the impression that Flynn was a bit of a benefactor who was driving loads of customers his way.

Somehow that made it even more admirable, that Flynn would go through all that trouble to donate blood. Who knows, maybe they really needed that rare blood type that Flynn happened to be producing that day.

I was sitting in the front room of his house while he was out. I was reading one of the books from his bookshelf, but now I was scrolling social media on my phone. I got a text from Kate and instantly felt guilty. She had texted me two days ago, and I hadn't responded. She was texting now to see if I was okay.

I typed:

Shit. I'm sorry, Kate. Completely forgot to respond.

Then I realised there was also a missed text from my mum. That one was four days ago. I thought I'd better respond to it quickly before she got worried and came down to Thivleton again.

After I'd dealt with all my missed messages, I went back to scrolling social media. And that's when I saw it. A meme. An innocent little meme telling an innocent little joke:

You can say you're a woman all you want, but one kick in the balls will show you just how wrong you are.

I ignored it and kept scrolling, but a few minutes later, another one: A girl saying to a boy, *Don't be upset. It's okay to have a small penis.* And the boy's response, *I still wish you didn't have one.*

I decided to look at a different social media app, which was a mistake because then I was shown some trending news that included some politicians calling all transgender people demonic, predatory, an insult to God and Mother Nature, mutants, groomers, and perpetrators of dangerous ideology. And somehow, they were met with thunderous applause, as if they'd just decreed that world hunger had ended.

I decided to just check my email instead. One of them informed me that there was a new comment made in the forum for translators I often check. The discussion was about a Korean book that involved a trans woman in the plot, and the new comment proclaimed that the notion that a man could become a woman by chopping off his dick and wearing a dress was the most laughable form of degeneracy.

I turned off my phone. I wouldn't escape it today.

"Hey, Ange, I'm back," said Flynn as he came through the door.

"Hey. How was blood donation?"

"Good. I'm A positive today."

He came into the front room and sat with me. Today

he was a man with light skin, strong arms, and curly brown hair.

"You all right?" he asked me. "You look upset."

"Yeah, I'll be all right."

I must not have sounded very convincing because he asked again. "What's wrong, Ange?"

"I'm fine. I've just reached my quota of how much anti-trans shit I can take from the Internet."

"Oh." He nodded, understanding. "It is quite bad, isn't it?"

"Yeah," I laughed. Bad didn't come close to describing it. "You know, it's actually pretty fucking incredible how hard it is to avoid all that. People make jokes online where people like me are the punchline, and everyone just laughs. No one calls them out; they just laugh. I see adverts online for documentaries discussing how people like me deserve to have our rights taken away, and somehow that's not flagged as hate speech by the stupid Internet algorithms. I think it's the lack of condemnation that gets me. People applaud this shit as if it's okay. People slander what it means to be transgender every day, as if it's okay to use human beings as scapegoats to push politics or get in good with your mates or whatever-the-fuck reason, as if no one is harmed by those actions." I forced the air out of my lungs to try and calm myself down. "I'm just so fucking over it."

Flynn pulled me in and hugged me. I felt at home in his arms.

"Ange, I'm sorry. I hate that you have to go through that."

I relaxed into his embrace, felt his chest move against my face as he breathed calmly. Today, Flynn and I were in sync—I was what he needed, and he was what I needed. We were harmonised, and it felt wonderful.

"I know what we should do," said Flynn, pulling away from me.

"What?" I wondered, fixing my hair.

"Let me take you out to dinner."

"Dinner?"

"Yeah. We can get dressed up, go out. Forget all that shit online and go have some fun."

"Where would we go?"

He thought for a second. "I've got a place in mind. It'll be a surprise. You in?" He smiled slyly. It was a smile new to this face, but I'd already become drawn to it. It was confident and cunning; it was dangerous and spontaneous.

"Okay," I said, trusting completely in his confident smile. "That could be nice."

I felt somehow more alive with this version of Flynn. He felt reckless, devious, and like he was holding back a much more dangerous man, while at the same time, trying to pull a much more dangerous woman out of me. He made me want him to succeed in that, because I knew he would keep me safe. I trusted him completely.

I tugged at his shirt to pull him closer and kissed him. I tried to make the action seem calm and controlled, but in reality, it felt urgent. My heart beat differently when Flynn and I were in sync—not just faster but stronger, and

I could feel every single pump of my blood. I lay back on the sofa, pulling him on top of me. He pressed his lips to my neck in the way he knew I loved. He made me feel alive when he kissed me like this. Everything before was living in a blunted dream, but this was sharp, intense. I could feel. I could breathe. I was alive.

Each time he kissed me, a warmth surged down my neck and throughout my body, but then he stopped, and the feeling was slowly fading.

"Come back," I moaned, still tugging at his shirt. "I'm not done with you."

He chuckled softly. "We should really get dressed so we can go."

He kissed my neck once more, and it satiated me for a second. "I'm starting to think we could just stay here, and you could keep kissing me."

"But then you'd never know what I have planned."

I watched him suspiciously—his knowing, cunning, smile that I trusted with my life. I groaned. "Fine. Let's go. But we're coming back to this later."

"Of course."

He kissed my lips and pumped life into me again for just a second, and when he pulled away, he took my hands and pulled me up with him. Then he whisked me into the walk-in wardrobe, where we spent a good hour or two trying on different clothes and making ourselves look fancy. I tried on things with sparkles, things with overly long sleeves, things with no sleeves, things that were long and went down to my shins … I found the wide-brimmed purple hat Flynn once wore and tried that on. It didn't really suit me.

I waltzed over to Flynn who was looking at himself in the mirror. He had his soft curls tied back into a ponytail but let a single spiral of hair hang down at the side of his face. He wore shiny, dangling earrings, an off-the-shoulder top, and a nicely fitted blazer.

I wrapped my arms around his bicep. "You look nice," I commented.

He sighed. "Thanks. I don't think this suits the body I'm in, though."

"Why not?"

"It's a little too feminine."

"So? You look great."

"I don't want to draw too much attention to myself. It's been a few days since I've changed; I'm due soon. I don't want to attract looks and have people notice something odd."

"Well, you said we were going to have fun, right, to forget about what people say and think? If you start changing, we'll leave. But until then, let's just have fun. Let's wear what we want and be who we are and not worry what others think of it." I rested my head on his shoulder and looked at us in the mirror. "I mean, we do look good."

He kissed the top of my head. "In that case, I need a matching skirt."

I settled on wearing chunky ankle boots; a long,

asymmetrical skirt; and an oversized top tucked into the skirt at the front.

And then we were off. We had to get a cab because neither of us could drive. I never learned because I like to walk, and most of the things I needed were within walking distance, but Flynn didn't drive because it was dangerous. If they changed while driving, if their eyesight suddenly got worse or anything like that, they could get into an accident.

We drove up to a part of London I'd never been to before, and when we arrived, Flynn paid the driver and helped me out of the vehicle. He led me down the street to a restaurant called Intergoût.

I looked at Flynn. "Intergoût?"

"The food here looks one way but tastes a different way."

I stared at him suspiciously.

He gave me that sly smile. "You'll see. Come on."

He led me inside. It was pretty dark except for the faint orange glow from the lights lining the ceiling. It was crowded, but the seating was very intimate and secluded from one another. And there was a lovely, savoury scent in the air, but I couldn't put my finger on what it was.

We got a table quite quickly and sat down across from each other.

"This is nice," I said, admiring the cosy, wooden design of the restaurant.

"You haven't experienced this place yet." He picked up the tablet that was on the table. "So, this place is all-you-can-eat, but there's a catch." He tapped away at the screen. "I'll order us some chicken, and you'll see what I mean."

After a few minutes, a waiter came by with a small portion of chopped-up chicken breast with two toothpicks stuck in them.

"Go ahead," said Flynn, grinning with his sly, confident grin.

I took a piece of chicken and popped it into my mouth. It was warm, it smelt like chicken, it felt like chicken in my mouth, but it tasted nothing like chicken. It tasted like a strawberry.

I looked at Flynn, shocked. "What the fuck?"

"Right?"

"This is chicken."

He nodded.

"But it tastes nothing like chicken."

"That's the idea, yeah. Here, order whatever you want." He handed me the tablet. "I recommend the watermelon-flavoured sushi."

I scrolled through the menu: kiwi-flavoured lamb, banana-flavoured pork, mango-flavoured steak; and there were other combinations: salmon-flavoured rice, orange-flavoured pasta, caramel-flavoured prawns, chocolate-flavoured French onion soup …

We ordered quite a few things. The portion sizes were small, so we could try loads of different foods without getting too full.

And just like that, I forgot about all that crap online.

Flynn was amazing. He could do the impossible. He could make me forget that the world isn't a nice place. He could make me forget that sadness and pain were things a person could feel. He could bring me to life and make me feel that everything before was just half-living.

After a great dinner, we went back to Flynn's beautiful old house, and when we stepped inside and he closed the door, I took his hand in mine and kissed him. I moved closer and kissed him again, closer and closer until he lifted me off my feet, and I wrapped my legs around his waist and my arms around his neck. I kissed him again, and he carried me into the bedroom. My heart was beating and my skin was tingling. I felt alive again. Somehow, even more alive than before. There was a tension inside of me that could only be released by my proximity to him. We were in sync. We were harmonised, like perfectly fitted puzzle pieces. Sometimes it felt like a long wait to get to this point—all the other versions of Flynn that weren't quite in sync with me—but now it was here, and it was amazing.

He dropped me onto the bed, and I pulled my shirt off over my head while he removed his blazer. As soon as I removed my bra, he was on me, kissing my lips, then my neck. I lay down and let him kiss me. The warmth was spreading from my neck again. I could barely control my body as I let that warmth take me. Harmony. We were two parts of a whole. Only this version of Flynn could turn a bad day this good. He kissed my nipples and ran his fingers over them as he moved down to kiss my stomach. The warmth had taken hold of me; it was spreading throughout my body, and I dug my fingers into the bed as he moved farther down my stomach.

Then he stopped.

I poked my head up to look at him. "You all right?"

He was frozen for a second, then he said, "We have to stop." He sat next to me on the bed, closed off.

I sat up. "What's the matter?" But when I looked at him more closely, I got my answer. There was a patch of olive skin on his cheek, and his eyes were two different colours.

My face fell, and I put my shirt back on. "Oh."

"We can't. The change is coming."

"No, I understand."

"I'm sorry."

"Don't be." I put my hand on his arm and looked at him. "Don't be sorry. I understand."

I understood, but I was still disappointed. Time was up. We were out of sync again. A broken clock is right twice a day, but then that time passes, and it's wrong again.

"Guess I should get my things, go back to my flat tonight," I said.

He nodded. "That's best. You don't want to be here when it happens."

"I just want to know you're okay, Flynn."

"I will be."

I hugged him tightly, saying goodbye. Not goodbye for tonight but goodbye for ever. This face—the light skin; the brown curly hair; the sly, confident smile—I'd never see it again.

Everyone changes. We're all different people throughout our lives, but no one more so than Flynn. And that's okay. It has to be. We must move on, move forward. But that doesn't stop us from remembering, and I will always remember when Flynn was him.

4 July

I was sat at the end of Flynn's bed early Tuesday morning. I had just woken up, and Flynn was taking a shower in the bathroom connected to her bedroom. I yawned as I wrote in my diary, reviewing some of the things I'd written about Flynn's condition. I hadn't written much on the midway changes yet. They were the in-betweens—the differently coloured patch of skin, the boobs that wouldn't shrink away, the voice that stayed stubbornly high-pitch. Flynn made it out to seem like those were the delayed changes, that they sometimes took longer than the rest, but they would assuredly change to match the rest of the body. But from my own experience with Flynn, that wasn't always true. These in-between changes sometimes stayed all the way until the next change.

I was looking at one of these in-betweens now, as I watched the naked, olive-toned woman step out of the shower through the open bathroom door. She tied up her thick, wavy hair, moving it away from her soft, warm face.

She was petite and had a model-worthy figure. Her boobs were firm, her bum was round, her thighs were toned, and she also had a penis—a small dangling knob between her legs. And it wasn't a man's penis; it was a woman's penis. I could tell. It was smaller. It didn't stick outwards; it curved inwards with the natural curve of her pelvis. And it was attached quite proudly to a woman's body. It wasn't the majestic antlers of a stag; it was the subtle stumps of a doe. She had a body like mine, and this was the first time I had seen it on someone other than me, portrayed so beautifully and proudly. This version of Flynn knew no shame for the body she had, not a single shred.

She caught my gaze and said, "Enjoying the view?"

"Yeah," I admitted shamelessly. "Tits and tail out and all."

She laughed as she wrapped herself in a towel, came over to kiss me, and then sat next to me on the bed. "Well, I know what tits are," she said, "but what's the tail?"

I smiled. "That's just my name for a woman's penis. Since, in French, *la queue* means *tail*, but it's also a euphemism for *penis*. And the word *queue* is a feminine noun, so it just sort of fits."

She smiled at me and then clutched her stomach.

I put away my diary. "You all right?"

She shook her head. "It's happening. Soon."

"The change?"

She nodded and took a breath. "This one feels like it's going to be rough."

"How can you tell? What does it feel like?"

"It's hard to describe. It's like a pressure in my head, like an invisible clamp squeezing me. The more pressure I feel, the worse the change will be."

She groaned and clenched her stomach. I guessed that held more of her attention than the feeling in her head at the moment.

"I guess I should go, then," I said, but she stopped me.

"No." She had her hand on mine. "I think … I think I want you to stay."

"Really? You're sure?"

"I'm ready if you are." She looked at me, waiting for confirmation.

"I'm ready."

She rubbed her temples. "Just know this won't be pretty, Ange, especially this change. I can feel it; this is gonna be hard."

"I'll help you through it," I promised. "Whatever you need."

"Do you know the recovery position? Like, for seizures and stuff?"

I shook my head.

She grabbed her phone from the bed and looked up instructions on the recovery position, which she showed me.

I reviewed the instructions. "Are you in danger of having a seizure?" I asked.

"Seizures, fainting … If you're gonna stay, it'll be nice to know you'll keep me from banging my head into something. That always tends to make things worse."

I didn't say anything. I don't even think I was breathing.

"I don't want you to worry," Flynn assured me. "I'll be okay in the end. Trust me. But you need to be prepared. I'm gonna be sick. A lot. There'll be blood. I'll be in pain …"

"I can handle it," I resolved. "I'm not going anywhere."

She looked at me as if she knew I had no idea what I was getting myself into, and she was right. But I would stay. I'm not leaving. Flynn finally trusts me enough to let me into this part of her life, and I won't let her down.

She unwrapped the towel from her body and cast it away. "It's easier naked," she explained. "Less to muck up."

She looked at her trembling hands and sighed. "You know, the worst bit is when I actually like the body I'm in. Sometimes I wish I could have just a little more time as I am." She ran her hands over her body, feeling every crevice, memorising her form with her fingers. Then she whispered sadly, "I don't want to go."

And then it began.

She drooped and would have fallen off the bed if I hadn't caught her. "Flynn?" I said. She didn't respond. She'd fainted.

It was silent, but fear screamed within me. Flynn was still breathing, and there was a strong pulse, but she was limp, unresponsive … dead.

I held her close to me and waited, feeling her body against mine. She would be different after this, changed, and she wouldn't come back, not ever. Her last words were

I don't want to go, and now she's gone.

I took a breath. Everything was fine; I just had to wait. Death and rebirth, that's change, that's Flynn. I just had to wait, and everything would be okay. I picked up my phone and looked up the recovery position, reviewing it. When I looked back at Flynn, I saw that there were patches of light skin forming, spreading like ink blotches and wiping away the previous olive complexion.

Then Flynn jolted awake, lurched forward, and spewed sick all over the floor. I held her up, stopping her from falling into it, and she mumbled hoarsely, "Toilet."

I helped her off the bed and carried her to the bathroom. Her feet dragged on the floor, and a strange crunching sound was made with every failed attempt to put weight on them.

We just barely reached the toilet when she dropped down and hugged the seat, filling the bowl with bile. She barely had time to breathe; she was puking nonstop. Her stomach was so clenched that I could see her ribs, I could see and hear them cracking under the pressure of her abdominal muscles.

Then she dropped. Her head hit the bowl, and she collapsed onto the bathroom floor, shaking. She was having a seizure.

I ran to the bed to get a pillow and placed it under her head. Then I tried to move her away from anything she could hit while she was convulsing.

I just watched, hoping the seizure would stop soon. Her

skin had now fully lightened, and each convulsive movement of her body shook the thick hair out of her scalp. When the seizure was over, she was bald and unconscious. I put her into the recovery position and hoped she would wake soon.

My nose was burning with the smell of bile. Curiosity made me peek in the toilet bowl. The sick was bloody and chunky. I couldn't really tell what most of the chunks were, but I thought that some of them were teeth. I could see the shape of them as they sank to the bottom of the toilet bowl.

When I looked back at Flynn, they looked a little older, more wrinkled. There was stringy, white hair rapidly growing from their scalp, chin, and upper lip.

Then they woke up and screamed.

"Flynn. Flynn!" I said. They didn't respond, but by the sound of the scream, their voice had gotten deeper, older.

Then there was a pop, like squishing a grape but louder, and I was splattered with Flynn's blood.

They were unconscious again. I wiped the blood from my face and stared at the mangled, androgynous body before me. They looked like a contortionist who'd contorted themselves a little too much and ended up breaking something. Flynn also looked taller, and upon closer inspection, I realised that their bones had grown, but the rest of them hadn't. There were bony protrusions at their joints where their skin struggled to stretch, but at their fingers and toes, the skin couldn't stretch far enough, and the blood-soaked bones just stuck out like a bud out of the soil.

It was silent again, except for the crunching that was Flynn's bones rearranging themselves. He was masculinising. His hip bones cracked into a narrower arrangement. His shoulders popped and broadened. His boobs deflated, and from the nipples, a thick, bloody liquid squeezed out with a squelching sound.

This was a different person now, an older man. And the woman from before, she was truly dead, screaming in a puddle of her own blood and bile until she was gone. For ever.

Flynn woke and sat up.

"Flynn!" I rushed over and put his arm over my shoulder, making sure he wouldn't collapse again.

"I'm sorry," he mumbled deeply.

"What are you sorry about?"

"I know how terrifying this all is."

The tips of his fingers and toes were starting to grow muscles, blood vessels, and skin to cover the exposed bone. Hair was growing on his arms, legs, and chest, and every time I looked, his stringy white beard had grown longer.

"Are you okay?" I asked him.

He nodded very subtly. "My joints hurt, but we're coming to the end of it, I think." He looked at me but failed to stretch his lips into a smile. He yelped and bent over, clutching at his crotch, and when he relaxed and removed his hand, I saw that his penis was bigger, masculinised. Then his eyes widened and he sighed. "I can't feel my legs.

Ange, I need you to carry me into the disability room. I need a wheelchair."

"Of course."

I carefully lifted him up. It took a few tries. He was a large man now, taller than me, and his legs weren't working, so I was carrying all of his weight. Once I found a good angle to be able to use my legs to lift him, we were up, and I was dragging him out of the bathroom.

I did my best to avoid all the sick and blood on the floor. There were still faint snapping sounds, which I assumed were Flynn's smaller bones snapping into their new places. I now understood why Flynn wanted me to leave so quickly the morning after we first slept together. Nothing could have prepared me for what had just happened. I felt like I'd witnessed a brutal murder, a murder so savage and violent that the victim could no longer be recognised. But it was also like a birth—the blood, the screams, the agony, and in the end, new life. Born in violence, killed in agony, and then born again in blood and bile. That was Flynn.

I took him into the disability room and sat him carefully on the bed. Then I searched through his collection of wheelchairs, looking for the right size for his new body.

"That one," he said, pointing to one of the folded-up chairs. "That looks like it'll work."

I got the chair he was pointing at and unfolded it. Then I helped him into it, and he was right; it was a perfect fit.

I sat on the bed and sighed. And then it was silent. Truly

silent. No bones cracking. No inner screaming. There wasn't a thought in my mind. Silence.

"How are you doing?" Flynn eventually asked me.

I opened my mouth, but I couldn't speak. I just smiled and shook my head.

"You're covered in blood," he mentioned.

"That's okay," I whispered. Then I sighed. "Lots to clean."

"Leave it for now. It still has to finish liquefying."

"What do you mean?"

"The solids—all the chunks in my sick—they're bits of my insides: organs, teeth ... They'll dissolve eventually, and then we can clean up the liquid, and that will be that."

I breathed. I felt cold, hollow. "So what now?"

"We've gone through the brunt of it. Should just be minor things now: hair growth, skin changes, eye-colour changes ... There is the possibility of another seizure, but that's unlikely now—they usually happen nearer the beginning of the change. I'd also like to not be naked, but best to wait until my body settles down a bit. Still feels like my insides are trembling."

I didn't look at him. I felt like *my* insides were trembling. I felt sick.

"Hey, Ange," he said softly. "Look at me." I did. "I'm all right. You were fantastic."

"I don't feel fantastic. I feel sick to my stomach. I mean, what the fuck was that? I knew it wasn't gonna be some magical transformation—your skin gets all shiny and then you're someone new—but I thought ..." I took a breath.

"Fuck, man."

He didn't say anything. He just smiled sympathetically. What could he have said, anyway? There wasn't a string of words in any language that could make me feel even one per cent better right now.

"You go through that every few days?" I asked.

"It's not usually that bad, but yes." He ran his hand over his head. "I do appreciate your help, Ange. Without you, I would have collapsed into my own sick multiple times, and I would have had a much harder time of getting into this wheelchair … But I understand if you never want to see that again."

"I don't *ever* want to see that again." I took a breath. "But I will. I told you I'd help you, that I'd stay with you, and I meant it. You don't have a choice; you have to go through that every time. But you won't have to go through it alone. Not anymore."

A smile broke through his long, stringy beard. "Right, so, be honest. How do I look?"

I appraised the skinny, wrinkly, naked man before me and grinned. "Old."

"Old? Well, shit. I was hoping I only sounded old."

I chuckled lifelessly. "Tough luck."

"Well, I hope I'm at least good-looking. Maybe a sixty-year-old silver fox."

"More of an eighty-year-old wizard."

He chuckled. "Well, I've had worse. I remember the day of the moon landing. I was so fucking old I was basically on death's door."

"Wait, what? You remember the moon landing? Like, you were alive when that happened?"

"Uh … possibly. I'm not sure. You know my long-term memory gets muddled with each change."

"Flynn, the moon landing was, like, five decades ago."

"Then I suppose these old bones and wrinkles are fitting," he chuckled, but he stopped when he saw that I wasn't laughing. "Is that weird for you?"

I looked at him. He seemed concerned. "In terms of you and me, no, I don't think so. But it does make me wonder. Your long-term memory is so unreliable; who knows how old you really are? If you're remembering correctly, and you were alive during the moon landing, you're probably over sixty years old. Maybe even older; who knows how much you can't remember? I mean, have you ever thought about that? Your body doesn't age, Flynn, it changes. You're an old man now, but in a few days, you might be a little girl. What's to stop you living for ever? How would you even know if you were? How much of your past have you forgotten? You could be 100, 200, 500 years old, and you wouldn't know it."

"Guess so," he said sombrely.

"What about a birth certificate? That would say when you were born."

"Don't have one. Not my proper one, at least. I have a few forgeries with different birthdays in case I need a birth certificate for something, but I don't remember what happened to my original one."

I stared blankly at the old man before me, the old enigma of a man. How did this happen? How did Flynn get like this?

LATER

By evening, Flynn had fully completed his change, and we had cleaned up all the mess. Flynn's legs were still paralysed, and we thought that would probably stick until the next change.

I was in the shower, finally allowing myself the time to relax and to clean the bloodstains off my face, neck, arms and legs. I closed my eyes and just let the water shower over me and caress my body.

After this, after what I'd seen today, I knew I had to make a decision. Either I was committed to this relationship, or I wasn't. Witnessing Flynn change was stronger than any proposal of marriage could ever be. That couldn't be unseen; it couldn't be ignored. This was the moment where, if I wanted to, I could walk away, never have to see that again, never have to worry like that again. I had a choice.

Or did I?

I'd already fallen in love with Flynn. Was there really any choice? Of course I would stay. Of course I would witness that horror a thousand times over.

I loved him.

It seemed Flynn thought the same as me. When we were getting ready for bed, he pulled something out of his pocket.

"What's that?" I asked.

"A key to my place," he said, "if you want it. Ange, you've seen a side of me that no one has ever seen. I trust you, more than anyone."

And with that, we were committed to each other.

7 July

It was noon on Friday, and Flynn and I were taking our weekly walk in Oak Corn Park. We tried to keep up my old little habit together, as we both enjoyed the nice stroll.

I walked beside Flynn as he rolled in his wheelchair. He was still an old man for now, but he was due for a change soon. I've had three days to recover from the last change, and it wasn't enough. I've had nightmares about it. I've been dreading the next change. But I haven't spoken to him about it. As hard as it is for me, it must be infinitely harder for Flynn. I needed to be strong, strong for him. I didn't want him to regret letting me into this part of his life by revealing to him how terrified I really was. I had to believe that the fear would pass. I had to know that I would get used to it. Flynn did; so could I.

I hadn't spoken to Kate in ages, or Mum, or Margaret. I've been spending a lot of time with Flynn, and I just didn't have the bandwidth right now, especially not since

I witnessed the change. I just needed some time, time for things to settle a little.

"Bit nippy today," said Flynn.

"Well, gramps, it is England. Summer comes just one week a year, don't it?"

He laughed. "Not sure how I feel about you calling me 'gramps.'"

"Well then, maybe you should get more young. I hear collagen is good for your skin. Maybe you can start there."

He tried to look offended, but he was smiling too much. "Well, that's a lovely idea, Ange, just brilliant. Too bad you've already cleaned out planet Earth with your supply of it."

"And it makes my skin look amazing. No complaints."

He shrugged. "Can't disagree with that."

I watched Flynn as he rolled his wheelchair effortlessly along the pavement. Despite how old he looked, he was spry and energetic.

"By the way," he said, "I finally started an audiobook."

"What? When?"

"On the way to renew my licence." That was what he said in public when he was talking about getting a forgery.

"Well, how'd you like it?"

"To be honest, whoever's narrating it sounds a bit robotic."

"They're not all made equally." I shrugged.

"The text-to-speech on my phone could have done a better job."

"Really? Why didn't you just use that, then?" I grinned. "Would've been free."

"Is it too much to ask for excellence?"

"Dunno. You might be pushing it there, gramps. Not everyone's as excellent as I am."

He chuckled. "I see what you did there."

"Yeah, thought I'd take the opportunity."

"Maybe you should get into voice-over work."

"Ugh, *non merci.*"

"Uh, *Oui.*"

"*Non. Ça sera très embarrassant.*"

"Well, that's the extent of my French knowledge," he laughed.

"That's what you should do; you should learn French."

He looked at me quizzically. "Ange, I can't even remember my own bloody birthday. You want me to learn a whole language?"

"Sure. Might be good. Help improve your memory. I swear that's what they say about Alzheimer's and stuff, that knowing a second language helps with that."

"Ange, look at me. I'm too old for that shit." He grinned, and I laughed.

"Maybe you should learn another language," he said. "Why stop at just French?"

"Well, I know a bit of Scots from my mum. Does that count?"

He shook his head. "I think you should learn Japanese."

"*Mou!*" I groaned.

"*Mou?* What's *mou?*"

"Like, the only Japanese word I know."

"Sounds like an exasperated grumble."

"That's exactly what it is." I grinned. "You can tell I come from a family of grumblers, innit?"

He laughed. "That's still a head start, though. I mean, you must know other things, too, like *konnichiwa* and *arigato*. Everyone knows those words."

"Sure, I guess. And I know *jii-chan* and *baa-chan*. That's what I call my grandparents."

"See? You've got a leg up on everyone else. You should do it."

"Yeah, okay, but I also know that Japanese has three different writing systems and, like, a million different ways to count something. I ain't doing that shit."

"Yeah, but you're smart. I think you'd pick all that up easily."

"*Mou.*"

"See? You're halfway there already."

I flicked him on the shoulder.

"As complicated as it is, though," I said, "I do think Japanese is quite a romantic-sounding language. People think French or Italian sounds romantic, but those people have never heard someone whisper to them, *Uun, kowakunai.*" I did my best to say it in a sexy whisper, and judging by the look on his face, I did it well enough.

"Right. Fair point," he said. "What does that mean?"

"I dunno. Heard it in a film once."

"And you're sure you don't want to learn even a little Japanese?"

"Why, so I can whisper seductively in your ear?"

"I wouldn't be opposed."

I chuckled. He opened his mouth to say something, but I stopped him. "That's not a giggle; I'm chuckling."

"Did I say anything?"

"You were about to."

"I didn't say anything."

We came up to the pond in the centre of the park and sat at a bench there for a bit.

"This pond is lovely," said Flynn. "I should paint it one day."

"You should," I encouraged, but I was grinning as well.

"What? You don't think I can?"

"No, you can, but you've not picked up a brush in how long?"

"What are you on about? I painted something last week."

"Really? Where is it?"

"Well, I didn't finish it."

I nodded. "You didn't finish it? Interesting."

"I'm a mood artist, Ange. I work when I feel inspired."

"You keep telling yourself that."

He rolled his eyes. "What was that word you used again? Moo?"

"*Mou.*"

He nodded. "Right. That."

Just then, a woman walked by and looked at us. She had

a huge smile that crinkled her eyes. "So sorry to bother you," she said. "I just wanted to say I think it's absolutely lovely that you're out with him. I love to see the younger generation spending time with their elders instead of cricking their necks looking at their phones." She eyed Flynn's wheelchair. "Just lovely." Then she left.

Flynn and I looked at each other and laughed. Then I stood behind him, wrapped my arms around his neck, and kissed his head. "Come on, gramps," I said. "Let's get you home so you can slip on your orthopaedics and complain about what this world is coming to."

19 July

Flynn and I were sitting across from each other on the sofa, as we often did. We were both doing our own thing: I was working on a new manuscript, and Flynn was painting (probably sticking it to me for what I said two weeks ago).

We usually had our feet intertwined when we sat like this, but Flynn was a teenage boy today, and that came with a teenage boy's sex drive. It was easier for him to manage if we weren't touching. As he once told me: *preferably, I'd like to not spend the* whole *day with an erection.*

The abstinence wasn't just because I didn't particularly want to sleep with a teenager, but also because having a sex drive that doesn't align with your sexuality can make sex difficult to enjoy. I understood how he felt. Sometimes I forget, but I was once tortured by a male sex drive, too, and back then, I didn't want to enjoy and explore my sexuality; I wanted it gone. Just one of the things transitioning has made easier for me.

I peeked at Flynn and smiled. He had a canvas propped up on his thighs, and the rest of his paint supplies were on the floor next to him. He reached down periodically to clean his brushes and switch paint colours.

"What you smiling at?" he asked me.

"You. Your pimples and ginger bumfluff. You're adorable."

He stuck his tongue out at me.

"How old do you think you are now, anyway?"

"I don't know. Seventeen, maybe," he squeaked.

"Mmm, that voice says thirteen."

He squinted at me. "So is this just gonna be our lives now, you slagging me off any chance you can get?"

"Well, that is my love language." I grinned. "What are you painting?"

He hesitated.

"What, is it a secret?"

"It's not very good," he argued.

"No, you can't pull that shit with me. I see your artwork hanging all over this house; I know it's good."

"This one isn't ready."

"So? You can still tell me what it is."

"You won't let this go, will you?"

"Not planning on it, no."

He sighed and turned the canvas for me to see. It was

me. He was painting a picture of me as he saw me now, working on my laptop.

"Doesn't matter how good I may be," he said, "this one will never look as good as the real thing."

I stared at my likeness for a little longer, and then I said, "Don't sell yourself short, Flynn."

5 August

My flat felt very alien these days. I'd been spending most of my time with Flynn, so this little flat didn't really feel like my home anymore. But I had to admit, it was good to have a place away from Flynn sometimes. I used to only really come here whenever Flynn would change, but now they've let me into that part of their life, I find myself coming back here every now and then to separate myself from those changes. To escape. Sometimes, I just needed a break. The changes weren't always as horrible as when I'd first seen them—sometimes it was just fainting, being sick, and the crunch of bones being rearranged—but it always felt like losing another version of Flynn, like a horrible, bloody murder. And those faces never came back. Flynn said once that they repeat rarely, but the most I've ever seen was a nose that looked vaguely familiar.

I felt like a war veteran. I had seen the people I love die so many times. Every few days: blood, sick, crunch, crack … grief. But don't grieve too long because you only have a few days to be with this new version of Flynn before they are killed in a violent contortion of the human body. I was having nightmares all the time. I couldn't stop thinking of the blood and bile. I never could have imagined that loving a shapeshifter also meant grieving them just as much. Being with them was so difficult, and yet, it was also so easy. I couldn't breathe, and yet, Flynn was the only reason I could breathe clearly.

I took these little breaks in my flat to de-stress. Maybe one day I would develop a tolerance for it like Flynn seemed to have, but for now, I needed time to myself, or else I just might scream.

There was a knock at the door. It was probably Mandip. I hadn't seen her in ages; she must want to catch up.

I opened the door and was met with a blonde, cross-armed woman.

"Kate?" I said.

"Where the fuck have you been?" she seethed.

"What do you mean?"

"I text you, and you don't respond. I call you, and you fob me off. The last time I saw you in person was two fucking months ago. And believe it or not, this is not the first time I've knocked on this door. You're never here, Ange. I was this close to going to that boyfriend-of-yours's place and paying him the fucking ransom."

"Kate, don't exaggerate."

She pushed past me roughly.

"Where are you going?"

She sat herself down on the sofa in a huff. "Come on.

Sit. You and I are gonna have this out. I'm not leaving until we do."

I closed the door and sighed, striding over to sit next to her.

"Why are you ignoring me?" she started.

"I'm not ignoring you, Kate."

"Then why aren't you answering any of my texts? Why are you avoiding me as if I've done something to you?"

"I'm not, Kate. I'm just busy."

"With him."

"Is that a problem?"

"Yeah, actually, maybe it is, if he's making you forget who your family are."

"He's not making me do anything. You're so fucking dramatic, Kate."

"Yeah, and you're a fucking bitch."

"What is the matter with you, Kate? How am I a bitch now?"

"When I started going out with Bridget, did I stop texting you? Did I stop ringing you? Did I ever cut you out of my life?"

"I haven't cut you out of my life, Kate."

"You may as well have. It's all about Flynn now, innit? You don't have time for me anymore."

"Oh, naff off, Kate." I got up.

"Don't walk away from me. I'm not finished."

"Yeah? Well, maybe I am. Maybe I don't feel like putting up with your bullshit. Knocking down my door and screaming at me, acting like I betrayed you or some shit."

"No, you didn't betray me, Ange, you abandoned me."

"Abandoned? You are so fucking dramatic," I scoffed. "Never changes, does it? Ever since we were little, you get one tiny thought in your head and dramatise the shit out of it until you've turned it into something it's not. Guess what, Kate, not everything has to do with you. I didn't abandon you; I'm just busy."

"Busy with what?"

"It doesn't matter."

She forced herself to take a breath. "You know what you are, Ange?"

"What?" I challenged.

"You're a shit sister."

"I'm a shit sister?"

"Yeah, you bloody well are."

That was it for me. That was the end of my tether. "You know what? I'm sorry you fucking hate me so much. I'm sorry I'm apparently such a bad sister now. I'm sorry I don't have the energy to keep up with Kate every two seconds. And I'm sorry I'm too preoccupied by the fact that I have to watch my fucking boyfriend die in front of me every three days!"

There was silence. And then Kate said, "What?"

Fuck.

I sat next to her and sighed. "Never mind."

"No, no, you can't take that back. Ange, what's wrong? What do you mean you're watching him die in front of you?"

I bit my lip. "It's not my place to say."

"But it is my place to know what's happening with my sister."

I looked at her.

"Even a shit sister is still a sister," she admitted. "Spill."

I took a breath. She wouldn't let this go, and I couldn't come up with a convincing lie. I had to tell her. "Flynn has an illness."

"What sort of illness."

"A weird one."

"It's not contagious, is it? Not like an STI or something?"

"What? No. No, I'm fine. He hasn't passed anything onto me."

"Then what?"

I took another breath. "I know you're not gonna believe me, but he's a shapeshifter."

"A shapeshifter?" she repeated suspiciously.

"Yes." I breathed again. I couldn't believe what I was saying. "He has an illness that makes him change every few days—age, sex, ethnicity, everything."

Kate looked at me very seriously and asked, "Are you on something?"

"No."

"I'm not fucking playing with you, Ange. Whatever shit you're on, it's fucking with your mind."

"I'm not taking drugs, Kate. Listen to me. This is why he kicked me out when we first slept together. He was being sick, and I even thought his voice sounded different then. That's because it wasn't his voice. He was changing, Kate, and he didn't want me to see."

Kate nodded and took out her phone, but I quickly plucked it from her hands.

"Ange, give me back my phone."

"No, you're gonna call emergency or something."

"Well, what do you expect me to do? You've clearly lost the plot."

I put the phone out of her reach. "Just listen. Can you do that?"

Her eyes locked onto her phone, and she suddenly lunged at me to get to it. "Kate! Kate, stop! Listen!" I yelled. I got the upper hand and held her down. "Just listen. Please."

Once I got her to calm down, I ran through everything with her, everything Flynn and I have been through, every detail about how gruesome the changes were, though my words could never do it justice.

Kate looked at me, mulling things over. "Ange, I get it; that sounds rough. But it doesn't convince me that you're not off your rocker."

"Oh, Kate, come on."

"I'm serious, Ange. I'm worried about you. People can't shapeshift. You know that. The fact that you would come up with this … really fucked-up story about a shapeshifter out of a fucking horror film, it's mental."

"Kate, please. I'm begging you, as your sister, trust me. I'm sane. I'm sober. I swear to you on both our mums. I swear to you on the time we lived together when my dad kicked me out … I'm struggling. I admit, I'm struggling. I never meant to make you feel like I'd abandoned you, Kate. I need my sister; I need you to believe me. I love Flynn so much, but I can't breathe. My insides are screaming. And I just need …"

"Someone to lean on," she finished.

I nodded, and she hugged me. And suddenly, I was a teenager again, leaning on the one person in the world who's always been there for me. And I cried because I'd abandoned her. I didn't mean to, but I did.

"I'm here, Ange," she said. "I'm not saying I don't believe you, but I think I need to see for myself. I want to meet him."

6 August

It was Sunday evening, and Flynn and I were snuggled up together on the sofa, watching a film. Today, Flynn was a muscular, South Asian man with subtle flecks of grey in his hair.

We were in sync today, and all I wanted was to just enjoy that, to feel alive with him. But I couldn't. I tried. I tried all day. But my argument with Kate yesterday loomed over me, and it meant I had to talk to Flynn about it. He wasn't going to like that I told her about his condition. I'd had my day with him, a day where we were perfectly matched, but now the day was over. Time to tell him.

"So, Flynn," I said, playing with his fingers, which he had draped over my shoulder.

"Yeah?"

"You know Kate? My friend?"

"Um, is she the one you stayed with when your dad kicked you out?"

"Yep, that's her. She came by my flat yesterday."

"Yeah?"

"Yeah, haven't seen her in a while, have I? And … she was not happy."

"Because you haven't been seeing each other?"

"She said I abandoned her."

He nodded. "Guess I can see that. We have been spending a lot of time together. And from what you've told me about your history with her, I guess I can understand why she'd feel that way. 'Abandoned' is a bit of a strong word, though."

"No, it's fair. I've barely been texting her. I've fobbed her off every time she's called."

"Why?"

I peeked at him. He was staring at me, concerned. "To be honest, I've been having a hard time with your changes. But I didn't want to say anything because I didn't want you to think I couldn't handle it. I don't want you to think you made a mistake in telling me. You didn't. But it's just so hard to see you like that, and I just need some space from time to time, from everything. I just needed time to myself, and I didn't have the energy to keep up with my relationship with Kate."

Flynn was silent for a second, and then he said, "I have a hard time with my changes, too. Sometimes I get nightmares about it."

"Me too."

"But I wanted to seem like it didn't affect me to help you feel more at ease about it."

"So you've been doing the same thing I've been doing?"

He nodded. "I understand, Ange. It's scary." He kissed the top of my head and sighed. "I'm not like other people. To share my life with someone is to subject them to my condition, to afflict them with the same pain I've always felt. And I'm sorry I've put you through that."

"No. No, you didn't put me through anything, Flynn. Don't blame yourself. I bumped into you, remember. I invited you out. I came back after you ghosted me. I'm here because I chose to be, Flynn. And I don't care how hard it is, how much it hurts to see you change, I don't regret being with you. Ever."

He held me tighter, and I relaxed into his embrace. But then he said, "Was your argument with Kate bad?" and I suddenly remembered why I'd started this conversation in the first place.

"Um, you know. Kate and I are like sisters, and sometimes we fight like sisters. It's no big deal, and she was right to be mad at me. We screamed at each other, she tackled me once, and I … told her about you." I whispered the last bit, but Flynn heard it loud and clear.

He pulled away from me. "You what? What do you mean you told her about me?"

"Not on purpose," I defended. "We were arguing; it just slipped out, and then she wouldn't let it go."

"You told her about my condition?"

"Yes?" I was too cowardly to say that as a statement.

He stood up. "Oh, fucking hell. Come on, Ange."

"I didn't mean to. I'm sorry."

"You know you can't tell people."

"I know. I know. I'm sorry. But Kate won't tell anyone else. You can trust her."

"I trusted you, and you still told her."

"Are you saying you don't trust me?"

He sighed and rubbed his eyes. "No. No, of course I trust you." He sat back down.

"Flynn, I'm sorry. It was an accident. I really didn't mean to tell her. But is it really so bad if other people know? I mean, you have an illness; you're not a demon."

"The slaves out of Africa weren't demons. Poor and disabled people, they're not demons." He looked right at me. "You're not a demon, Ange. But that doesn't stop anyone from trying to get rid of the people they don't like, does it? You slipped up and told Kate, and maybe Kate understands. But what if she slips up and tells someone? And what if that someone tells someone else? Before you know it, it gets out that there's a witch in Thivleton. A monster. Someone who is undetectable. Someone who could rob a bank, rape a child, murder a family, and never be found. You can't catch a person who can change their face, their voice, their thumbprint. Then people get scared. They become afraid. And suddenly it becomes justifiable to attack a human being's right to exist based on a hypothetical fear."

I looked at him, at how serious his expression was. "That's not a hypothetical, is it? That's actually happened to you."

He considered for a second and then shook his head. "I don't know. I can't remember. Maybe some of it happened, maybe all of it, or maybe I just dreamt it once. But it's not an absurd fear, Ange; you know that."

I thought about the prejudice I've faced in my life due to my being trans. I knew all too well what fear and hatred could make people do, what lies ignorance could make people believe. "I know. You're right. I get it … Look, Flynn, I'm sorry. I'm so sorry. It was an accident. But Kate's my sister; she cares about me, and that means she cares about you, too … and she wants to meet you."

He looked at me dubiously.

"What's done is done, Flynn. I can't take it back. Kate's just worried about me. She wants to know the person I've given my heart to. You can trust her. I promise."

12 August

It was Saturday, and Flynn and I planned to meet up with Kate in Thivleton Centre, the largest shopping centre in town.

Today, Flynn was a middle-aged South Asian woman with a very serious expression that was largely undermined by her cute button nose. She was also quite a bit taller than me. I'm sure people thought she was a model.

We met Kate in the food court, and she instantly hugged me and kissed my cheek. Then she stepped back to appraise the tall woman next to me.

I introduced them. "Flynn, this is Kate. And, Kate, this is Flynn."

Kate's eyes were wide. "Whoa. Nothing like the guy you described to me, Ange."

"No, not at all," Flynn agreed with a smile.

"All right, so, am I to still consider you a man, like, use he/him?" Kate asked Flynn.

"Think of me however you like. I don't really care."

"She's just Flynn," I added. "I change the pronouns I use for them all the time, so join the club."

"All right, then, Flynn," said Kate, "shall we get something to eat and have a little chat?"

"Sounds very menacing," said Flynn. "Lead the way."

We all queued up to get some Indian food and then sat down at a table, Flynn and me on one side, and Kate on the other.

"Right," said Kate, tying her hair up as we all started to eat. "Let the grilling begin."

"Kate, you don't have to interrogate her," I said.

"You stay out of this, kitten."

"Please, interrogate me all you want," said Flynn. "Ange says you're trustworthy, so ask me whatever you need to."

"Do you love her?" asked Kate quickly.

"Yes." Flynn's answer was just as quick.

"And you understand that she is my sister, and if you hurt her in any way, I will find you and cut you?"

Flynn smiled. "Noted."

"Are you satisfying her in the bedroom?"

"Kate!" I snapped.

"The grown-ups are speaking, kitten. Hush. Flynn, is she satisfied in the bedroom?"

"I certainly hope so," Flynn chuckled.

Kate raised her eyebrows. "You don't know?"

"Well, I imagine that's something you'll have to ask her. As far as she's told me, though, she's very satisfied."

Kate smiled. "Good answer."

"Kill me," I grumbled.

"You don't have to be here if you don't want to be, kitten. Why don't you pop off and get yourself some sweets."

"I'm not going anywhere, Kate. I have to mediate this exchange."

She laughed. "Oh, it's cute you think you have any authority here."

I went red and shut up.

"Good girl," Kate praised. "Now, back to it, Flynn. Ange tells me you have an illness."

"Yes," Flynn nodded.

"Contagious?"

"Not that I'm aware."

"Then how were you affected?"

"Don't remember."

"Yeah. Ange mentioned it affects your long-term. That's quite convenient, innit?"

"Depends on your perspective. I find it quite inconvenient most of the time."

"Do you now?"

"Well, how would you like it if you couldn't remember how old you are or where you were born?"

"You don't know how old you are?"

"No."

Kate stared at Flynn. "So you could be really old, then. Like, ninety."

"It's possible, yes."

"What's the oldest memory you have?"

"I don't know. When were flip phones a thing?"

"That's the oldest thing you remember?"

"I think so, yeah."

Kate sat back. "Interesting. Because Ange told me that you remember the moon landing."

"No I don't."

Kate looked at me.

"Flynn gets her memories muddled with each change," I explained. "She did say to me once that she remembered being alive during the moon landing. She's probably just forgotten."

Flynn stared at me, absolutely astonished.

"You did tell me that," I confirmed. I could only imagine how strange that must have felt for her. Before, if Flynn forgot something, then she forgot it. But now I was here. Now I could remember the things she couldn't. I could know things about her that she didn't.

"All right, muddled memory," said Kate, seemingly convinced. "So I see. What about your changes, Flynn? How does that work?"

"Every few days, I change into someone new."

"Yes, Ange has already told me that. You're age changes, too, yeah?"

"That's right."

"What's the age range?"

"Um … nine-ish to eighty-ish, maybe. But who knows what I can't remember?"

"And your whole physiology changes? So, if you're nine, you are biologically a nine-year-old?"

"I keep the same mind, but yes, my body is nine years old."

"So you don't age, then? You're just reborn like a phoenix?"

Flynn shrugged. "It's not that glamorous, but I suppose so."

"So you'll never live to death like the rest of us. You'll outlive us all."

Flynn shrugged again. "It's possible."

"It's possible?"

"I'm not sure. Maybe one day I reach an age limit and

die, or maybe not. I really don't know."

Kate thought for a second. "If you were to get hurt, and then you changed, would your injury heal, or would you still have it on the next body?"

"It would heal."

I looked at Flynn curiously. I never realised that.

"So, your changes are sort of like regenerating," said Kate. "You're like a lizard shedding its skin or growing back its tail."

"I suppose."

"So I wonder, then, if this isn't like some sort of natural defence mechanism."

Flynn pondered. "I'd never considered that."

"What happens if you catch cold?"

"Usually … forces a change. Shit, I think you're on to something."

Kate relaxed into her seat. "I read a lot of mystery novels."

Suddenly, Flynn held her stomach and groaned.

"You okay?" I asked her.

"Yeah." She groaned again. "I think maybe this food's not agreeing with me. I'm gonna pop to the loo. I'll see you two in a bit." She got up and left us.

"Right, first things first," said Kate after Flynn was gone, "Flynn is mad fit."

I chuckled. "Better take her in while you have the chance. That body won't last long."

"How's that working for you, then, babes? You going ambisextrous on me?"

"No, I'm still straight. But I like Flynn, you know? It doesn't really matter to me what they look like."

"Do Flynn's genitals change, too?"

"Come on, Kate, behave."

"Make me, kitten." She winked at me and then stared me down with a grin.

"Yes, their genitals change," I admitted.

"Well, that's quite something." I could tell she was imagining the implications of that.

"Oi, stop it, or I'll tell Bridget you're fantasising about another person."

"Go ahead. Bridget doesn't care who I think about. She knows I love her, and she's not the jealous sort."

I puffed the air out of my cheeks. Kate just loved to wind me up.

She grinned at me.

"What?" I asked.

"Nothing. Just thinking about you and Flynn, and how you have the audacity to say you're still straight."

"I am straight."

"Babes, if you're dating the woman I just saw, your 'straight' has a kink in it. You're straight with added seasoning."

I smiled. "Are you done?"

"My little sister was in a rut, and now she's found a shapeshifter to fall in love with," she said. "That is quite the story … if it's real."

"Seriously? You're still doubting it? Flynn looks

nothing like how I described before."

"How would I know? This is the first I'm seeing them."

"I'm not lying to you, Kate."

"I'm not saying you are. And I do believe something's going on here, but shapeshifting? I want to see it first."

"Trust me; you don't."

"Not the change itself … your description was enough." She shivered. "I just want to see the next body for myself. Then I think I'll have enough to believe this whole thing."

I got a text then. It was Flynn:

Can you come to the women's for a second? Need your help.

I got up. "I'll be back, Kate. I have to go check on Flynn."

"Everything all right?"

"Not sure."

"Well, you'd better not be sneaking off to shag her in the cubicle. I ain't fucking waiting for that."

"Do one, Kate," I yelled back at her as I made my way to the women's toilets.

When I got there, all I saw was some woman washing her hands. I didn't see Flynn anywhere. I looked at the woman and thought for a second. "Flynn?" I said. She didn't respond; Flynn wasn't her. But there was a tap at one of the cubicle doors.

The woman finished washing her hands and then walked over to me, whispering, "Whoever's in that cubicle over there isn't doing so well. Proper sick, that one. Maybe that's who you're looking for?"

I looked at the cubicle she was pointing to. "Cheers."

She patted my shoulder and walked out.

I went over to the cubicle and knocked. "Flynn, you in there?"

"Ange, we have a problem."

Oh no.

Oh, no, no, no, no.

"Can I come in?" I asked.

Flynn simply unlocked the cubicle.

I opened the door, slipped inside, and closed it back. The toilet was full of sick and a little blood, and there was an old man with long, greasy hair sat at my feet.

I shook my head. "No."

"I'm afraid so," he said deeply.

I shushed him quickly. "Stay quiet. We're in the women's, remember, and you sound like Father Christmas."

He nodded silently.

I looked at him. His clothes weren't too feminine. That was a good thing and a bad thing. Good because it would attract less attention; bad because they didn't make him pass for a woman, and we still had to get out of this bathroom.

I rubbed my face. "Flynn, I thought you could tell when the change was coming."

"So did I," he whispered. "This is new."

"Are you finished changing, do you think?"

"Not sure. Most of it's done, but not sure if these will

stay." He put his hands to his sides and pumped out his chest, displaying his plump, round boobs.

"Oh, fuck," I sighed. "Are they bigger than before? I didn't think that happened. That's an in-between change; isn't it supposed to be halfway between male and female?"

"I never said that. Everything changes separately from each other. It's biological, natural, and nature doesn't play by society's rules. If it wants me to have a masculine body with a feminine chest, then I'm a man with boobs and that's that. Actually, can you help me get my bra off? It's a little tight."

I shook my head and sighed. "Stand up."

He did so, and he turned his back to me. I lifted his shirt and unhooked his bra.

"Oh, that's better. Thanks." He sighed and looked at the toilet, at all the blood and sick in it. "Kind of looks like one epic period, innit?"

"Can we not joke about this, Flynn?"

"Sorry."

I could hear someone coming into the bathroom.

"We have to get you home," I said.

"Right. I could use a binder, though."

I looked at his boobs. "Yeah, you could. I'll text Kate. There's a shop called Queer Corpus here. She can buy you a binder and bring it to us." I started texting her. "What size do you think you are?"

He took some rough finger measurements. "I don't know. Maybe a large?"

I shrugged and took his word for it. I knew nothing about chest binders.

When I finished texting Kate, she responded with:

No problem, baby girl. Can't wait to see this.

"Right, Kate's on her way. But even once we get your chest under control, you still look like a guy."

"Do I look old enough to be your grandfather?"

"I guess so."

"Okay, so maybe I'm your grandfather, and I got a little confused. You came in here to help me out."

"Okay. Okay, yeah. Let's go with that."

We flushed the toilet and cleaned up a little. Luckily, this change wasn't as violent or messy as it could have been.

"Ange," called a voice. It was Kate.

I opened the cubicle door a crack and beckoned her over.

"Do you have the binder?" I whispered.

She handed it to me discreetly while I eyed the other women glancing over to see what was going on.

"Thanks, Kate. Granddad just got a little confused, ended up in the wrong place. Wait here for a bit. Just need to help him out."

My eyes filled in the blanks of that story for Kate. She nodded.

I closed the cubicle door. "All right, gramps. It's okay; you just got a bit turned around. Let's get you home."

As I helped Flynn into the binder, I whispered to him,

"How are you, though? You in pain?"

He shook his head. "This one was quick."

"Thank God. It could have been so much worse."

I pulled his shirt back down and appraised his chest. "Flat enough," I said, not at all confidently.

He held my shoulders and kissed my forehead. "Let's go."

I opened the door. "Come on, gramps. You're not supposed to be in here."

I walked out the cubicle holding Flynn's hand, and Flynn acted as though he wasn't entirely certain where he was.

"Fuck me!" said Kate when she saw the old man I walked out with.

Everyone immediately looked at us.

"Kate," I whispered harshly.

She instantly realised what she had done and said, "Uh … there you two are. Got lost again, granddad?"

"Seems so," said Flynn.

Kate took a second to take in how deep his voice was now, then she turned to the women looking at us. "Sorry if our granddad made any of you uncomfortable. He's a little sick. Come on, granddad."

Then we all walked out.

Kate offered to drive us home, and when we got to her car, she took me aside as Flynn was getting in and hugged me.

"All's forgiven," she said. "I believe you."

18 September

Things have been really good now that Kate knows. She and Flynn have become friends. Sometimes they even talked and spent time together without me, which defo meant they were spending at least some of that time talking about me. What are sisters for, I guess?

Flynn gave Kate permission to tell Bridget about their illness. Bridget took it pretty well. She was full Bridget about the whole thing—laid-back and go-with-the-flow. Guess it's easier to believe when both me and Kate can back up the same story. Unlike either of us, though, she didn't demand proof. She took it all at face value. Just Bridget being Bridget.

So now Flynn and I weren't alone in all this. The four of us were a little community that stuck together to make dealing with Flynn's illness a little easier. I had people I could talk to without Flynn, and Flynn had people they could talk to without me, and that really helped ease the stress in our relationship.

So things have been good, or as good as they can be. It's still hard sometimes. I don't like waking up and finding Flynn passed out on the floor in a puddle of sick with an exposed neck bone from where the skin hadn't finished growing. I didn't like when Flynn was unhappy with the body they had. They say they're fine with whatever body they're in, but sometimes I notice they don't talk as much because they don't like their voice. Or during sex, they seem distant, and I can feel that. There'll always be challenges with Flynn, but we were in a good place now.

We've also discussed Kate's theory, how Flynn's changes might be some sort of defence mechanism. Flynn got a stomach bug a week ago and started changing instantly. I wondered if a similar thing had happened when we were at the shopping centre with Kate. We talked about it multiple times until one of Flynn's changes came with a memory: The illness wasn't natural; it was done to them. Flynn suddenly remembered one day, and it wasn't an event they wanted to remember. I couldn't get anything more out of them. They didn't want a conversation; they didn't want to think about it. It must have been a painful memory. But now I knew that shapeshifters weren't born, they weren't even infected, they were created. By who? Why? We haven't talked about it since, and Flynn has changed again, so the memory is gone.

Today, Flynn was a young teenage girl with lanky arms and freckles. She moved a little awkwardly, not yet used to the body. It was late Monday evening, and we were watching Bridget's stream together, casting it from my phone to the television screen.

"All right, chat," said Bridget, swivelling in her chair with her feet up. "How are you lot doing?" She read the responses. "'*Good.*' '*Good.*' '*Better now you're here.*' Aw, thanks. '*Good.*' '*Excellent.*' '*Terrible.*' Well, don't tell people that." She winked and flicked her hair back. "Anyway, chat, we're gonna have fun today. We'll talk, I'll get dressed, maybe react to some things. Good fun … '*First time here. Had no idea you were British.*' Yep, Thivleton, England: the shithole no one's ever heard of. '*Where's Kate?*' The bitch wife is currently playing a new game, but I'll get her to come to stream later on."

"So this is Kate's wife?" asked Flynn.

"Girlfriend," I corrected. "But honestly, they're basically married in every way except on paper."

"Why does she keep winking and flicking her hair back?"

"They're tics. She's got Tourette's."

Flynn looked at me, concerned, and I immediately knew why.

"Yeah, she does blurt out random shit sometimes," I explained. "She's very unlikely to blurt out that she knows a shapeshifter, but even if she does, people will assume it's not real. I mean, she used to have a tic where she proclaimed she was a Nazi. People know she doesn't always mean what she says. You're fine."

"Okay. If you say so." Flynn's face was uncertain, but she trusted me enough now to follow my lead. If I trusted Bridget, then so would she.

"All right, chat," Bridget continued, "I am going to get dressed now. Well, I'm gonna do makeup, actually. But I'll also put on this punk jacket with spikes on the shoulders, so kinda getting dressed.

"Anyway, got a story for you while I do the makeup. So,

contrary to what you may think, between me and the bitch wife, I am a total pussy when it comes to bugs in the house. I know, I may call her my bitch wife, but Kate saves my scared arse all the time—Pop your trainers on!—Sorry. So we were watching television the other night, and when I say a massive spider showed up, like, clearly escaped from the laboratory of a mad scientist. And, chat, I was so fucking scared, I literally leapt into the air, and she caught me in her arms … Exactly, chat, like a damsel in distress; proper off-brand for me and my patented masculine femininity.

"So there I was, in Kate's arms, but, chat, don't get me wrong, I was the fucking hero here. I stuck out my legs and said to Kate—Pop your trainers on." She laughed at her own tic. "No, sorry, didn't say that. I said, 'Kate, I'm your weapon. Aim me.' And, you know, chat, I was one brave fucker. I let her just launch me at the wall, foot in the air, and I crushed the spider with my jacked heel."

"Bullshit," came Kate's voice as she entered the stream, sitting down in a chair next to Bridget.

"Ey, look, chat, it's the bitch wife. Everyone, say hi to Kate."

"Hey, chat." Kate waved to the camera. "Don't believe a word Bridget tells you. She's a fucking liar. What actually happened is—"

"Exactly what I said, obviously," said Bridget, but Kate flicked her on the head, and she shut up.

"As I was saying, she jumped into my arms, kicking and

screaming like a scared little child, and I just moved her forward, and her kicking feet squished the spider."

"That's not what happened," Bridget grumbled.

Someone donated and had their comment read out loud: **Sorry, Bridget, but it sounds like you were the bitch wife in this scenario. Kate was definitely wearing the pants in the relationship there.**

"Thanks for the ten-dollar donation," said Bridget. "And fuck you; I was brave."

"What's ten dollars in sterling?" Kate whispered to Bridget.

"Depends whose dollars it is. Let's see … looks like CAD. Canada."

"Is that good?"

Bridget shrugged. "It's all right. Not as good as USD."

"All right, chat," said Kate, "any Americans out there, if we get enough donations in USD, maybe I can convince Bridget to wear a packer."

"What? No. No, don't promise that." She flicked her hair back.

"Yes. Where are Bridget's mods at? Set up a donation goal for, say, 1000 USD, and if we reach that, I'll get her to wear a packer. And not just stuffing a sock down her pants, I mean a proper silicone penis."

"Kate, don't promise that. I'm not doing that."

The thousand-dollar donation goal was posted.

"What the hell? Mods, which one of you did that? I'm the one who pays you, remember, not Kate. I'm the one you take orders from."

The first donation to the goal was made, and the comment was read out: **Looks like Bridget is the real bitch wife. Kate just took control of the stream and is a good businesswoman to boot. Giving chat what they want. Let's get Bridget wearing a packer.**

"Looks like you'll be wearing it after all," said Kate as the donation goal got closer to being reached.

Bridget crossed her arms. "This is such bullshit."

"Oh, shut up, acting like it's so terrible."

"It is terrible, actually."

"Oh yeah? Then why do you even own any packers if you didn't want to wear them?"

"'Cause someone in chat sent one to me; I didn't buy that shit."

"The fuck are you on about? You own five of them."

"Pop your trainers on—Same answer." She folded her arms.

Kate looked at the camera. "Really, chat? You've sent her five packers?"

"Most of them are massive, too," Bridget complained. "I'm a pretty small girl. Even if I did have a dick, it wouldn't be that big, I mean, come on."

"You saying you don't have big-dick energy?"

"Absolutely not. More like little knob vibes."

Flynn laughed at that, and I couldn't help but laugh, too.

A donation was made to have a comment read out

loud: **Bridget is far more likely to have big-dick energy because she'll never have big-tits energy**.

Bridget put her hand to her heart, pretending to be offended. "Wow, man, right to my core. Thank God I don't have big tits, though. It would be so much harder to cross-dress if I did."

Kate started laughing.

"I don't know what you're laughing about. You love my tits."

Kate couldn't stop laughing. She shook her head and pointed to something on the screen.

The thousand-dollar donation goal had been met.

"Oh, fuck me," Bridget grumbled.

"Nice one, chat," said Kate. "You should wear the one you can pee out of, Bridget. Stream just started; you're gonna be wearing it for a while."

Bridget got up begrudgingly to rustle through her stuff off-camera, and after around twenty minutes, she had fully changed into her guy fit, complete with fake beard stubble and a bulge in her trousers from the packer.

"All right, chat, here's the fit. Full guy mode … with the bloody packer."

I watched Flynn watching with intrigue. After this, she started watching Bridget's streams all the time, often donating and commenting. I liked to imagine it made her feel seen. Bridget was a cross-dresser, and even though that wasn't the same as Flynn's shapeshifting, it was close enough.

We were both really grateful to have Kate and Bridget in our lives. They had our backs, and they understood us. They were family.

30 September

It was Saturday, and Flynn and I had invited over Kate and Bridget for dinner. Today, Flynn was a pleasant-looking, dark-skinned Asian woman—the closest we've ever gotten to looking related. My skin was darker than hers, and she had more typically East Asian features than I did, but maybe we could pass quite easily for half-sisters.

We told Kate and Bridget to come around three, as we planned on cooking together. They didn't get here until half-three, though. Kate's fault; she likes to spend too much time getting ready. Unlike Bridget, who would just throw anything on and call it an outfit.

When they did arrive, I hugged Kate in greeting. Bridget shook Flynn's hand; this was the first time they were meeting in person. Bridget looked at the patch of milky-white skin on Flynn's arm—leftover from her last change—and nodded, saying, "Sick."

"This house is sick," said Kate, staring at the stone walls.

We were all going to make a big, French meal. Well, we'd try at least. There were a few open cookbooks and a few open recipe websites. We wanted to make quiche, croissants, soupe à l'oignon, and a chocolate soufflé. We also added some leftover steak that we chose to call *bœuf* to fit the theme.

When we realised how long some of that shit takes to make from scratch, we had to send Kate out to the shops to get some pre-made pastry dough. Some of the food (like the croissants that came out of a can) turned out well; others (like the soufflé) were a disaster. But it was fun all the same.

We all sat down at the table together, basking in our cooking victories and suffering in our culinary defeats.

Bridget scrunched her nose as she ate, the only one of her tics I'd seen tonight. She must have been having a light tic day.

"So, we didn't do too badly, did we?" said Flynn, taking a bite of her quiche.

"Better than my brother's cooking, innit, Kate?" said Bridget.

That made Kate almost choke on her food. "I should hope so. Your brother cooks like a fucking caveman."

"My brother is a fucking caveman," Bridget corrected.

"What's that make you Bridget?" I asked.

"Hey, believe it or not, I work hard to pull off this no-fucks-given masculine persona. Dane's just naturally gross and dumb."

"No love lost between you two, then," said Flynn.

"Oh, no," added Kate. "We love when he pops in unannounced needing a place to crash for the night. Really keeps us on our toes."

"How's your brother, Ange?" asked Bridget.

I shrugged. "Only ever hear from him when a big life event happens, so I guess same old."

"I didn't know you had a brother, Ange," said Flynn.

"Yeah. He lives in Ireland with his wife. He kinda does his own thing; doesn't keep in touch with the family too much. Short of pregnancy or something like that, I probably won't hear from him till Christmas."

"What about you, Flynn?" asked Bridget. "You got siblings?"

Flynn thought for a second, and Kate and I watched intently, wondering if she would unearth a new memory from her past, but we weren't so lucky.

"Don't think so, no," she said. "Just my parents who passed a while back."

"Oh, man, sorry to hear that."

"Don't be. They were horrible to me."

That was something. Flynn doesn't always remember how she feels about her parents or anything about what they were like, really. Those memories only come up every once in a while. I wanted to delve into that, especially since Flynn would likely forget by tomorrow, but we all silently and collectively agreed that that wasn't an appropriate subject to discuss.

After dinner, Kate and I were doing the washing-up while Bridget and Flynn were talking about Bridget's stream.

"I'm translating a pretty steamy romance," I said to Kate. "We matching?"

"Sorry, babes. Haven't done any voiceover stuff since last time."

"Damn."

"Them two are getting on, aren't they?" said Kate, looking over at Flynn and Bridget.

"Yeah," I agreed. "I knew they would, though. They're very similar people—just laid-back and living their lives. And they both have chronic conditions. That probably creates some innate understanding between them."

As if on cue, Flynn asked Bridget about her Tourette's.

"No, man, I don't mind," Bridget said to Flynn. "It started when I was a teenager. I was in school, and I suddenly couldn't stop turning my head. It freaked me out because I couldn't explain to people why I was doing it. That made me anxious, and that seemed to make things worse. Thought I was fucking possessed, didn't I? I mean, I didn't think Tourette's because I wasn't swearing uncontrollably, and that's all I knew about it at the time."

"So when did you figure out it was Tourette's?" Flynn asked.

"Not for a while. My mum didn't believe that I couldn't control it for the longest time. She thought I was putting it on to get out of going to school or seeing family or whatever."

"That's horrible."

Bridget shrugged. "Honestly, I was a shit kid. Very rebellious. Anything I could do to piss an adult off, I would do. So my mum didn't trust me much at all. My rebellious nature kind of backfired on me. She didn't take my tics seriously until this …" She lifted back her fringe and showed Flynn a scar on her forehead. "Got that as a souvenir from my very first proper tic attack. She was starting to believe me when I couldn't stop hitting myself, but she definitely believed me when I smashed a glass over my head and had to go to hospital."

Flynn covered her mouth, shocked.

"But, hey," Bridget continued, "made it easier when I brought home my first girlfriend. I didn't even come out to them; I just did it. Before the Tourette's, they would have said I was attention seeking, but all they ended up saying was, 'Guess she's a lesbian now.'"

She shrugged and Flynn laughed.

"All worked out for the best, though. They learned to trust me, and I became less of a shitty kid when I stopped suppressing my love of women. Just goes to show: Don't suppress who you are on the inside because it can make you a real bitch on the outside." She and Flynn laughed.

"I'm actually happy you two know about Flynn now," I said to Kate as we finished with the washing-up. "Flynn doesn't have any friends or family, no one who really knows them. It was just me for a bit. But this is better, the four of us. As apprehensive as they were before, I think Flynn really appreciates having you and Bridget to talk to."

"Yeah, it is nice," said Kate. "I've been waiting for a day like this to come."

"What do you mean?"

"Well, when we were kids in primary, we were so close, people used to think we would start dating in future."

I laughed at that. "People see a boy child and a girl child acting close and just assume romantic feelings will eventually develop."

"Innit, though? But then we became sisters when you started your transition. I punched a lot of guys in the balls for you, and one girl in her newly budded breasts."

I grinned. "Yeah, you did."

"We're family, Ange, and I love that. But now we're adults. We don't live together anymore. We don't see each other at school every day. And I met Bridget, and she's become my family as well. I really wanted the sister I love so much to have that, too. And now," she glanced over at Flynn, "now you have. I feel like the four of us are one big family. Imagine us all when we're older. Your kids will call me Aunty Kate."

"Who said I'm having kids?"

She looked at me with no humour at all. "Come on, baby girl, between the two of us, it's defo more likely to be you than me. I can't stand those little boob-suckers. But I'm sure I'll love your kids."

"You're thinking too far ahead, Kate. Flynn and I haven't even really discussed kids. I don't even know if either of us wants them. I mean, can you imagine a kid being around for Flynn's changes?"

"Can you imagine a kid *with* Flynn's changes?" Kate countered.

I'd never even thought of that. "All the more reason it probably won't happen."

"You can adopt. I'm adopted; it's great."

I shook my head and grinned. "Maybe, Kate. I don't know."

"I'm calling it now, kitten. Put down fifty quid on it."

I chuckled.

"But this is nice, though," she continued. "Who would've thought that our primary school friendship would turn into this little family?"

I looked at Flynn and Bridget, and then at Kate. "Yeah. Who would've thought?"

3 October

Today, Flynn was a tall, curvy woman with a warm, brown complexion and beautiful long hair. She had one hand on my foot and the other between my legs as I lay on the bed, one leg bent, the other outstretched. We were in sync. It happened more often these days, maybe because we were both more used to switching roles, or maybe because Flynn's condition wasn't as stressful now that we weren't the only ones who knew. Either way, things weren't so fleeting anymore. The clock was right more than twice a day; in fact, it only ever broke down occasionally.

"Ange, your feet are twitching. You're distracting me."

"Can't help it; your fingers are in me."

"Do you want me to stop?"

I closed my eyes and exhaled softly. "No. No, keep going. You're doing good."

Usually, sex between me and Flynn was a game of exploration and discovery on my part. Flynn always had a new body, so what they liked changed, and their reaction to different things we'd do would change also. We had fun constantly figuring things out. But this time, Flynn was the explorer. She wanted to try fingering my tubes, and that was a part of the human body she didn't know existed until I told her a few months ago. She took her attempts very seriously, focusing and paying attention to how I was reacting. I knew my twitching feet weren't helping her, but it was quite a sensitive area, all things considered; how else was I going to react? The first time we tried this, she had trouble even finding my tubes, and when she did, it kind of hurt. Then she started getting lucky here and there, but now, now she was getting good at it.

She rhythmically moved her curved finger in and out of me, brushing the tips of my nervous system, filling me with a tingling warmth. Her other fingers rested atop my penis, and I reflexively pressed against them. My body twitched with each brush of my nerves. Flynn chuckled and held down my foot, but she could never hold back what I felt within me. My foot pushed against her hand and my pelvis pressed against her fingers, and suddenly, I was alive again. Everything felt sharper, stronger. Something was pulsing beneath my skin. I was hyperaware of every touch, and at the same time, I was numb. And then

I relaxed, and I breathed.

"Looks like I'm getting better," Flynn said as she moved closer to me, running her fingers lightly up my stomach.

"Much better," I agreed with a pleasant sigh, outstretching my bent leg.

She leant in to kiss me and then sat herself atop my pelvis. She slowly rocked back and forth, tracing lines down my stomach with her fingers, and only occasionally stopping to massage her breasts or run her fingers over her clitoris.

This version of Flynn liked to take control of her own sexuality. For someone who's only had this body for two days, she remarkably seemed to know everything about it. Even when I started brushing simple circles into her inner thighs with my fingers, she took my hand by the wrist and moved it to her lower back. She knew exactly where to direct me because she knew me, and she knew herself.

She relaxed deeper with each rocking motion, sighing faintly. She didn't fail to hold back any force from within; she simply flowed like a river. The juxtaposition between us was what put us in sync—two opposing parts that worked together.

There was a time when I thought Flynn had to be a man for us to be fully in sync, but that wasn't true, not really. It was more about understanding who Flynn was with each change and understanding who I had to become. Now we were rarely ever out of sync, and everything felt so much better.

Flynn lay down beside me, kissing my neck in the way I loved. She drew a pleasant moan from me as she draped her arm across my stomach. I placed my hand over hers, interlocking our fingers.

"I like this body," Flynn breathed into my neck.

"I like it, too. Your hair's beautiful."

She took some of her hair and threw it over my face. I laughed, brushing it away.

"I meant how it feels," she explained. "Everything feels so muted and mellowed."

"Is that a good thing?"

"It's comfortable, relaxing … peaceful."

"You do seem very comfortable in this body."

"Mmm," she agreed, sighing and relaxing even closer to me. "I'm going to miss it when it's gone."

That reality was always a sobering note in our enjoyment together.

"It's not gone yet," I said. "Try to keep your mind in the present. That's what helps me. I mean, last week, you didn't know how much you'd enjoy the body you're in now, did you? And who knows how you'll feel about the next body?"

She kissed my neck again, and I gripped her hand tighter.

My phone went off then. I flopped my arm over to the nightstand and felt around for it.

"Oh, shit. No way," I said with a smile when I read the text.

"What?" Flynn asked.

"Sydney just texted me. You don't know her. She's an old family friend who lives in Canada."

"Oh. She all right?"

"Yeah, she's good. She says she's coming over to England to visit family in Milton Keynes, and she's making the rounds to see all her old English friends."

"Did she used to live here?"

"She was born here. Moved to Canada when she was twelve—her parents had work there—then when she was much older, her parents moved back to England, and she decided to stay in Canada."

"Don't know if I could manage that. It's cold over there." Flynn shivered.

"Actually, I hear it's quite warm in the summertime. But, anyway, she's wanting to come to Thivleton to see me."

"That sounds fun."

"Yeah. I'm excited; I haven't seen her in a few years." I looked at Flynn and then at the bedroom around me. "I'm thinking this should probably just be a me thing, innit? If she comes here, and you change, we'll have a lot to try and explain."

Flynn nodded. "Yeah, you're right."

"I'll invite her to my flat, and we can catch up like old times."

"Sure. Sounds good."

"Will you … be all right?"

"Yeah, I'll be fine. Why wouldn't I be? She's your friend, Ange; go catch up with her."

"Well, what I mean is, what if you change and you need me?"

She pulled away slightly to look at me. "Ange, I survived before I met you."

"But your changes are getting more unpredictable, like that time with Kate at the shopping centre."

She kissed me. "Ange, you've made my life infinitely better, but I think I'll survive just fine without you for a little bit. Please don't let my illness keep you from living your life."

I smiled. "Okay. I won't. But you'll ring me if you need me, yeah?"

"Or I could ring Kate."

"Or you could ring me."

She kissed me again. Longer this time; she was trying to relax me. "You don't need to worry about me, Ange."

I may not have needed to worry, but she couldn't stop me.

12 October

I opened the door of my flat and let Sydney in. She was a tiny woman with a jet-black pixie cut and turquoise-rimmed glasses.

"Hey, girl," she said, hugging me. "I've missed you."

"Yeah, you too, Sydney."

She walked around my flat. "This is a nice place, eh?"

"It serves its purpose." I closed the door.

"Apartment life, huh? Last time I was here, you were just moving out of your mom's house."

"Yeah, I've been here a while now. Mum moved back to Scotland."

"Oh, did she? I'll probably just call her, then. Don't know if I'm up to going to Scotland to visit her. This is just a short trip to see some friends and family." She yawned loudly. "Oh, sorry."

I grinned. "You knackered? Still jetlagged?"

"Probably. I got here on the tenth. Left right after Thanksgiving. Bad idea. So much food and then straight on the plane to England. I felt so nauseous."

"I thought Thanksgiving was in November?"

"No, that's American Thanksgiving. Canada's is the second Monday in October."

I nodded.

"You want a cup of tea?" I offered.

"Oh, yes, please. I am a keener for British tea. I've gotta drink as much as I can while I'm here, eh?"

I put on the kettle. "I think that's the most Canadian I've ever heard you sound."

"I know, right? Welcome to the Great White North. Been living there too long."

Sydney sat on the sofa, looking over the back of it with her head resting on her arms.

"What sort of tea do you want?" I asked her.

"Do you have English Breakfast tea?"

"Uh … yes I do."

"Cool."

I took out the box of teabags and got them ready for when the kettle finished boiling. "So how are your family? Have you seen them yet?"

"Yeah, they're good. I'm actually staying with them while I'm here. Saves money, you know?"

"Sure." I nodded, pouring the boiled water into a cup and steeping the teabag. "So how's Canada?"

"Oh, getting colder. Almost toque weather."

"What's that, some sort of winter coat?"

"What, a toque? No, that's a hat. Like a knitted one for the cold."

"Like a beanie?"

"Yeah, you got it."

I walked over and handed Sydney her cup of tea.

"Thank you," she almost sang as she took it from me. She really liked her tea.

I sat next to her.

"You're not having tea?" she asked.

"Nah, I'm good."

"All right." She shrugged and sipped her tea. "So, listen, Josh and I are thinking of moving."

"Yeah? Where to?"

"Not sure yet. Probably close to where we are already, so Mississauga, Markham; I don't know, maybe even Etobicoke."

I stared at her, confused.

"Those are all places in or around Toronto."

"Oh, okay."

"But Josh has been throwing around the idea of getting out of Ontario altogether, maybe go to BC."

I looked at her again.

"Those are provinces."

"Oh." I nodded. I wasn't following the foreign geography, but I thought I had enough to work with.

"My issue, though, is moving away from everyone we know. Say we do go to BC; it'd be so much harder to see everybody."

"Is it a really long drive?"

She looked at me, shocked. "Drive? Who's driving? That'd take days."

"Days?"

"Dude, Canada's the second biggest country in the world. Going to BC from where I am is like going to Russia from the UK. It's far."

"Wow. Really?"

"Oh yeah. Plus, there're the different time zones to consider. It's a real hassle. I don't think we'll end up doing that."

"If I were holidaying in Canada, I'd want to go to Montréal," I said. "I hear some of the architecture there is beautiful. I'd love to see it."

"Oh, well, that'd be easy for you, girl; you speak French. You'd be right at home in Montréal. Me? I'd feel like a fish out of water. The only French I know is what I can remember from school: *Je m'appelle Sydney. Comment ça va ? Ça va bien.* Montréal's just not as much fun if you only speak English."

"Maybe we'll go together one day," I suggested. "I can do the talking for you: *Hi, this is my friend Sydney. She's Canadian, but she doesn't speak any French. She had to bring me, her English friend, to interpret for her.*"

Sydney laughed. "Look, girl, I'm totally fine with that. As long as you can order me a nice, authentic, Montréal poutine, I'm totally on board."

We both laughed.

Then she put her tea down on the table and turned to face me. "So, I've got a dump for you."

A "dump" is what Sydney and I started doing a few years back, when she visited the time before last. Since she's in Canada and I'm in England, and neither of us keeps in close contact with the other's family, we "dump" any secrets or anything we've been holding onto, knowing that we'll keep that knowledge in our respective countries and not cross borders, as it were.

I faced her attentively. "Go ahead. Dump."

She hesitated, and then said, "I'm pregnant."

"What? No way. How long?"

"Oh, it's barely been two months. Haven't really told anyone yet."

I eyed the cup on the table. "Should you really be drinking tea, then?"

"Who are you, my doctor? It's fine. I'm monitoring the caffeine."

"Oh, well, I'm happy for you." I hugged her.

"Yep. Fingers crossed I haven't jinxed things by telling you so soon."

"Don't be superstitious. It'll be fine. You'll be a great mum, I'm sure."

She pulled away and smiled at me. "Thanks, Ange. I'm excited, but, you know, the nervous kind, the kind that makes you wanna shit yourself."

"You'll do great," I assured her. "Have you told the fam yet?"

"Oh, yeah, I had to. They were starting to wonder why I was vomiting all the time. I did want to wait until, like, three months to tell everyone, but I'm already here. I think they all would have been pretty pissed if I went back to Canada and told them over the phone when I was just here, you know?"

"Yeah, they probably would. That's great, though, Sydney. I'm really happy for you."

She smiled and picked her tea back up, taking another sip. "So, have you got a dump?" she asked.

I considered whether I should tell her. I mean, I'm sure she'd respect the sacred nature of the dump; plus, there's no way she'd believe me, anyway.

"All right. In actual fact, I do," I said. "I am dating a shapeshifter."

She grinned. "Okay. What does that mean?"

"Like, I'm going out with a real shapeshifter. They've got an illness that makes them change bodies every few days."

"Oh yeah?" She sipped her tea again. "Whose bodies are they changing into?"

"No one, in particular, I don't think. Just new, unique bodies each time."

I could tell by her expression that she was just humouring me; she wasn't believing any of this. But it felt nice to talk about it with a friend as if this were a normal thing.

"So what's that like, dating a … *shapeshifter?*" she made it sound so sensational.

"Honestly, wonderful … and terrifying."

"How so?"

"Every time they change, it's violent. There's sick and blood, and you can hear their bones breaking and shifting into new places."

"Oof." She shivered. "You should write that down, girl. Sounds like it would make an excellent horror book; I'd read it."

I glanced at my diary, which was lying on the table, and muttered hopefully, "Yeah … or maybe a romance.

"Honestly, Sydney," I continued, "I find I'm really curious about them, about how the changes work. Their illness affects their long-term memory, but every now and then, they remember something like being alive during the moon landing or the fact that they weren't born a shapeshifter; it was done to them. I wish I could know more. In the back of my mind, I'm scared that one day my lack of knowledge will be a detriment, like something terrible will happen that neither of us was prepared for, something we won't know how to fix."

"Well, why don't you just talk to this shapeshifter? Go to therapy or something. See if a doctor can help drudge up some of those old memories."

I shook my head. "Can't. They think it's too dangerous to let anyone know, especially a doctor. And I don't think that the past is something they want to remember either. I just have a bad feeling, every time we get close to touching on a memory from too far in the past, like when they remember their parents. I feel like, one day, my ignorance just might cost me."

Sydney grinned and then laughed. "And you told me not to be superstitious. That's a neat story, Ange. You should totally write that down."

7 November

I woke from a nightmare. It was a nightmare so close to reality that it shook me right to my core. It terrified me. But it wasn't real, and that calmed my beating heart. All I had to do was open my eyes, and it wasn't real.

I turned over in the bed to snuggle closer to Flynn, but they weren't there. I was alone.

I got my phone and checked the time: 2:00 a.m.

"Flynn?" I called.

No answer.

My heart was beating fast again. The nightmare wasn't over yet.

I rubbed my eyes and got out of bed, begging not to see what I thought I might see. I headed for the bathroom; my mind moved me quickly, but my body moved me slowly. The bathroom door was open a crack, and the light was on. My mouth was dry, and I could feel my heart in my throat, in my dried-up tongue. I pushed the door open, and that's when I realised I was wrong before. It wasn't that the nightmare hadn't ended yet; it was that it had only just begun.

There was a limp body sprawled out on the floor in a pool of thick blood. Flesh was peeling off from almost every part of it, exposing so much bone that it looked like a skeleton wearing a tattered skin suit. The eyes hung out of the sockets by just a few ligaments.

I immediately felt sick and rushed to the toilet to boak, adding to the sick that was already there. I usually had a pretty good stomach, and I'd handled myself quite well when it came to Flynn's changes, all things considered. But not this time. When I ran out of bile to throw up, I felt weak. I slipped down to the floor and looked at the unmoving body beside me. I just sat there for a second, catastrophising. Then I inched over and felt for a pulse …

I adjusted my hand, felt again …

I checked a different pulse …

Please.

It wasn't until tears were streaming down my face that

I felt something: a single beat. One heartbeat. That's it.

I kept my finger on Flynn's pulse and waited, waited, waited … Another beat.

Their heart rate was slow, maybe one or two beats a minute. What should I do? Flynn's heart rate is usually rapid during the change. Should I call an ambulance, or trust that Flynn will be fine? Do I expose Flynn's condition to everyone in A&E, and thus, the world; or do I sit here quietly and trust the process?

I couldn't decide. I didn't know what to do, and it wasn't fair that it was up to me to make this decision in the middle of the night. I was angry; angry at Flynn, angry at myself, and angry that if anything bad happened, it would be my fault.

I stood up and went to get my phone. That's when I realised I'd been sitting on the bathroom floor for an hour. A whole hour of indecision, and Flynn hadn't moved. A regular change usually took an hour, the bigger parts of it anyway. But Flynn was still just a body in a pool of blood.

My thumb trembled over my phone screen; I still didn't know what to do. I ended up calling Kate. Luckily, she picked up.

"Ange?" she said sleepily. "What time is it?"

"Kate," I whispered shakily. "Kate, I don't know what to do."

"Ange? Ange, what's wrong?"

"It's Flynn … I don't know what to do."

She must have heard the fear in my voice because she

said, "Ange, hang on. I'm on my way."

In just fifteen minutes, there was a knock at the door, and I let Kate in. I led her into the bathroom, and she covered her mouth when she saw it. She turned away and leant on my shoulder for support.

"You okay?" I asked her.

She nodded. "Yeah. Just swallowed my own sick. I'm good."

She straightened up, and we just stared at Flynn's body for a second.

"How long have they been like that?" Kate asked.

I shook my head. "Not sure. I woke up at two, so at least since then."

"How long does it usually take?"

"An hour, maybe. I don't know what to do, Kate. There's barely a pulse, and it's never been this bad before."

Kate looked away again; she couldn't take the sight. "Should we call 999?"

"I don't know. Flynn always says that no matter how bad it looks or how much it hurts, they'll be fine in the end. But it's never happened like this before. I don't know if Flynn's okay. But if we take them to A&E, we'll be revealing to the world that there's a shapeshifter in Thivleton. And who says they'll even be able to help? Flynn's said before that painkillers make things worse; what if they give Flynn some drug they think will help, and it kills them?"

Kate hugged me, and I cried. I was so scared, paralysed

by the fear of making the wrong choice.

Then there was a crunch.

Kate and I both looked at the same time. Flynn's shoulder had moved, and it was a little smaller.

"They're still changing," said Kate. "Maybe … maybe we should just let it happen. We can just keep an eye on them."

All I could do was nod.

"Come on." Kate put her arm round me. "Let's go sit in the front room. We'll hear if Flynn moves. Staying here and watching isn't doing us any good."

I conceded, and Kate took me into the front room and sat me on the sofa. Then she sat beside me, and we were silent.

I've described witnessing Flynn's changes before as feeling like I was a war veteran. Now, it felt like Kate was my sister-in-arms. We didn't need to speak; our shared experience did the talking.

I leant my head on Kate's shoulder, and she rubbed my arm, comforting me. She took out her phone and started typing.

"What're you doing?" I asked.

"Texting Bridget. Letting her know what's happening."

"I'm sorry I worried you."

"No, don't be. I'll always be here for you, Ange. Always."

We heard another crunch, and I instantly jumped up and ran back to the bathroom. It took me a while to notice any changes; it was the same limp body bathed in blood. When Kate came to check on me, I pointed at Flynn's feet.

"Look. Their feet are smaller," I said.

Kate looked, but she couldn't for long. The exposed bones and muscles were too much for her to stomach, and the smell of sick didn't help things. "Come on, Ange. I can't be in here. Let's wait in the front room."

I silently conceded yet again, and we went back to the sofa.

After a few silent minutes, I said, "I have to get Flynn to a doctor."

"You want to go to A&E?"

"No, I mean some sort of specialist. We can go private, find someone who's willing to help us—study Flynn's condition and keep tight-lipped about it. I can't do this, Kate, the not-knowing. I'm not asking for a cure; I just need help."

"Will Flynn be on board with that?"

I shook my head. "I'll have to convince them."

"You'll have to convince the specialist," Kate pointed out.

"I'll video the change, start to finish. That should be proof enough."

"And nightmare fuel," Kate muttered. "What sort of specialist did you have in mind, anyway?"

"Dunno. Maybe a geneticist? Shapeshifting probably changes your DNA. That's genetics, innit?"

Kate shrugged.

There was another crunch, and I visibly shook.

"Okay, so we'll look for a specialist," Kate agreed. "But

what about now? Are we still gonna wait and see, or do we go to A&E and see if anyone there can figure something out?"

I sighed forcefully. "No. We wait. Too many people in A&E. Too easy for it to get out. We just have to hope that Flynn will get through this. And if they do, then I'll get down on my hands and knees and beg if I have to. We need a doctor."

The hours ticked by, and suddenly, it was afternoon. Bridget came over, and we all ordered some food. Bridget and I searched online for specialists who might be able to help Flynn and also keep quiet about everything, while Kate took a nap on the sofa. But I couldn't sleep … because Flynn was still on the bathroom floor.

"Yo, Ange," said Bridget. "Is there another bathroom in this house? I need a wee."

"Yeah, down the hall. It's split, though. Loo's on the left, bathroom's down there on the right."

"Right, cool. I'll be back."

She left, and I continued searching on my phone for doctors. I found a few good write-ups for a few doctors who had dealt with rare diseases before.

Then there was a scream, and it woke Kate up. She looked at me, and then we both ran straight for the bathroom to see Flynn's body. They were still unconscious, but the body was in a different position. They must have woken up for just a moment.

"What's wrong?" said Bridget, rushing in. When she saw

Flynn, she was almost sick right there. Kate had to take her away.

I could hear Bridget muttering, "Jesus, Fuck. Fucking shit, man."

Bridget hadn't seen Flynn like this before. When she got here, Kate forbade her from looking, and she was clearly right to do so.

After Kate got Bridget to calm down a bit, she came back into the bathroom to get me. I didn't have the strength to remove myself from Flynn's side, even though I knew staring wouldn't help anything. That's why I called Kate; that's why she's here.

She pulled me into the front room and sat me on the sofa again. Bridget was pacing around, clearly shaken. She was sniffling a lot, too; the anxiety was aggravating her Tourette's.

Evening came quickly, and Kate and Bridget decided to stay the night. They slept together on the sofa, but I was up all night. I sat in the bedroom, not wanting to look in the bathroom but also not having the strength to stay away.

8 November

It was 2:00 a.m. Twenty-four hours, and Flynn was still on the bathroom floor. It had also been twenty-four hours since I last slept.

Then I heard someone being sick.

I rushed to the bathroom to see a little boy hugging the

toilet seat. He was weak, dazed, and he looked up at me, flesh hanging from his bloodied face, saying, "Ange … water."

I nodded and ran to the kitchen, filling a glass with water so fast I could have broken a record. But when I got back to the bathroom, I knew I wasn't fast enough. Flynn was unconscious again.

I was sad. I hated myself for not running to the kitchen faster. But I wasn't scared anymore. I knew now, seeing the mangled but recognisable features of a little boy, that Flynn would be okay in the end. But would I be okay? I didn't think so, not without the assurance that something would be done about this. I had to find a good doctor, and I had to make a good case for going to see this doctor. I had to convince Flynn to do this.

I took out my phone, pointed the camera at Flynn, and hit record. Just in case I didn't get another chance. Just in case I needed this recording. I just had one of those gut feelings that I needed documented proof of what was happening here. This wasn't the recording I would show a doctor, I wanted that one to be from the very beginning to the very end, but if I couldn't get that, at least I would have this.

When morning came, Kate and Bridget woke up, and Bridget ordered in some breakfast for all of us. Flynn was still changing, but he looked like a normal, unconscious boy now—no visible bones.

Kate and I were in the front room, looking for doctors.

"I may have found someone," said Kate. "A geneticist who seems to treat a lot of rare genetic disorders. Looks like he's written a few research papers as well based on experience treating his patients. And one of those patients praised his openly asking consent to use them as a case study, and also their discretion and maintaining the anonymity of the patient."

I pulled on Kate's hand, making her show me her phone screen. "Who is he?"

"Dr Jacob Murphy. He's in a multidisciplinary clinic that's got endocrinologists, cytopathologists, gastroenterologists, ophthalmologists … Sounds like that would cover a lot of bases."

"Okay. Where is he? Close?"

"Birmingham."

I sighed. "That's almost a three-hour drive."

"I'll drive you. Don't worry about it. You just have to worry about convincing Flynn."

I sighed. Now we had a good candidate for a doctor, I was able to relax a little. I sat on the sofa and instantly fell asleep. When I woke up, it was afternoon, and a little boy was sat next to me.

"Flynn," I said, and I hugged him before he could respond.

And for the moment, the nightmare was over.

The rest of the day was spent cleaning up all the sick and blood. Kate and Bridget stayed and helped, though Bridget didn't help much, as her stomach couldn't take it.

But she did point something out that I hadn't noticed before: The blood hadn't dried. Even though it had been there for over a day, it was still liquid. Granted, it was a lot of blood, but that still seemed odd.

By mid-evening, we'd finished cleaning, and Flynn ordered everyone dinner. And then Kate and Bridget left. I hugged Kate tightly on her way out and whispered to her, "Thank you for coming."

She rubbed my back and said, "Any time. Let me know about Birmingham."

And then they were gone, and it was just me and Flynn.

We were sat on the sofa, enjoying the warmth from the fireplace. I was shattered. I must have looked like a zombie; I certainly felt that way. But Flynn looked the same as usual—relaxed and go-with-the-flow. That irritated me. After everything I'd been through, it was over now, and we were just to move on? No. I couldn't.

"So, Flynn, listen," I started.

My drained face was reflected in his innocent, blue eyes.

"While you were changing, Kate and I were looking for a doctor."

"What sort of doctor?"

"A specialist. For you. Someone who can help us understand this, maybe offer a treatment, anything to make it easier."

He sighed. "Ange, we've been through this. It's dangerous. If what I am gets out into the world—"

"This doctor is known for his discretion. He cares for

his patients more than he cares about being famous for dealing with rare cases."

"What doctor? Have you already found one?"

"His name's Dr Jacob Murphy. He's a geneticist. He works in a multidisciplinary clinic that will cover a lot of bases in figuring out why you change and how to help."

"Ange…"

"Flynn, please."

"How would you even get a doctor to believe any of this?"

"We video the change, start to finish. Maybe talk through what's happening while it happens."

He sighed again. "Look, Ange, I get you're scared, and I'm sorry. But this isn't safe. I mean, short of tying him up and threatening him, we can't guarantee his discretion. What if we show him a video of a shapeshifter, and he tells the whole medical field? Everyone will be curious at first, but then everyone will be afraid. They'll come for me. That's always how it goes."

"I'd take that chance," I mumbled.

"Ange, don't be like that."

"Why not? Flynn, you don't know what it's like. I die a little every time I see you like that. I got up in the middle of the night, and you were soaked in blood on the floor, flesh hanging off you like you'd been attacked by wolves. Do you know what that feels like, to see that? I sat with you for an hour, and you'd barely changed. That's never happened before, Flynn; it's never taken this long. All I kept thinking was: 'This is it. This is how you die. Your illness just takes you, violently, in the middle of the night.'"

"But, Ange, you know I'll be fine. I'm always fine."

"I don't know shit, Flynn. And neither do you. It's changing; we can't predict this illness anymore. You were out for two days. That's not supposed to happen. And I was this close, Flynn, this close to calling an ambulance and outing you to anyone who would listen on the off chance that someone in A&E could help. This has to stop. I can't take it anymore. Please, let's just try."

He looked at me, opened his mouth but didn't speak. Then he shook his head, but before he could tell me no again, I got my phone, pulled up the video I took of him changing, and shoved it in his face. He watched quietly. It wasn't the worst of the change, but there was some exposed bone and hanging flesh in the recording; it was grotesque enough to make my point. You could hear me crying in the background as well, and that made Flynn cry. He pushed the phone away before the video even finished and said, "Okay. I'll do it. We can try."

11 November

It was Saturday evening. Flynn was still a little boy, but he was feeling a change coming on soon. I'd gotten an appointment with the specialist. I told the lady on the phone that this was a special case that required the doctor's discretion, and she sounded like she understood. I got the feeling we weren't the first to ring up about something like this. Hopefully, that was a good sign.

We invited Kate and Bridget over. We were going to record Flynn's change to show the doctor. Kate was going to record, I was going to tend to Flynn and narrate what was happening for the video, and Bridget … Bridget was just moral support, really. Kate wouldn't let her stay for the change, and Bridget didn't argue. She was in the front room, there if we needed her.

The rest of us were in the bedroom. Flynn was sat on the bed, naked except for a towel on his lap. I sat with him, and Kate stood with my phone camera pointed at us.

"Are you sure about this?" Flynn said to Kate as he rubbed his temples. "It won't be pretty."

"Can't be any worse than what Ange made me walk in on in the middle of the night, mate."

"Sorry," I said to her guiltily.

She shook her head and made a face that said, *Don't worry about it. We were all freaking out.*

Flynn smiled. "Shouldn't be that bad this time … Hopefully." He bent over and cradled his head.

I kissed him and asked, "Soon?"

"Soon," he confirmed.

I took a breath and looked at Kate. "You ready?"

She nodded. "Let's do it. Pressing record."

"Right, so, this is usually how the change will start," I said to the camera. "Flynn will get a heady feeling or a stomachache or something. That's how we know the change is coming."

Kate moved to get a better shot of Flynn. Flynn smiled painfully and looked at her. Then he looked at me and said, "Well … whoever the next me is going to be, I guess … tag, you're it."

Then he fell into my arms.

"Now he's fainted," I explained to the camera. "He'll stay like this for a few minutes, maybe. This is usually when small changes happen, things like skin colour or texture, eye colour, maybe body-hair changes or fingernail growth."

Kate moved to get a good shot of Flynn's eyebrows, which were becoming bushier.

"It's possible that he'll have a seizure at this point as well," I continued to explain. "We'll have to wait and see."

Suddenly, he woke up and jolted backwards onto the bed, and there was a cracking sound.

"Flynn?" I said.

He didn't answer. He rolled off the bed as fast as he could, heading for the bathroom. But he didn't make it. Weakness in his legs pulled him to the floor, where he was sick just before falling unconscious right in it.

I rushed over, moving him off the sick and cleaning him up a little with his towel, which had fallen off him when he started bolting for the bathroom.

"There'll be a lot of sick," I explained. "This is just the start of it. The sick will have solid chunks in it. Those are bits of Flynn's insides: teeth, organs, and that. When the change ends, those solid bits will liquefy. We're not sure why."

Then Flynn started convulsing. I folded up the towel and placed it under his head, keeping the side with sick on it away from his face.

"So, now you can see that his skin has some cooler undertones to it, and he's growing a bit more body hair. He's probably gonna end up with a man's body by the end."

The seizure stopped, and I put Flynn in the recovery position. Then we waited. A few minutes went by, and then another seizure started. This one shook out some of Flynn's hair and replaced it with hair that was shorter and coarser. Then he was still again. It was silent. And then …

Pop.

Blood splattered as Flynn's bones broke and shifted.

"Oh, fuck!" said Kate. Then, when she remembered she was supposed to be a silent camera person, she said, "Sorry," and quietly wiped the blood off her face.

"That happens sometimes," I explained to the camera. "It's like a big shift in skeletal structure or something, and it all happens so quick that something pops and there's blood." I wiped the blood from my eyes and mouth. "Flynn's blood type changes with each new body. Personally, I wonder if the blood that comes out during the changes is a way of flushing out the blood from the old body." I shrugged.

I looked at Flynn. Despite the blood that had just splattered, there was no exposed bone, just some torn skin which was already starting to heal. This was going to be an easier change. It could have been so much worse.

Flynn woke, and I quickly helped him up and took him into the bathroom. I was used to how this went now; I knew Flynn would need to be sick, and I had to get him to the toilet. The second we got there, he hugged the seat and started throwing up.

"This will go on for a little bit," I explained as Kate videoed Flynn being sick. "There's also blood in the sick, as you can see."

I held Flynn up, as I knew that after he was done being sick, he would either faint or have a seizure, and I didn't want him to hit his head. He ended up fainting, and I laid him nicely on the floor in the recovery position.

"Bridget!" I called. "Can you get us some water?"

"'Kay!" she called back.

"Leave it at the door!" Kate called to her. "Don't come in here!"

"Wasn't planning to!"

The crunching and cracking had begun now. Flynn's bones were being ground up, mixing and mincing into a new flavour.

"This is the main bit," I explained. "Flynn's bones will rearrange, and this is where the big changes happen: size, fat distribution, primary and secondary sex characteristics …"

Flynn's legs snapped and popped, and suddenly they were longer. His skin was holding strong, though; it hadn't torn again.

"Water!" called Bridget.

Kate handed me my phone while she got the water from Bridget. "Cheers, babe," she said to her.

"I'll be out here if you need me," said Bridget. "Please don't need me."

"We'll try not to."

Then Kate came back and took the phone from me, getting a good shot of Flynn's now-long arms.

I continued my explanation. "I don't think he'll be changing sex this time, but if he were, this would be when it would happen. His penis would shrink into a clitoris and his scrotum would open up into labia. But sometimes it stops in-between, and he might have more intersex characteristics: an enlarged clitoris, a scrotum with no testicles, breasts on a male body …"

There was a huge crunch, like stepping into thick snow and twigs, and Flynn was writhing, screaming out in a deep voice. He was still unconscious, though, so all we could do was endure it. Kate looked at me from behind the phone, asking with her eyes if I was okay. The answer to that was complicated, but I would go on. I nodded to her.

When Flynn had calmed down again, we could hear some of Bridget's vocal tics in the background—repetitive whistling, mouth clicking, and the occasional 'Pop your trainers on.' The crunching and screaming in here must have been freaking her out.

"You can go check on her if you want," I whispered to Kate.

She shook her head. "She'll be fine."

Then, Flynn woke up, groaning as he pushed himself off the ground and into a sitting position. I immediately handed him the water that Bridget brought us, and he gulped it down.

"So, the change is nearing its end now," I explained. "As you can see, Flynn's older, maybe early twenties. He's got more body hair—chest and back hair, arm hair, bit of stubble. There's also a bit of mixed ethnicity here: You'll notice that this time round, his skin has remained pale, but his hair has gone from straight to coily. It's much shorter, too, and some of the longer bits of Flynn's previous hair are now on the floor."

Kate moved the camera to look at the clumps of hair on the floor, some of which were soaked in chunky sick.

"That'll … that'll liquefy in the end," said Flynn hoarsely.

I looked at him. "You all right?"

He nodded solemnly.

"Bridget!" I called. "Can you bring us a towel?"

After repeating the same whistle tic for the umpteenth time, she yelled back, "Sure!"

"I've already got a towel," said Flynn.

"You were sick on it," I explained.

"Oh … sorry." He covered his eyes and rubbed his temples.

"He's usually a little disorientated immediately afterwards," I explained to the camera. "That'll go away soon. There will continue to be minor changes throughout the day, maybe some more hair growth or slight colour changes in skin, hair, or eyes. It also takes him a second to get used to his new nervous system and regain his dexterity."

"Towel!" called Bridget.

Kate handed me the phone to get the towel from Bridget. I turned the camera to face both me and Flynn.

"That's probably about it," I said to him. "D'you think?"

He nodded and said in his new, deeper voice, "It'll have to do."

I ended the video, and when Kate came back with the towel, she handed it to me as I pocketed my phone.

"You ended the recording?" she said as I wrapped Flynn up in the towel.

"Yeah. We've got what we need, I think."

She paused for a second before saying, "Fuck, Ange, I don't know how you do that all the time."

I shrugged. "You get used to it."

And in that moment, I felt somehow closer to Flynn, parroting something he would say in that very same situation. How similar we'd become … or how similar we already were.

I helped Flynn up, and we all sat on the bed.

"We all ready?" I asked, as I took out my phone and prepared to review the video we'd just taken.

Flynn and Kate nodded, and I hit play.

Only a minute into the video, Flynn said, "I can't. I'm gonna sit in the front room with Bridget." He stood.

"Wait," I said. "Don't you want to check it, make sure you're comfortable with showing this to the doctor?"

"No. You lot do what you like with it. I trust you." Then he staggered off.

Kate and I continued to watch. She put her arm round me midway through because I was tensing. The woman I was watching on the screen was on duty. She didn't have emotions; she just tended to her loved one. But that same woman watching herself now felt sick to her stomach, tortured by this forced overtime.

"So what d'you think? Good?" said Kate when it was finished.

I wiped my eyes dry. "Good enough. It'll get our foot in the door. It's hard to deny that, video proof of a real-life shapeshifter." It was more sensational in my head than I made it sound when I spoke.

"So what now? Do we send this to Dr Murphy?"

"No. We can't risk this video getting out. We've already got an appointment with him; we'll show him in person."

Kate kissed my cheek and hugged me. Now all we could do was wait.

4 December

It was Monday evening, and I was in the shower, cleaning the sick and blood off of me. Flynn had changed today, and that was lucky because we had our first appointment with Dr Murphy tomorrow. Since Flynn's changed so recently, we won't have to worry about that for the long drive to Birmingham.

I got out of the shower, dried myself off, and put on a long T-shirt. Then I went into the bedroom and saw Flynn sitting at the end of the bed. Today, he was a young man with soft, olive-toned skin and curly, ginger hair.

"You all right, Flynn?" I said.

He was looking at me, but I didn't think he was actually seeing me. I approached and kissed his forehead.

He looked up at me. "Big day tomorrow."

"You worried?"

He looked down and gave a slight nod.

I pulled him in, resting his head on my chest. "It'll be okay. I've got a good feeling."

"A good feeling?"

"Sure. There's something to be said about a woman's instincts, isn't there? Or is that just me?"

"Dunno. Next time I'm a woman, I'll let you know if I get that feeling, too."

I smiled and stroked his head, threading my fingers through his curls.

"Will you be in the room with me when we speak to the doctor?" he asked quietly.

"Flynn, I will be with you, always, until the day you turn me away."

5 December

Kate came early in the morning, and I opened the door to let her in.

"Hey, baby girl," she said, hugging me. "Hey, Flynn." She nodded at him from over my shoulder.

"Hey," he said. "No Bridget?"

"Nah, just me. Bridget had a long stream last night; she needs to sleep. Sorry. I know she's your work wife."

Flynn blushed. "Well, uh, no, uh, I mean … We made breakfast." He squirrelled off into the kitchen.

Kate grinned at me as she let me go. She now had the dangerous knowledge that she could make Flynn blush just as easily as she made me blush.

We ate breakfast—eggs, bacon, and toast—and then we were off on the long trip to Birmingham. I sat with Flynn in the back of the car as Kate drove. I was grateful to Kate for doing this, but about half an hour into the drive, I started to feel some of the anxiety Flynn had been feeling since last night. This was it. We were finally going to get some answers—potential answers, at least. That was exciting, but it was also scary. There was just as much chance of hearing, *Here, take this. This will cure you*, as there was of hearing, *This illness is very dangerous, and I believe it will eventually kill you*. And of course, there was also the possibility of, *I'm afraid I'll have to report you to the authorities. Your condition is extremely dangerous to the world, and the public have a right to know of your existence.*

It was afternoon when we arrived at the clinic, and from there, everything felt mechanical. We parked, locked the car doors, entered the clinic, took the lift to the second floor, entered reception, filled out some forms, waited in the waiting room, and then …

"Flynn Smith," someone called.

I took Flynn's hand and walked into the doctor's office with him. Kate stayed in the waiting room. We sat down in the hard chairs facing the backs of the computer monitors that obscured the doctor's face.

After a few seconds, he stood from his desk and came to greet us: "Hello, hello. I am Dr Jacob Murphy. Nice to meet you both."

Dr Murphy was an older man with large glasses and wiry hair. He seemed like the sort of man who only ever got excited about very special circumstances, and he seemed quite energetic now.

We introduced ourselves, and then he sat back down and said, "So, how can I help you? I hear you have an interesting case for me."

I looked at Flynn, encouraging him with my eyes.

"Um … first," he started, "it's really important to me that everything about my condition is kept quiet. Just between the people in this room. It's a matter of my safety."

Dr Murphy grinned. "I understand. In fact, I once had a patient very similar to you, in that they asked me to keep things quiet. With their permission, I can tell you now that they were born with a condition which made their cells age backwards. I know, utter madness. But from birth, they had wrinkly old skin, aged eyes—just the most well-worn newborn you could imagine. The parents wanted this all under wraps, you see. I'm sure you can appreciate the value of de-ageing cells to the medical community. People would want to study this individual. So they came to me, and I did what I could, and of course, kept it quiet. As far as anyone else is concerned, it is impossible to age backwards, and if either of you speak a word of this, know I will deny it."

I looked at Flynn. He gave me a nod and said, "Show him." And from there, everything went more organically.

I pulled up the video on my phone and went to hand it to the doctor, but before I did, I warned him: "This might be a little hard to watch."

"Well, I appreciate your concern, lass, but I think I can manage."

I gave him my phone, and he watched. I went to hold Flynn's hand, as I knew this would be difficult for him even to just hear the video. When the sick started, we had the doctor's interest, but when the crunching and cracking started, Dr Murphy's eyes were as wide as marbles.

When the video ended, he said, "Bloody hell." Then he looked up from the phone, seeming to remember he was in a professional setting. "Pardon me," he said, and he gave me back my phone.

He rubbed his face and pondered for a second. "That was remarkable. I mean, a little boy becoming a young man in an instant. Wow. I would very much like to meet this man."

I looked at Flynn, and he said, "That would be me."

Dr Murphy looked at him, astonished.

"I've changed again since then," Flynn explained, "a few times, actually."

Dr Murphy covered his mouth. "My god. You're a shapeshifter, an actual, real-life shapeshifter."

Flynn reluctantly nodded.

"Well, I understand your desire for secrecy. I assure you, my only interest is aiding in your quality of life. I will not abuse the trust you have given me."

"We appreciate that," I said. "That was a big concern."

"Of course, of course. Are you the wife, if you don't mind me asking?"

"No. Girlfriend."

"I see. I imagine he's very lucky to have you."

"I am," said Flynn.

The doctor relaxed into his chair. "Right, so, tell me everything. How often does this usually happen?"

"Every three days or so," said Flynn. "Sometimes a little longer, sometimes a little shorter."

"And I see your ethnic features shift with the transformation, as well as your age. Sex too?"

"Yes," Flynn confirmed. "Everything Ange explained in the video is true."

The doctor nodded pensively. "Have you noticed any sort of pattern, like how often you become a woman versus becoming a man?"

"No, no pattern. It just seems to be random."

He nodded. "If I could ask, why did you come to me? It seems these transformations are quite painful, so have you come for me to ease this pain, or are you perhaps looking for a potential cure? I'm not saying I could, but if I were able to give you something that would stop you ever changing again, is that what you're after?"

I looked at Flynn. He didn't answer.

"Perhaps that requires some thought," said the doctor. "Losing something, even something bad, there'll be a grieving process. Maybe we need to have a think about whether this ability you have is something you'd really like to get rid of.

"Um … I think it might be helpful to get some more background here. How long have you had this condition?"

"I don't know," said Flynn quietly.

"When did onset of the symptoms begin?"

"I don't know."

"Do you know how this all began? Did your condition always manifest as it does today?"

"I don't know."

"The illness affects Flynn's long-term memory," I explained. "He won't be able to answer much about his past."

"Well, that will admittedly make things harder," said the doctor.

"Also," Flynn added, "you should know that my information on file isn't actually correct. I don't know my date of birth. I don't know how old I am. I don't know my birth sex or the names of my parents. Smith isn't my real surname. I don't know what my surname is, or if I even have one."

Dr Murphy interlocked his fingers. "Very curious."

"Flynn's memories come and go with each change," I said. "He forgets the things he remembers, but since I've been with him, I know that he's old enough to have been alive during the moon landing and that this illness didn't develop naturally. It was done to him somehow."

Flynn looked at me, shocked, as he always did when I reminded him of something he'd forgotten. I found it interesting that, by the time he changes again, he'll forget I ever reminded him of anything, as if my reminder didn't count as a short-term memory because what I'm reminding him of happened in his long-term memory.

"Also," I added, "our friend believes that this is some sort of defence mechanism. Any time Flynn is injured or catches a cold, he'll immediately change."

"Hmm, that's very helpful. Hang on …" He started typing on his computer. "I apologise. I should have been taking notes from the beginning. Your video just caught me off guard."

We went over everything again, and the doctor watched the video a few more times until he had written up some good notes. (He watched the video with the volume off for Flynn's sake.)

"Right," he said. "I think we should begin with a few tests: blood work and maybe a neurological exam. Give me a chance to look over the results and see if we can't figure something out." He stood. "It was a pleasure to meet you both, truly. You can talk to the lady at reception about a follow-up appointment. Whereabouts do you lot live anyway?"

"Thivleton," said Flynn.

"I'm not familiar."

"It's a small town just south of London," I explained.

"I see. Quite the trip getting here, then. Tell you what, I'm thinking we'll be seeing each other quite a bit as we try to figure this all out. But I think we can make most of those appointments over the phone. Make it easier on you lot."

We shook Dr Murphy's hand, and that was it. It was maybe the best-case scenario. He believed us, and he understood the need for secrecy.

"All right. Flynn Smith," said the receptionist when we went to see her. "Looks like you've got a few tests to do. The neurological exam as well as the follow-up with Dr Murphy will probably be early next year, but we can get the blood work done right now. If you come out of here, and then go down the hall to your left, three doors down is blood work."

"All right, cheers," I said.

We paid for the appointment and then regrouped with Kate, telling her everything. She decided to wait in the car while we got the blood work done.

We got to the blood work room, and Flynn wanted me to stay with him while they drew his blood. Then I realised something. Flynn donates blood all the time, and to do that, a needle had to puncture his skin, thus injuring him. Yet it didn't force a change. There must have been a certain extent to which he had to be sick or injured for it to force a change, because clearly a small puncture from a needle wasn't enough. More pieces to the puzzle.

I watched Flynn as the lab technician prepared the needle. He seemed a little off, nervous. But he shouldn't have been; he's done this many times before. When the technician tied the band around his arm, he jumped.

"Are you all right?" she asked.

"Yeah. Yeah, sorry."

I held his hand to comfort him, and the technician was able to draw his blood.

Then we returned to Kate's car and started the long journey back to Thivleton. Flynn bought Kate dinner and petrol as a thank you. And then we were home by early evening. Kate had already left, and Flynn and I were snuggled up together on the sofa.

"So, how're you feeling about the doctor?" I asked him.

"Good, I guess. It went better than I could have hoped."

His words were positive, but I was paying more attention to the sound of his voice. "What's the matter? Why do you sound upset?"

He sighed. "You know when I had my blood drawn?"

"Yeah."

He scrunched his face. "It seemed … familiar. I don't really remember, but it felt like … like I was strapped to a chair once … someone … did something." It looked like he was scraping the ends of his mind to find this memory, but he failed all the same. He sighed and shook his head.

"It's okay," I said, and I kissed him. "Doesn't sound like something worth remembering, anyway."

8 December

It was Friday afternoon, and Flynn and I were just getting home from our weekly walk in the park. Today, Flynn was an old woman with pale, wrinkled skin that drooped a little at her cheeks. She was also using a cane.

"I'm just gonna pop to the loo," she said.

"Sure."

Immediately after she left, I got a phone call. It was my mum.

"All right, Mum," I answered.

"Hello, Angelina. How are you?"

"I'm good."

"Been a wee while, hasn't it?"

"Yeah, a little over a month since we last spoke. What's up?"

"Well, you know, it's that time of year again."

"Oh, right." I sat down on the sofa. "Christmas."

"Yes. It'll be at mine this year. Sixteenth of December. Are you coming?"

"Um …" I thought about Flynn. "I'd love to, but I'm not sure I'll be able to make it up to Scotland. I've got a lot on at the moment. How about I let you know?"

"Oh, I'm sure you can find the time. All the relatives will be glad to see you, as well. You should bring that lad you've been going out with. What was his name again?"

"Flynn. We'll, uh … we'll have to see, Mum. I'll let you know."

"All right, Angelina. Nice speaking to you."

"You too."

"Speak soon. Love you."

"Love you, too."

I hung up and sat quietly.

"What are you thinking so hard about?" asked Flynn as she returned from the toilet.

I looked at her. "Nothing. My mum just rang me. She invited me to the annual Christmas family gathering, but I don't think I'll go."

"Why not?"

I hesitated. "Busy."

"Do you want to go?"

"I mean, sure, I guess."

Flynn looked at me with her aged eyes. "You know, Ange, I know you well enough to know when you're telling me a half-truth."

I smiled bashfully.

"Let me guess," she sat next to me. "Your being 'busy' is you wanting to stay with me to make sure I'm okay."

"Is that bad?"

She put her hand on my thigh. "I'll be fine, Ange, I

always have been. Go see your family."

"Actually, Mum's invited the both of us."

"Oh. To Scotland?"

"West Dunbartonshire, yeah."

We both sat silent for a moment, and then Flynn said, "Let's go."

"Let's go? What do you mean *let's go?*"

"It'll be fun. I can meet your family. We'll have a good time."

"Okay, I hate to point out the obvious issue, but isn't that dangerous? Scotland's a long ways away; what if you change?"

"We'll have to figure that out, but I think I can manage it."

"How? I mean, we'd need a means of travel that's easy to exit in case you change. That means no plane, which also means it will take at least eight hours to get there, and the more time we spend travelling, the more likely it'll be that you'll change during the travel. And even if we figure out the travel situation, what about when we're there? We'll need to book a hotel or something, especially because we'll need somewhere to go if you change at my mum's. And then what if you change at the hotel and they don't recognise you as the same person who booked it in the first place?"

Flynn considered this. "When is it?"

"The sixteenth."

"Okay, here's the plan: We leave for Scotland right after

I change within three days of the sixteenth. We hire a cab to take us there so we can get out if we need to. In Scotland, we rent out a place for a few days, where we can stay and I can change if need be. We stay until the sixteenth, go to your mum's, and then come back to England."

"What if you change at my mum's?"

"We say I'm feeling sick and go back to the rental."

"What if you're a girl when we're there? I've told my mum I've been going out with a bloke."

"I'll wear a binder and be a very effeminate man if I have to be."

"What if you're not an appropriate age?"

She sighed. "Look, Ange, every plan has holes if you poke it. My point is: If you want to go, then I want to go with you, and we can make it work."

I thought for a second, and then a smile grew on my face. "Okay, yeah. Let's do it."

16 December

It was Saturday, the day of the annual Christmas family gathering. Flynn and I arrived in Scotland yesterday, and we were lucky because today, Flynn was a tall, lanky man with dark skin and strong cheekbones. His voice was a little high, but it still sounded male enough. He was also hard of hearing and had to wear hearing aids. That bugged him a little, but it wasn't the end of the world.

Scotland was cold, colder than England, anyway. There

was even a light dusting of snow on the ground, which really helped it feel like Christmas, even though actual Christmas was still a week away. My family always did the big annual gathering a week or two before Christmas Day so that actual Christmas could be celebrated with friends and more immediate family. I usually spent Christmas Day alone, as Kate and Bridget would go to see Bridget's family most times. But some years, Bridget's family wouldn't be able to host them, and they'd go see Margaret instead. I would usually join them in that case.

Flynn and I picked up a cheese platter on the way to Mum's, and when we got to her house, she opened the door and smiled.

"Angelina," she said. "So glad you could make it." She hugged me and took the cheese platter off my hands. "And I presume you're Flynn."

"I am. Nice to meet you." He shook Mum's hand, and Mum was taken aback by his voice for a minute, but she got over it.

"Let me just put this platter in the scullery. Come ben, you two."

She ushered us in, and we entered. Mum's house was very colourful. She liked fancy wallpapers, and the house reflected her indecisive nature. There were quite a few people already here as well, but the house was big enough to not feel crowded. As we went around greeting everyone and saying *Merry Christmas*, I remembered what I always tend to forget about coming to these gatherings: I'd have to deal with my family's various reactions to my transition. Every time an aunt would say, "Merry Christmas, Angelina," a cousin would say, "All right, Adri—Sorry, I mean, Ange." Or even worse, an uncle who would just say, "Nice to see you, Adrian."

"Why do people keep calling you Adrian?" Flynn whispered to me.

"That's my old name."

"Oh," he said simply. Then he thought about it. "Oh! Right, of course. Is that weird for you?"

I sighed. "What do you think? I do love seeing everyone, but I always seem to forget it will come with this part of it."

I had to talk closer to Flynn's ear while he had the hearing aids in. He had trouble hearing me if there was too much background noise or echoing sound, and this was a large house with a lot of people talking at once.

We continued on until we bumped into my grandparents.

"Oh, Angelina, how are you?" said my grandmother, crinkling her face into a smile. "I've not seen you in ages."

"Nice to see you, too, Baa-chan. I'm good."

"Is that Adrian?" said my grandfather, looking up from his newspaper.

"Angelina," my gran swiftly corrected.

"Oh, aye. Angelina. How's work, then?"

"Work's good, Jii-chan," I said. "Editing at the moment."

He nodded. "Good. That's good."

Despite my grandparents having grown up in Japan,

they sounded as Scottish as anyone else here. Not only had they picked up the English language remarkably well, but they even spoke the local dialect, too. I always wondered if it was a little easier for them because the Japanese R and the Scottish R sound so similar. Either way, I've always been impressed by that.

"Who's this, then?" said gran, smiling at Flynn.

I introduced him. "This is Flynn, my boyfriend."

"Oh. Boyfriend," said gramps, making a face like he was surprised. "Let's see, then."

He offered his hand, and Flynn shook it. My grandfather believed you could tell a lot about a person by shaking their hand. He said it was something someone explained to him years ago.

Gramps nodded and said, "Good grip. Good lad. I like him."

I chuckled. "Glad you approve."

He winked at me, and then we left them.

Flynn and I continued making small talk with my various relatives. Someone spotted me from across the room and said, "Hi. Havenae seen you lot around before. My name's Jake." He shook both my and Flynn's hands.

"Angelina," I introduced myself hesitantly. "And this is Flynn."

"How do you lot know the family?"

"Well, Flynn knows me, and I'm … Andrew's friend."

"Fae Ireland?"

"No, no, friend from when he lived in England."

"Oh, aye? Yeah, I suppose that makes sense; you sound English. You actually look a wee bit like him."

I grinned. "Yeah, I get that a lot."

"All right, well, nice to meet you both." Then he left.

"Who's Andrew?" asked Flynn.

"My brother."

"Then why'd you say you were his friend?"

"Because Jake is my cousin, and he clearly doesn't recognise me. We used to hang out together when we were kids, well before I transitioned, but I haven't seen him in ages. He doesn't know who I am."

Flynn laughed. "Why didn't you tell him who you were, then?"

"Can't be arsed. I'll have to explain to him that I transitioned just for him to potentially give me the look that says: 'Oh, you're one of those transgenders,' and then walk away awkwardly."

"Maybe it won't faze him," Flynn suggested.

"Honestly, I would sooner stumble upon a unicorn."

"Well, we are in Scotland."

I smiled and rolled my eyes.

We talked with a few more people until we ran into Andrew. I could spot his muscular body anywhere.

"All right, stranger," I said, hugging him.

"Ange," he said. "Been bloody ages."

"Andrew, this is my boyfriend Flynn."

They shook hands.

"All right, Flynn," said Andrew. "How'd you meet my

sister, then?"

"Sorry. Come again." Flynn leant in closer. There was too much background noise again.

"I asked how you met Ange."

"Oh. Nothing remarkable, really. She bumped into me in a café."

"Is that right?" Andrew looked at me. "I'm pleased for you, Ange. You look happy."

"Yeah, I am." I smiled. "How's Saoirse? She turned you Irish yet?"

"Well, I've taken to calling the loo the jacks, but other than that, still English. Saoirse's in the kitchen with Mum. She likes to cook, so she gravitates to wherever the food is, you know?"

"She still doing culinary school?"

"Yeah, she's cracking on. Listen, I'm gonna mingle a bit more, but we'll catch up later, yeah?" He leant in closer to Flynn so he could hear him. "And I defo want to get to know you better, Flynn, if you're going to be dating my sister."

"I look forward to it," said Flynn.

Andrew patted me on the shoulder and went to go mingle.

Flynn and I continued sauntering around and chatting with different people. I noticed that there were a lot of family pictures on the walls, false family pictures, really. They didn't represent our family as it was now; it was a window into how it was before. I wasn't happy that they were still up.

"Is this your dad?" asked Flynn as we looked at one of the false family pictures.

I sighed. "Yep. I don't know why Mum's still got these pictures up. He doesn't deserve the fucking wall space."

"Well, you do all look quite happy," Flynn countered. "Makes for a nice picture."

"It's fake happiness."

Flynn put his arm round me and pulled me close, and I wrapped my arms around his waist. He pointed at the people in the picture. "So this is your mum. And this is your brother. Who's this one, another brother?"

I giggled. "That's me."

His mouth dropped. "No it isn't."

"Yeah, that's me pre-transition. Cute, huh?"

He pulled away to look at me, and then back at the picture. He did this a few times. "Holy shit. That's mental."

"Why do you think my cousin didn't recognise me?"

"Yet I'm the shapeshifter?"

"Shut up, you." I snuggled up closer to him.

He stared at my younger self in the picture for a while. "What?" I asked him.

"Nothing. You just seem … sad, even though you're smiling."

I grinned. "All in the eyes, mate. They're the windows to the soul, and when you're living as someone you're not, like I was, the eyes are always how you can tell."

He kissed my cheek. "Does it bother you that there are

old pictures of you all around here?"

"It used to, back in the day. I wanted to escape that version of me so badly, and I hated anything that reminded me of it. But now, I don't really care. I feel so far removed from 'boy' me; it doesn't even really feel like I'm looking at me. I feel like I'm looking at someone I used to know, someone who got me to where I am now but who I no longer need."

He was quiet for a long moment.

"What you thinking about?" I asked him.

"Just the things we have in common. With your cousin not recognising you and how different you look from your younger self, you may be the only person I've ever met who could understand first-hand what it's like to have my illness. Well, you and maybe Bridget."

"I don't know if I'd say that."

"I would. You know what it's like to live in both a male and a female body. You know what it's like to be in-between. You know what it's like to have to conform to gender norms, or to not want to conform, or to have the way you feel about yourself not match the body you have. You know what it's like to not be recognised by people you know. I honestly think you're the only person who gets it, Ange."

I considered what he'd said. I'd never really thought about it before, but Flynn understood all my trans issues. I never really had to explain to him why I felt dysphoric one day, or why something someone said was transphobic, or whatever else. He got it. He always got it. His experience as a shapeshifter made it easier for him to understand me, and my experience as a trans woman made it easier for me to understand him.

"We understand each other," I said to him, and he smiled.

We continued mingling for a while, and then I told Flynn I wanted to speak to my mum alone for a bit. I left him with my brother, and they chatted. I wasn't worried; Andrew wasn't one to pry. It'd be nice for my brother and my boyfriend to connect a little.

On my way to the kitchen to see Mum, I overheard two of my aunts talking.

"Have you been hearing the news lately, about all these transgenders?" one of them said.

"Oh, aye. I have been," said the other.

"What do you make of them?"

"Ah, you ken, I don't care what you want to do in the privacy of your own home, as long as you're no hurting anybody."

"Exactly."

"But I think it aye crosses a line when you involve other people, especially the weans."

"I agree. And let's be honest, all this shite is just an easy way for predatory men to get into women's spaces."

"Aye, it is. I think it all has much to do with upbringing."

"Really? I've being hearing it's a social contagion."

"Oh, aye, that as well. But these things start somewhere,

don't they? They start in the home. Take …" She lowered her voice a little, but I could still hear her. "Take young Adrian."

"Miko's bairn?"

"That's the one. He's a girl now, intit? And where's the father? I reckon all this has a lot to do with that. Now, Andrew got lucky. He was older and had a better head on him. But Adrian? Well …"

"Excuse me," said a tall, blonde woman, bending over to speak with my two seated aunts. "If you old gobshites are going to talk shit about someone, at least get your feckin' facts straight. *Ange*, transitioned before her dad left, not after."

That was Saoirse, the only person in the family who not only had zero issue with my being transgender but who actually said she expected me to transition eventually. Apparently, I never really seemed like much of a boy to her.

She came over to me. "Hey, Ange. It's been ages."

"All right, Saoirse?" I hugged her.

"You look good."

"You too."

"So, what's the craic with you? You been doing okay?"

"Yeah. Been working, living life, you know. I got a boyfriend, too."

She smacked my arm. "No feckin' way."

"Yeah. He's over there with Andrew."

"Oh, well I have to meet him."

"Yeah, go ahead. I'm gonna go see my mum for a bit,

but I'll catch up with you."

She patted my shoulder and went to talk to Flynn and Andrew, and I went into the kitchen.

"Hey, Mum," I said. She was the only one here, and she looked back at me quickly while pulling chicken out of the oven.

"Angelina. Good. Do me a favour and put this on the worktop for me."

"Sure." I got some oven mitts and took the chicken from her, putting it down on the counter.

"You all right, Angelina?" she asked, too busy now tending to the potatoes to look at me.

"I'm fine."

I lifted myself up to sit on the counter, but Mum swiftly said, "Off the worktop, Angelina."

"You're not even looking at me. How did you know?"

"I see everything ahint me, Angelina. I've got eyes at the back of my head."

I got off the counter and rolled my eyes.

"I saw that, too," she said.

"*Mou*," I grumbled.

"Don't you *mou* me."

I looked around the kitchen; there were "fake" family pictures in here, too.

"Where's your boyfriend, Angelina?" asked Mum.

"Oh, he's with Andrew and Saoirse."

"Oh, is he? Left him alone with Andrew, did you? You must really like him. You know Andrew's got some embarrassing stories about you."

"Yeah, but he wouldn't tell any to Flynn."

"You think so, do you?"

Maybe I'd made a mistake leaving them two to chat.

"Either way, I'm happy for you," said Mum.

"Thanks."

I looked at her; she was still tending to the potatoes. "Mum, can I ask you something?"

"You may."

"Why do you still have pictures of Dad up?"

She paused for a second, and then continued as if I'd asked her what she thought of the weather. "They're pictures of the family."

"Fake pictures."

"They're very real, Angelina, you were there."

"You know what I mean."

"They're happy memories, Angelina. That's why they're up."

"I wasn't happy," I countered.

She slammed her hands down. "Well, not everything's about you, Adrian, is it?" She sighed. "Angelina."

I nodded, understanding. "You blame me, don't you? That's what it is at the end of the day. You blame me for breaking up the family."

"No, I don't blame you, Angelina."

"I think you do. You think my transition broke up the family. Well, for your information, Dad left because he didn't really love us. Andrew moved to Ireland because he wanted to live his life with Saoirse; it had nothing to do with us. And you chose to move back to Scotland. I'm the only one who stayed in Thivleton. So don't blame me for splitting up the family. It just happened. That's life. People move on to different things."

She put the potatoes in the oven and approached me. "All right, calm down, hen."

I stared at her. That stopped me in my tracks. "What did you just call me?"

"Hen."

I hesitated. "That's the first time you've ever referred to me with a feminine term."

"No it's not."

"Yes it is."

"If you say so."

"Well, I think I would know, wouldn't I?"

She took my hand. "Look, Angelina, I dinnae blame you for your father leaving us. If I'm being honest with myself, that man was aff his heid from the start. I keep the pictures up because they're happy memories for me. I was happy in them. I was happy with the idea of our family as it was. That doesnae mean those were good times, and that doesnae mean I'm not happy now."

"If you know that, then why are they still up?"

She sighed. "I don't know. They make me happy. I just like to remember that time fondly. It was simpler. But I do understand that you weren't happy, and I'm sorry about that. I understand your father left us because he didn't love you enough to love the real you. I just miss him sometimes. I have a lot of grief from what happened, and that's not your fault, Angelina, it's not. He made his choice, and I made mine. I chose to love my daughter."

I hugged her. "I love you, too, Mum."

She held me for a second, rubbing my back. Mum and I weren't always on the same wavelength, and she really got on my nerves most of the time, but at the end of the day, even if we didn't always get each other, she loved me, and I loved her.

Then she suddenly pushed me away and said, "Now, aff you go; out the scullery. Leave me to cook."

I shook my head and smiled, and then I left her.

I went to join Flynn, Andrew, and Saoirse. We all talked for a half-hour, and then dinner was served. The food was all laid out on the long table, and everyone took a paper plate, piled on whatever food they wanted, and found a spot where they could sit and eat while chatting amongst themselves.

After Flynn and I got some food, we sat with Andrew and Saoirse and continued chatting. But soon, Flynn said, "Sorry. Where's the loo?"

"Just down there. I'll show you," said Saoirse.

"You all right?" I whispered to Flynn.

"Yeah, just need a wee."

"Okay. Good."

He and Saoirse left, and then I said to Andrew, "So? What do you think of Flynn?"

"I like him. You picked well, Ange."

I smiled. "You, uh … you didn't tell him anything embarrassing, did you?"

He smirked. "Embarrassing like the lemon story?"

"Fuck off. You didn't tell him that."

He shrugged. "Just welcoming him to the family."

Fucking mortified.

"I notice Flynn's got a few memory issues, though," Andrew continued. "And he was very evasive in discussing his family or his childhood. There trauma there?"

"You could say that."

He nodded. "I see. Well, I'm proud of you, sis. Good to see you doing well."

"*Sis?*" He'd never called me that before.

He shrugged again. "Trying something new."

"All right, then. Thanks … *bro*."

17 December

Flynn and I left for England in the morning. Flynn was a young, teenage boy today; he changed last night. Luckily it happened when we got back to the rental house, so we were alone. But it also meant neither of us got much sleep. We pretended he was my younger brother, in case anyone wondered what I was doing with a teenage boy. He looked enough like me for no one to really question it.

In the cab, I asked Flynn if he enjoyed himself.

"Yeah," he said. "It was lovely seeing everyone …

Remind me to get new hearing aids at some point. I think the ones I had in yesterday are probably a bit old."

I smiled. "Will do."

"What about you? Did you enjoy yesterday?"

"Yeah. Bit exhausting dealing with everyone's opinions and reactions to me—somehow I always manage to forget that inevitability—but it was nice seeing the fam."

We both kipped a little in the cab, but when we made it home, we instantly jumped into bed. Just before I was about to fall asleep, Flynn said, "So, your brother mentioned something to me yesterday about some lemon story …"

I threw my hand straight over his mouth. "Not a word. Just go to sleep and forget it. I never want to hear you mention that again. Not now, not ever."

I took my hand away from his mouth, and he chuckled. "I thought it was a cute story."

"Ugh, kill me," I groaned.

17 January

The Christmas season was over, and the new year had begun. Kate and Bridget went to see Bridget's family on Christmas Day, and Flynn and I just had a quiet day, not doing much of anything. The family gathering in Scotland had been enough for us. Flynn also had a neurological exam about a week ago. It was with a local neurologist who would send the results to Dr Murphy. The exam seemed to go well, but I guess we'll find out what Dr Murphy thinks soon. Our next appointment with him is on the thirtieth. Despite what he said about making most of our appointments over the phone, this one, he said, needed to be in person. He wanted Flynn to take an eye exam, and he wanted it to be done at his clinic. Kate offered to take us up there again. She didn't have to, we could get a cab, but she wanted to. She felt that she was a part of this now, ever since I had her come over that night to help me with Flynn's change. I guess she had a point, really. Bridget even agreed to go with us this time, so it would be a big family affair. Though, she stipulated that if Flynn showed any signs of an impending change, she would be removing herself from us until it was over, even if that meant jumping out of the moving car. I was glad Bridget was coming, though. She and Flynn really got on, and I know all this doctor stuff makes Flynn nervous; they could use a friend around.

Today, Flynn was a woman with curly hair, chubby cheeks, and skin that was like melted milk chocolate. We were eating dinner together in the kitchen, and she said to me in her very quiet voice, "Ange?"

"Yeah?"

"You know how, last time we saw Dr Murphy, he said I should have a think about what my treatment goals are? Whether I want to be treated or cured?"

"Yeah."

"I think … I think maybe I want to be cured."

I looked at her; she was biting her lip. "You sure?"

She gave a small nod. "I want to be in one body and grow old in it, with you."

I smiled at first, but after some thought, I said, "But wait, Flynn, we don't know how old you actually are. What if Dr Murphy does cure you, and then you die the next day of old age?"

She frowned. "I hadn't thought of that … But I can't be that old, can I? I mean, I don't feel old."

"Your body's young, and you can't remember further back than the past twenty years or so, but that's all the illness, innit? Strip that away, and for all we know, you very well could be that old."

She smiled darkly. "Well, it doesn't really seem like an illness, then, does it? It seems more like a miracle."

"Until you're writhing in pain, covered in your own blood and sick and turning into an old woman who's paralysed from the waist down," I countered.

She sighed and cradled her head in her hands, her curls falling to cover the sides of her face. "What do you think I should do, Ange?"

My breath came out hollowly. "I don't know that I can make that decision for you. It's your body."

"I'm not asking you to make the decision for me; I'm asking for your opinion. If you were in my place, what would you do?"

That was in impossible, unfair question. I could never imagine being in Flynn's place because I was playing the part of Angelina: the woman who fell in love with a shapeshifter. I could never endorse a decision that would take Flynn away from me, but I also couldn't endorse a decision that would force them to suffer eternally.

"I don't know," I admitted. "Maybe we could stop the changes but get you to stay in whatever body you're in. We could freeze your illness and keep you in whatever body you want to be in for ever." That was the best I could do, picking an option that wasn't even on the table.

Flynn sighed again, peering at me through her fingers. "Yeah. Maybe."

30 January

It was the day of our appointment with Dr Murphy. Kate had driven us all to his clinic in Birmingham. We did Flynn's eye exam first, which Dr Murphy was in the room for. He was observing and discussing things with the ophthalmologist while she performed the examination.

When that was done, we went to Dr Murphy's office. Kate and Bridget sat in the waiting room.

"All right," said Dr Murphy, closing the door. "If you don't mind, Flynn, before we begin, I'd just like to take a quick look at you. Is that all right?"

"Sure," said Flynn.

Dr Murphy bent down to examine Flynn in her chair. He looked at her straight, blonde hair; her large, round eyes; and her square jaw and strong cheekbones.

"I'd like to feel your face and hair if that's okay?" said the doctor.

"Sure, I guess."

Dr Murphy pressed his fingers to Flynn's face like he was examining a sculpture he had just made. Then he ran his fingers through her hair and asked, "How long have you been like this?"

"About a day," said Flynn.

"And how did you look before? Anything like you do now?"

"Not at all. I was a man, older, East Asian."

"And yet you wouldn't be able to tell. Remarkable."

He took a seat at his desk and continued. "All right. So, we've done some tests, looked over the results, and unsurprisingly, I can confirm that you are biologically a shapeshifter. There're no ifs and buts about it; your body changes at a cellular level into a completely different configuration. Now, obviously, as far as I'm aware, this is a condition that has not ever been observed or studied. But for all we know, there are other doctors in the world like me who are willing to keep things quiet to protect the safety of their patients. Nonetheless, this is a real, observable condition, and I've taken to calling it cellular metamorphosis disorder, or CMD. You see, all cells have a life cycle—they live and die. There are cells in the human body that live for only a few hours, and there are cells that live for a few years. When a cell dies, it is replaced with a new cell, until the person dies, of course. But with your cells, Flynn, as someone with CMD, they all instantly die at more or less the same time and are then replaced with new cells in a completely different configuration. In essence, your cells are regenerating, but they are not regenerating into the same sort of cells they've always been. They're becoming different cells. So the question is: why? What is causing this to happen?

"Well, unfortunately, I'm not entirely sure. It does, however, seem to be based on self-preservation. We know that if you are sick or injured to a certain extent, that will force a change. Your body seems to regenerate your cells at this accelerated rate in order to keep you alive. And I imagine, barring some unforeseen circumstance, this means that an individual with CMD can live indefinitely."

"Are you saying I'm immortal?" asked Flynn.

"Quite possibly, yes." He continued without giving us time to digest that. "So, every time you regenerate, your phenotype changes—that is, the characteristics expressed by your cells: the colour of your hair, the shape of your nose, etc. But where are your cells getting this information from? How do they know how to arrange themselves into a white, European woman one day, and a black, African man the next? My first guess would be DNA. For example, let's say your mum had brown eyes, and your dad had blue eyes. And let's say you have blue eyes, too. That doesn't necessarily mean your mum's brown eyes are not still encoded into your DNA. It's just that your body has chosen to express the gene for blue eyes instead of brown eyes. Your cells seem to be able to re-read the instructions in your DNA with each change and select a different trait to express. What's interesting is the extent to which you can do this. It suggests an extremely diverse family history on your part. But I don't believe that is the whole picture. A diverse genotype does not explain your ability to change your sex and age as well.

"When it comes to sex, a lot of that can be influenced by sex hormones: oestradiol, progesterone, testosterone, etc. But some things cannot be changed. Once you've grown breast tissue, you cannot un-grow it. You cannot grow a uterus or make ovaries become testicles. These things happen in the womb, and once you are born, they cannot be changed. However, this rule of nature does not seem to apply to you. You claim you have had female sex organs and even menstruated on one day, yet on a different day, you were able to produce sperm with your male sex organs. This ability to completely change your sex is absolutely remarkable and cannot be explained by my previous DNA theory.

"And then there's your age, how you can go from being postpubescent back to being prepubescent in the span of a night. Absolutely remarkable."

He took a second to shake his head in disbelief before continuing. "You've also complained about premonitory headaches and seizures, as well as long-term memory loss. And the young lass here has said that you have minor changes in your personality when you change as well. This all suggests to me that there is also an effect on your brain, even if your mind doesn't change in the same way your body does.

"So, here's my current theory: Upon review of the results of your genetic testing, your genome seems to suggest that the photoreceptors in your eyes are quite odd. That is to say, the cells in your eyes that convert light to signals for your brain to read don't act like the rest of your body. These cells don't appear to change like the rest of you does, and their structure is unlike that of any I've ever seen. So I wonder if they have anything to do with all this. You see, all cells have a sort of memory. An example of this is when you stop exercising for a time and then go back to it. Your muscles will have an easier time rebuilding themselves than they would if it were your first time exercising them. Your cells can remember how they used to be in the past. So I think—bearing in mind this is just a theory—I think the photoreceptors in your eyes can observe and remember certain traits you see in other people and copy those traits to your DNA so that you can express them when your cells regenerate. Have you ever noticed that you sometimes resemble someone you've actually met?"

"No," said Flynn. "The faces are unique; I don't resemble anyone."

Dr Murphy rubbed his cheeks. "Interesting. There must be some involvement with the cells in your eyes. That can't be a coincidence. Perhaps your eyes must be triggered into remembering a specific trait; perhaps you have to see a person many, many times before it is engrained within you."

Flynn shrugged.

"Well, that's neither here nor there, I suppose. Let's discuss treatment, shall we? I have a few ideas, but I need to know what you would like to get out of this treatment. Have you given any thought into whether or not this is something you want cured?"

Flynn looked at me, and I nodded. I didn't want to sway her decision. This was *her* decision, not mine. But I silently hoped she wouldn't choose something that took her away from me.

Flynn looked at Dr Murphy. "I don't want to die," she said quietly. "Not yet, at least."

"I don't believe you can die," said the doctor. "Even if you were stabbed through the heart, I imagine you would just regenerate into a new body."

Flynn looked down. "So, really, I could outlive everyone—everyone I know and love … and, with my memory problems, eventually, I could forget I ever knew them. I could've already forgotten someone I used to know."

"Yes," the doctor confirmed. "That is quite possible."

Flynn looked at me as I tried not to look as anxious and worried as I felt. We had already suspected a lot of what Dr Murphy was telling us, but to have it confirmed now, it was a different feeling. It wasn't hypothetical anymore. It wasn't guessing at things we knew nothing about. This was real. This was how things were. And it was terrifying.

"I want to live," said Flynn. "I want to live in one body, a young one, that will age at a regular rate, and then I want to die when I'm old, with the people I love."

Dr Murphy sighed. "Well, I can't guarantee anything, but we can certainly try. I'm going to write you a prescription, and we'll take it from there."

14 February

It was the fourteenth of February, Valentine's Day, supposedly the most romantic day of the year. But Flynn and I weren't doing anything special. Actually, *we* weren't doing anything at all. Flynn was asleep. It was a side effect of the medication Dr Murphy prescribed for them. It made them tired, like, properly knackered. Every day, Flynn slept longer and longer, and their changes hadn't really stopped either.

I spent the day working and reading. I was actually reading manga at the moment. And I was reading it in French. English girl reading Japanese manga translated into French—the life of a rebel. Too bad Flynn was still asleep; they would've found that funny and impressive.

After I ate dinner alone, I realised Flynn had been asleep for over twenty hours. I had to wake them up and give them water and some food.

I went into the bedroom with a glass of water and a slice of bread. Flynn was usually a bit nauseous when they woke up, ever since starting the medication, and bread was about all they could stomach.

I rubbed the arms of the little girl passed out on the bed. "Flynn. Flynn, wake up."

She grumbled and turned over.

I bent down and kissed her cheek. "Come on, Flynn. You need to eat something."

She yawned and sat up, drunk with tiredness.

"What time is it?" she asked in a small voice.

"Quarter to eight."

"Ugh. Then why are you waking me? It's too early."

"No. Quarter to eight at night. You've been asleep all day."

"Oh." She was too tired to be shocked by that. Her body was teetering, desperate to lie back down and sleep some more.

I handed her the glass of water. "Here. Drink this. You can't go back to sleep yet. You need to eat and drink and probably use the toilet."

She nodded, too tired to speak.

She ate the bread, drank the water, and then trotted off to the loo. After she'd been in there for ten minutes, I said, "You all right in there, Flynn?" She didn't answer, and I guessed why. I walked into the bathroom and saw her asleep on the toilet. I knelt down beside her and woke her again.

"I don't think these meds Dr Murphy's given you are working," I said.

She yawned. "They are making me pretty knackered."

"Plus, they haven't really helped your CMD at all, have they?"

She yawned again. "Nope. Still changing."

I smiled at her. "I'll ring Dr Murphy tomorrow."

19 March

"So how are you, baby girl?" said Kate as she looked through the period-product section of the pharmacy. We were here to pick up my oestrogen prescription as well as some other miscellaneous supplies.

I shrugged. "I'm all right, I guess. Little knackered."

"Yeah? What about Flynn?"

"They're pretty depressed, honestly."

"New meds?"

"Yep. Flynn's been irritable and just sad all the time, and the changes haven't stopped. I don't know if these meds are working either."

"Sounds rough. Here, catch." She threw me a box of panty liners.

"Oh, crap, yeah, I do need these. Cheers."

She winked at me.

"You know, it's a little odd that you always seem to know when I'm low on liners."

Kate chuckled a little. "That's because you're always low."

"Not always."

"Oh, yes, you are. You're a very leaky girl." She winked at me again.

"Shut up. No I'm not."

She kissed my cheek. "Oh, kitten, you're so adorable when you're embarrassed. But a little daily excretion's nothing to—"

I threw my hand over her mouth before she even finished her sentence. "That's not fair, Kate. I haven't done anything to set you off yet. Shut up." She kept moving her lips underneath my hand and mumbling; she was going to finish what she was saying regardless of whether I could hear it.

When she finished, she looked at me expectantly, and I removed my hand from her mouth. She smirked and said, "Someone's feeling a little bratty today, aren't we?"

"Oh, yeah? Well, let's see how you like it. Let's talk about what comes out of you."

"I'm not as leaky as you, babes."

"Maybe not all the time, but there is a certain time of the month when you're *way* leakier than I am."

She grinned. "You want to talk about my period? That's cool."

"Oh, please, Kate, you hate your period. Don't act so nonchalant about it."

"I do hate my period, but I'm not ashamed of it. What do you want to talk about? Where I am in my cycle? My flow? Texture? Colour?"

She grinned even wider when I hesitated. No matter

what I did, I could never beat her at this.

She kissed my cheek again and said, "I'm not ashamed of anything that comes out my fanny. Actually, I'm quite proud of some of it." She winked.

Then she moved to the cough medicine section, calm and unaffected.

"You just love winding me up, don't you?" I said, following her.

"It is a highlight of my day, yeah."

"You know, for the record, I started wearing period pants, so I don't need to buy liners nearly as much as I used to."

"That's good. Very environmentally conscious. But you still keep a stock of liners handy when you wanna wear something sexy, which is most of the time now Flynn's around, innit?"

"Well, I mean …"

"Don't worry, baby girl, I've got your number."

I must have been blushing this whole conversation, and Kate was just drinking it in like she was milking a golden cow. I sighed. "I really hate you sometimes, Kate."

"That's what sisters are for," she chimed.

"Anyway," she continued, "back to the situation with Flynn's meds. These things just take time, babes. You've got to find the right meds."

"Yeah, I know," I sighed. "I just wish the wrong meds didn't always have to make things so much worse."

"Well, it's a process, and sometimes it just doesn't work

out. Take Bridget. She's tried a lot of different medications for her Tourette's, but nothing really seemed to help, and anything that did help came with pretty bad side effects. The only thing that ended up helping her was learning to listen to her body—getting enough sleep, keeping her anxiety down, breathing exercises. You've just got to keep trying things until you find what works."

"I guess you're right. I just hope everything will work out in the end."

"It will, babes."

"Flynn's just so …"

Kate put her arm round me. "I know. That's why we're out together. Good to take a break from the partners and have some sister time."

"So you can milk my embarrassment."

"It's so much better winding you up in person. I can't see how red you get over the phone."

I rolled my eyes. "Anyway. I guess you're right. I do need a break from Flynn every now and then. As much as I love them, it's hard sometimes."

"I get it, kitten. I need my breaks from Bridget, too. She can get very chaotic. Even without the tics, she keeps weird hours because of her work, and she can get really keyed up at the wrong times. Gets on my nerves. It's good to take a break. Plus, I'm sure Bridget needs her breaks from me, too. She may not turn as red as you, but she's fun to wind up as well."

"Well, it is true that distance from you is the only thing

that makes me forget how much I hate you." I smirked.

She gave me a bear hug and said, "Space does make the heart grow fonder."

8 April

My hands were soaked in Flynn's blood as I dragged her limp, unconscious body to the bathroom. I hadn't slept properly all week, ever since we switched Flynn's medication. It's had the complete wrong effect: It's sped up Flynn's condition. Now, she was changing twice a day, and my nose had become so used to the unique smell of old parmesan cheese and iron that was Flynn's sick and blood that just going outside for some fresh air burned my nose like poison. I felt broken, like a woman at war. I was numb—no feeling, no emotion. I just had a duty of service to this remarkable human being.

But it did take a toll. That wasn't Flynn's fault, but it was because of them. I've been taking a lot of breaks, going outside and trying to rediscover myself, my emotions, who I am without being Flynn's keeper. And Kate came by to help sometimes; occasionally, she would even take over for me, even though I wasn't entirely comfortable subjecting her to Flynn's condition alone. But those moments to myself were few and far between; I had to take care of Flynn.

Once in the bathroom, I took off Flynn's blouse. It was covered in blood and didn't fit her anymore. She'd grown a more muscular frame in the span of a few minutes. Nowadays, she always looks like two different people. She was just changing so quickly—two different skin colours, two different eye shapes, one large foot and one small foot. The changes were becoming more violent as well. There was always blood to clean, or sick to clean, or chunks of flesh on the floor. I could hear Flynn's bones crunching and cracking almost constantly. I couldn't take it. My nerves were being plucked and prodded all the time, but I felt so dead inside that I couldn't even cry.

Flynn came to and was sick all over the bathroom floor. I lifted her over the toilet bowl, and she continued being sick into it. All I could hear was the sound of her strained oesophagus squeezing out her insides and spewing them from her mouth. It was like white noise to me, and I just carried on.

In the evening, a few hours after the change was over, Flynn went to take his medication, but I put my hand over the pill bottle and shook my head.

"This isn't the one," I said.

He sighed. "Guess we'll have to ring Dr Murphy again."

23 May

It was Thursday evening, and Flynn and I were snuggled up together on the sofa. Today, Flynn was a tall man with white skin and blond, shoulder-length hair, and he'd been like that for nine days. It felt like a marathon, but we'd finally found the right meds.

Now that Flynn wasn't changing, we both had time to learn and get used to his new body. Talking to him was great. Being next to him was great. Being in his arms was great. Kissing him was great. Sex with him was great. Life together was great.

The only issue was the headaches—a side effect of the new medication. They were getting worse every day, and more frequent. It used to be only a few minutes a day, but now it was constant. We'd discussed telling Dr Murphy about this. We had a phone appointment with him in a few days. Maybe he could prescribe something that could get rid of the headaches. And then this would be over. Flynn could stay in one body, stable, present. Dr Murphy would still have to do some tests to see if Flynn was ageing normally now or if his cells were stagnant. Or maybe his cells were still regenerating but taking on the same shape. Either way, we were almost there. Just a few tweaks, and this shapeshifting shit would all be over. Finally.

Flynn bent over and pressed his hands to his head.

"You all right?" I asked him, pulling away.

He shook his head. "My head. It hurts."

"Do you need something? Water? Ice?"

He groaned. His eyes were closed; I wasn't sure he'd heard me properly.

I took the initiative to head to the kitchen and fill a small bag with ice, making up a little ice pack. When I came back into the front room and pressed the ice pack to his forehead, I felt how hot his skin was. He was running a fever. I wondered if maybe he was sick—caught a cold or something. He never gets sick; he just changes. But now he's not changing, maybe that's what it was. I wondered if painkillers would work on him now, or headache tablets, anything. And then …

Pop!

Instantly, I was covered in blood. Flynn's body was just bones and dripping, bloody flesh.

He was dead.

I knew. I knew it in the back of my head. It was too good to be true. His condition was just biding its time until it could literally explode and spew pieces of him all over me.

It was quiet aside from the blood that dripped off my face or the chunks of intestine that fell off my hand. Then I heard a crack and saw a bone move, and I knew Flynn would be okay. He wasn't dead. It was just the man I'd come to love for the past nine days; he wasn't coming back. And then there was me. Each day, I came closer and closer to becoming a casualty of this war against Flynn's illness.

I stood in a very calculated way, no sudden movements, very slow and decisive. I walked myself to the bathroom and looked at the woman in the mirror. I couldn't see her dark skin behind the red, chunky blood. I couldn't see the natural wavy texture of her hair because it was messy, and she was too bloody knackered to comb it. And I couldn't tell how she felt, because her face was just dead, emotionless.

I couldn't tell how she felt, but I knew how I felt. I grabbed the rim of the sink with both hands to steady my shaking body, and I screamed as loudly as I could. I screamed and screamed. Louder. Louder. I wanted everyone to hear me. I wanted the mirror to crack and shatter at the sheer volume of my whaling. I was done. I hated this. I hated everything. Fuck, I wanted to explode. I wanted to explode like Flynn just did. I wanted to shower all of Thivleton in my blood and guts, just so everyone would know that I CAN'T FUCKING TAKE IT ANYMORE.

Fuck.

FUCK!

I took a breath. Another one. And another one. I wiped the blood off my face. No one heard me. No one saw me. No one in this town gave a shit. It was just me and the woman in the mirror. If I broke; I broke … But I wouldn't break. I couldn't. Even if I secretly wanted to. Even if I thought it would be the easiest escape … Flynn still needed my help. It was time to get back to work.

7 June

Flynn and I were taking our weekly Friday walk in Oak Corn Park. We just walked silently. Flynn was a bald, middle-aged woman, and she was also pretty irritable and difficult to talk to these days, ever since we changed her meds again. I guess we were both a little irritable. Never a good combination.

Flynn was also a little shaky—her dexterity wasn't as good as it could be. But with regard to her illness, she was doing a little better. She was still changing, but it was a bit milder—not as much blood, and it didn't take as long. The changes were also every four days now, most of the time. Progress, but not enough.

When we got back home, Flynn stumbled on her feet. I went to help her steady herself, but she pulled away.

"I know how to walk, Ange," she snapped.

"All right, fine. I was just trying to help."

"Well, you're not helping, are you?"

"What the fuck's the matter with you?"

"Nothing. Absolutely nothing except the same bloody thing that's always been wrong with me." She stumbled again.

I went to go help her, but she still pulled away from me. "Don't touch me."

"Flynn, just calm down."

"Calm down?" she scoffed. "Easy for you to say. Poor little Angelina doesn't have to deal with changes. She has no issue keeping calm." She rolled her eyes. "It's not the same for you. You can walk away. You can take breaks. I don't get a break from being me. No matter how hard I try, I can't turn my condition off."

I shook my head in disbelief. "Flynn, you don't know what the fuck you're on about. Who do think cleans your fucking blood and guts off the floor? Who do you think drags your limp body to the bathroom? Do you know how many times I've been covered in your fucking blood, how many times I've watched different versions of you die, over and over and over?"

"And do you have any idea how that feels, Ange? Have you ever broken every bone in your body just to have them reattach themselves in different configurations? Have you ever had your skin peeled off you, piece by piece? Of course you don't think about that. Everything's about you, innit, Ange? It's all about how much of a strain this is on you. Well guess what, I never asked you to be here. I never asked you to dote on me."

"You don't have to ask me, Flynn," I yelled at her. "You need me, so I'm here. I'm here because I bloody well choose to be, despite the fact that you're being such an arse these days. I am not that wishy-washy, Flynn. I have stuck around because, despite my better judgement sometimes, I love you. Your pain is my pain. And you don't get to invalidate that after everything I've seen, everything I've been through."

Flynn stumbled again and fell into my arms. I sighed away my rage and stroked her head.

"Ange," she said softly.

"Yeah?"

"I don't think these meds are right for me."

"Me neither."

I kissed her and held her close. Back to the drawing

board.

1 July

"I'm back," I called as I entered Flynn's house. I was at Kate's for some sister time, time to decompress and get away from all the CMD stuff—just some space from Flynn.

We still hadn't found a treatment that worked, but Dr Murphy wasn't giving up yet, and neither was I. We just had to stick through to the end. This will all be something we'll laugh about once Flynn is on the right meds and everything's fine. But for the moment, it's just hard.

I went into the front room. Flynn was sitting quietly on the sofa. Today, he was a teenage boy, slender, lots of acne, and a bit of bumfluff.

"Did you hear me?" I asked when I realised he hadn't responded.

He looked at me and said, "Come sit. I want to talk to you."

"Okay." I sat myself down next to him. "What's up?"

He didn't look at me; he kept his gaze straight ahead. "This isn't working."

"What's not working?"

"This. These meds. Trying to cure me. It's not working."

"We just haven't found the right ones yet."

"Ange, it's been six months. We keep trying and failing. We're both stressed. We're at each other's throats more often than not ... I just don't think we're going to find something that works."

"You're being negative, Flynn."

"No, I'm being realistic. How long are we supposed to go on like this? How long do we have to struggle with this before we admit that I can't be cured?"

I shook my head. "I'll never admit that. I won't. We just have to keep trying."

"Ange, it's not worth it. It's draining the life out of both of us."

I sighed. "So, what? You just want to give up?"

"It's not giving up. It's accepting the things neither of us can change."

"Says the one who can't stop changing," I scoffed.

"Ange, don't be difficult."

"I'm not being difficult. Flynn, you can't … you can't honestly tell me that you're okay. I'm not okay. Your illness—"

"Is familiar." He put his hand over mine. "I knew how to handle it. You knew how to handle it. Maybe that's okay. We have to know when to stop. Let's just focus on perfecting how things are, instead of trying to change them into something unfamiliar. It's not working."

"Okay, sure, maybe we did know how to handle things before, but that doesn't mean it was easy."

"No. But that's how it is. That's who I am. And I think we just have to live with that."

I didn't say anything. I was not okay with that. I didn't want to give up. After all the blood and sick, after all the times I'd watched the person I love die in front of me, I was not okay with that.

"Ange, please. We need to stop."

I forced out a sigh. "Fine. We'll let Dr Murphy know at our next appointment."

I didn't agree, but who was I to dispute? It wasn't really my decision, was it?

23 July

"So I think we just cut our losses," said Flynn.

We were in Dr Murphy's office. Today, Flynn was a round-faced woman with massive dimples whenever she smiled. But she wasn't smiling much now. We were here to end treatment with Dr Murphy, to admit that this wasn't working. To admit defeat.

Dr Murphy rubbed his face and sighed. "Well, I won't lie to you, I'm very sorry to hear you say that."

"Me too," said Flynn. "But we have to face it; this isn't working. My reactions to the treatments have been mildly bad to drastically worse, and nothing's even come close to making things better."

Dr Murphy nodded. "I understand. It's not like there's any standard of care for cellular metamorphosis disorder; as far as we know, you are the first person to have it."

"I'm the only person who has it," said Flynn.

"Maybe. You never know. The world is a strange place when you look close enough." He interlocked his fingers and rested his chin on them. "All right, so, I know you don't want me to tell anyone about your condition, and I have no intention of sharing the details of your case with anyone. I give you my word. However, with your permission, I wonder if I could tell your story to anyone else who comes to me with similar symptoms as you? Anonymously, of course."

Flynn considered this. "As long as you keep everything completely anonymous—don't use my name, don't say when you saw me, don't mention where I live. But on the off chance you find someone else like me, and you think it would help them to know about me, then you can tell them. Anonymously."

Dr Murphy nodded, and then he got up and shook both my and Flynn's hands. "It's been an absolute pleasure meeting you both. Thank you for bringing this remarkable disorder to my attention and allowing me the opportunity to study it. If you'd ever like to try treatment again, just give me a ring."

Kate drove us back home from Birmingham, and as usual, Flynn bought her petrol and a takeaway. Kate stayed with us for a bit, and then she went back home, and Flynn and I were alone.

I hugged Flynn tightly and held her in my arms. This was the reluctant end to this chapter of our lives. I didn't want it to be, but it was the end all the same.

18 August

So life was back to normal now. Well, I suppose "normal" is a relative term. Flynn was back to changing every three days, sometimes less, sometimes more. The changes themselves ranged from mild to violent, but they never got as violent as that time Flynn hadn't changed for nine days straight. For Flynn, this was life as usual, but for me, it still felt like war. Sure, things weren't as tense as they were before, and we weren't arguing as much, but that was only because I was staying quiet. When I first met Flynn, all I wanted was to be used to the changes. Now I was used to them, and all I wanted was to not have to be used to them. It wasn't fair, on me or Flynn. But Flynn was fine living like this, so I had to be fine with it, too. If I was going to be a shapeshifter's girlfriend, I had to be okay with it. I had to be. And someday, I would be. But that day wasn't today.

Today, we had Kate and Bridget over for a little dinner party, as we often do. Flynn was a bald man with a bushy moustache and sparkling green eyes. He was chatting in the kitchen with Bridget as they did the washing-up.

I was in the front room with Kate, and we drank cranberry juice. (At her request. She wanted to look like she was drinking red wine, but she had to drive home. Bridget doesn't drive.)

"So how are things going, kitten?"

I sighed. "I dunno, Kate. I feel like I can't say anything. Flynn seems happy, but it's false, you know? He's just sort of settled. But I can't settle. I know if we keep trying, we can solve this. But now I'll have to convince him again. After all we went through, he'll never go for it."

"Maybe you don't have to solve it. Maybe he actually is fine, and you just have to get on board."

I looked at her. "Whose side are you on?"

"Why are there sides to begin with?"

"Kate, come on. You were here. You saw what I saw. And Flynn told me himself that he wanted to grow old together in one body."

"Maybe he changed his mind."

"Because it was too hard to achieve. He gave up. But why should that mean I have to?"

Kate put her hand on my shoulder. "Ange, I'm gonna tell you something, as your sister who knows you better than you'd like."

I rolled my eyes. "What?"

"You're nosing your way into things that don't concern you."

"This concerns me quite a bit, thank you."

"Ange, you always get like this."

"No I don't."

"Yes, you do. You think you know best, and you don't accept when someone tells you otherwise."

"Kate, this is a completely different situation."

"How?"

"Because I don't think Flynn's able to see how much he's suffering. He's been like this for so long, he doesn't know what it's like to live without his condition. It's like me before I transitioned. I lived so many years as a boy that I didn't realise how much I was suffering. That was just life to me. I assumed every boy hated being a boy as much as I did. Then you told me that your mum was trans, and just knowing that that was possible, that I didn't have to be stuck as a boy and grow into a man, suddenly I really started to feel how much it hurt me every day to live like that."

Kate let out a single, slow breath. "And you think your gender dysphoria is in any way comparable to Flynn's shapeshifting? Is that what you're saying, Ange?"

"Yes."

She snorted.

"What?"

"I think you're being pretty fucking liberal there."

"Oh, do tell."

"All right, since you've forgotten, I remember the days when you would be dead depressed if someone called you handsome or complimented you in any way that made you feel like they viewed you as masculine. Or the days when you used to wish you had erectile dysfunction. D'you remember that? You wanted to cut the blood supply off from your penis; you even used to look up ways to make it atrophy. And I seriously thought back then that you were one unwanted erection away from chopping your knob off."

"Okay, can we stop talking about my tail? I get it."

She gave me an exasperated smile. "Just relax, Ange.

Okay? If Flynn says he's fine, then he's fine. Even if he is suffering like you were, which he isn't, but if he were, he has to realise that for himself. I didn't out you as trans before you were ready, did I? Even though I knew you were a girl way before you figured it out."

"You didn't out me, but you told me about your mum. You helped me realise it. I just need to help Flynn realise."

"Except this is not the same situation, Ange. Fuck, man, you are such a control freak."

"And you're a fucking drama queen."

I flicked her ear, and she gave me a bear hug.

Later, after Kate and Bridget had left, I was looking through Flynn's book collection, looking for a new book to read. I'd made it my duty to read every book he owned, just to save them from his negligence. I'd gotten through a lot of them already, and I was afraid I might have run out of the books that interested me. But then I found one I hadn't seen before. It had an old, green spine.

I pulled the book off the shelf. It didn't seem to be a novel; it looked like a journal or a notebook. I flicked through it. The pages were yellowed and crinkled, and it was full of messy but legible writing. There were also diagrams and equations. What is this thing? There was a date on the first page: *Wednesday, 22 April 1931*. Shit, this book was over ninety years old.

I skimmed some of the writing: "Today is a day of birth. As I write this, my wife is in labour, and our son will soon be here. Concurrently, my wife and I have decided to continue the research we started during the Great War. Immortality will soon be within our grasp, just as we welcome new life to this undeserving world."

"What're you doing?" said Flynn as he came into the front room.

"Just looking for a book to read. I found this really old notebook, from the thirties, apparently."

Flynn's eyes widened. "Don't read that."

"What is it?"

"Ange, put it back!"

"Okay. Fine." I carefully put the book back on the shelf. "What is it?"

"My father's journal."

My jaw literally dropped. I was bombarded with a million questions all at once, but the one I asked first was: "You remember your father? Like, you remember that he kept a journal?"

"I don't want to remember."

"But you do."

He looked at me. "What does it matter?"

"What do you mean *what does it matter*? If we had more information on your life, your family history, we could give that information to Dr Murphy. He could figure all of this out, find a better treatment. Your father wrote about some sort of research, about immortality, and—"

"I don't want to hear it!"

He rubbed his face and sat down heavily on the sofa. I sat next to him.

"Flynn, how much do you remember?"

"Enough to know I don't want to remember it."

"Tell me."

He shook his head.

"Flynn, if you don't tell me, you'll forget next time you change."

"Good."

I thought for a second, piecing bits of information together. "Did … did your father do this to you? Did he make you into a shapeshifter?"

"I don't want to talk about it, Ange."

"Fine. I'll just read the journal, then."

I got up, but Flynn put his hand on my wrist, stopping me. "Ange, please just leave it."

"Flynn, if we could find out how you got like this, if we could give that information to Dr Murphy, maybe he could find a cure. Didn't you say to me that you wanted to be cured, that you wanted to grow old together in one body?"

He sighed. He couldn't even look at me. "It's not worth it, Ange. We can't always get what we want. Sometimes, life just has different plans."

And that was the end of it. We didn't speak about it for the rest of the evening. But now I had found that book, it stood out on the bookshelf like a sore thumb.

19 August

It was two in the morning. I was sitting up in bed, and

Flynn was fast asleep beside me. I couldn't sleep, not when I knew that there were answers in the bookshelf in the front room. I didn't know what to do. Clearly, Flynn didn't want me to read it, and I should respect that. I should. But … If the information in that journal can solve the mystery of Flynn's illness, if it can cure him, allow us to grow old together, does that make it okay to betray his trust? Whatever happened is something he doesn't want to remember, so maybe I need to take some initiative and handle this for him. That's my duty, as his girlfriend, as the shapeshifter's keeper, in the war against his illness. Isn't it?

I looked at Flynn as he turned over in the bed. If I love him, if I really love him, what should I do? Trust him enough to respect his wishes, or betray his trust and take the situation into my own hands to stop his suffering for good? Will he forgive me if I read it? If he doesn't forgive me, will I be able to say that I did the right thing, that I helped him, even if he hates me afterwards? Maybe that's what this is about in the end. Will I be selfish or selfless? Will I do nothing and save our relationship, or do something and destroy it?

I thought, and I remembered the time when Flynn exploded right in front of me, and I was covered in his blood. I remembered all the times Flynn had been disappointed by the body he was in. I took a breath. I had to do it.

Slowly, I slithered out of bed. Flynn was still asleep. I tiptoed into the front room. Silence. He was still asleep. I plucked the green book from the bookshelf and sat on the floor. I didn't want to sit on the sofa in case it creaked and woke Flynn up.

I held the book in my hands for a second. Last chance to change my mind. Last chance …

I took a breath and opened it.

I continued the entry I'd already started reading yesterday:

"Today is a day of birth. As I write this, my wife is in labour, and our son will soon be here. Concurrently, my wife and I have decided to continue the research we started during the Great War. Immortality will soon be within our grasp, just as we welcome new life to this undeserving world.

"The research we started years ago was meant for the soldiers, but now our son is about to be born, I find I want to protect him. Should a war that big ever happen again, should England be invaded or should some other unforeseen threat to his life occur, I want my boy to be protected. I want him to be able to survive anything. My boy: Flynn Jones Riley."

That entry was dated *22 April 1931*. If Flynn was born then, that would make him ninety-three years old.

I flipped through the book. There were a lot of maths equations I couldn't understand and lists of letters and numbers, maybe names of genes. The journal was very unorganised. There was no structure at all, just random scribblings all over the place.

There was another entry from 1940:

"Flynn isn't taking well to the testing. I can no longer sedate him as I need him awake to gauge his reaction to the treatment. This means we can hear his screams when we give him the injections. But he will understand in the end why this must be done.

"We are running out of time. Somehow, the world has been plunged into war yet again. They've started bombing the city. I'd like to move all our work to the family home in Thivleton, if we can make it. Less chance of losing all our research in the bombings. Nothing to gain from bombing a small town.

"We've almost discovered which genes to mutate for the experiment to work. Soon, the secret to immortality will be unlocked."

There were still more equations and diagrams, and I wondered if they somehow explained how this experiment worked. It seemed like Flynn's parents mutated his genes to make him like this, to make him immortal.

There was another entry without a date:

"As our experiment progresses, I find myself wondering if I should make this discovery known to the masses. Frankly, they don't deserve it. After the Great War ended, I came home. I was lucky. I was mostly unscathed comparatively. I thought I would live the rest of my days happily with my wife and our son. But war has come again. And now I know that, when this one ends, if it ends, there will be another. People never stop finding reasons to kill other people. They forget the lessons we learned the first time. This world is going to Hell, and I will not play a part in handing it off to Satan himself. This research must stay within the family.

"I've already been contacted by the British Army. They recalled I began my research on immortality during the Great War and wanted to know if I'd made any progress in cracking it. They want me to make enhanced soldiers capable of regrowing limbs and surviving explosions. But do you know what would happen if I gave them my research? The British would never die. We'd be an unstoppable force. And there's only one place to go when you're that high up the food chain: down. If they think the Germans won't figure my research out once they're shown its potential, they're mistaken. Soon, everyone will have immortal soldiers. And then the most coveted research will be deciphering a way to kill the unkillable. Then we're all mortal once again.

"It will never end. I told them I abandoned my research. Immortality was a bastard of nature, and therefore impossible.

"No. This research stays in the family. There will be only one immortal in this world. My son will not become a victim of war."

Another entry had a date with no year. 28 May:

"Flynn has taken to the treatment. His genes have been successfully mutated. But it now occurs to me that, in order to test his immortal properties, we'll have to hurt him. Mary is being difficult. She wants to go on faith that we've succeeded and that our son is for ever safe from humanity. But I will not bet Flynn's life on something as fleeting as faith. The efficacy of the treatment must be certain.

"We'll begin with electric shocks, painful but non-lethal. From there, we'll play it by ear. We must subject him to many different forms of pain to see what he can endure. My current ideas are starvation, poison, illness, extreme blood loss, suffocation, and, if he survives every time, I'll put him into an explosive belt and blow him up. Then, if we were successful, I'll watch our good work as he pieces himself back together. Flynn must be subjected to all these horrors if we are to be certain of the efficacy of the experiment."

I threw up a little in my mouth at the thought of Flynn being put through all that. No wonder he didn't want to remember. If this was done in 1940, Flynn would have only been nine years old.

The next entry was undated:

"My son has become like a chameleon, able to disguise himself. But unlike the chameleon, he cannot control how he changes, and he does not always blend in. All tests were a success. Even the explosive belt proved unable to kill him. Flynn is capable of changing his physical form, rewriting his own DNA to be reborn as a new individual, while also maintaining most of his faculties.

"However, there is an oddity. Flynn seems to have

developed, as a side effect, hermaphroditic qualities, able to change his sex partially or indeed entirely through cellular regeneration. Indeed, this phenomenon is far more potent than any sex change boasted about in the press. My son, born with unambiguous, male reproductive organs, has since calculably regenerated into a female body older than his chronological age and capable of menstruation. This, of course, is an unforeseen and undesirable outcome, for my son to become biologically female, or indeed, intersex, and thus be subject to a feminine predisposition. I reject this outcome entirely—that my son could become the fairer, weaker sex and be rendered incapable of adequately defending himself in the face of opposition.

"But I fear it cannot be altered. Flynn only has a small threshold for pain and cellular damage before his biology forces a regeneration. I'm afraid more experimentation will be impossible, as the body will change, thus wiping the slate clean. Regrettably, this side effect shall have to be lived with."

I had my "historical context" shields up, but reading some of these thoughts on women and intersexuality was a bit jarring.

Another entry was dated *August 1948*:

"I have discovered another interesting oddity: Flynn, now seventeen years of age, does not remember his mother. Mary left us shortly after it became necessary to physically harm Flynn to test the efficacy of his mutation. Now, as time has progressed, there are times when Flynn cannot recall ever having a mother. This suggests to me that cellular regeneration also affects the boy's memory. However, he has not forgotten me. I have been with him all along, and that appears to make some sort of difference. The effect, I suppose, is only on his long-term memory.

"In order for Flynn to remember things, those things must be part of his everyday life. And so, we quite often have forgeries of legal documents made for each of his new faces. We make it a habit to do this. We discuss the importance of secrecy regarding his mutation. We discuss the benefit of anonymity for protecting oneself from the vile ways of mankind. All to instil certain touchstones in his life that he will not forget.

"I've also been able to set certain affairs in order. I've moved us out to the family home in Thivleton, private, secluded. I've been able to collect quite a sum of money for him to inherit, as well as a lucrative stream of passive income, making us quite well-to-do. Flynn is, for all intents and purposes, a shapeshifter, and he will be a bloody good one if I have anything to say about it. His form of immortality will blend so seamlessly into society that no war will ever be able to harm him, and his immortality will not be flaunted for the unworthy to study.

"This is the gift I leave my son. It belongs to my own blood, not the masses. The world do not deserve what I have created."

Another undated entry read:

"There seems to be a biological rhythm to Flynn's

regeneration. If left unharmed, he will usually regenerate every three days. Sometimes he will last longer—four or rarely five days. Sometimes he will last shorter, especially if affected by illness or harmed in any other way.

"This suggests an inherent life cycle to the boy's cells, all lasting the same amount of time. As for what determines this time, I imagine it is not dissimilar to a body's usual biological rhythms, though it does not align with any I am aware of.

"I also observe that there is a violence to his regenerations which alters with each go. There seems to be a swift and dramatic rejection of all old cells in favour of new ones. This results in a lot of blood and sick to clean, as well as solid chunks which appear to be organ and muscle tissue. Remarkably, these solid tissues liquefy by the end of the regeneration process."

Another entry from 1942 filled in a few gaps:

"Mary has left me, just when our research has finally come to fruition. I thought her quite emotionally strong for a woman, but it appears I was wrong. She was too frail to handle the pain we needed to put Flynn through to achieve immortality. I will miss her dearly.

"In other concerns, I find it necessary to fake Flynn's death in order to protect his new-found anonymity. I will destroy his original birth certificate and any other identifying documents. Flynn Jones Riley will now just be Flynn, and any necessary legal documentation will have to be frequently forged to match up with the boy's current appearance."

Another entry from 1950 read:

"It seems, whilst I've been so engrossed in my work with Flynn, I've forgotten about myself. You see, once Flynn's immortality, and thus his safety, was assured, Mary and I always intended to repeat these results on ourselves. But Mary's gone, and Flynn is an adult, though he doesn't look it at the moment. It seems, in all the goings-on, I've forgotten that part of the plan.

"But I find the natural decline of the human body over time has reminded me of this plan. Indeed, I am beginning to feel my age. I will have to get to work at adapting my research to mutate my own genes. I, too, shall be a shapeshifter."

A shapeshifter? Was Flynn's father still alive? Could he still be out there somewhere?

"Ange? What're you doing?"

I whipped my head back. It was Flynn. It was bright all of a sudden. It was morning. Flynn was awake. Shit.

He looked at me sitting on the floor with the open book in my lap, and he shook his head. "You didn't."

I closed the book. "Flynn, I'm sorry, but I had to—"

"You read my father's journal, even though I told you not to?"

"Flynn, you don't understand. There are diagrams in here, equations, notes."

"I don't want to hear it. I couldn't care less what's in that book."

"But if we give this to Dr Murphy, I bet he could understand it. He could help us."

"And that was worth betraying my trust?" He spoke quietly, and it confused me.

"I don't … Flynn, I did this to help you; this book can help you."

"But you betrayed me to do it. Is that how this works? I let you into the most vulnerable part of my life, I trust you with the knowledge of who I really am, but you can betray my trust if you feel you need to?"

"To help you, Flynn."

"I don't care how you justify it, Ange. That was your choice, not mine. Your judgement takes priority over my trust in you in a situation that involves *me*. Not you, Ange, me."

I stood up. My heart was beating way too fast. "You know what, Flynn, I resent that. This isn't just about you. I'm involved in this, too. I'm the one who is by your side, always."

"I didn't ask you to be."

"Bullshit! You came up to me, all that time ago in the café. From that moment on, you involved me in this shit. And I'm glad you did, Flynn, because I love you, but this isn't just about you anymore. I can't choose not to care about you; I do care about you. I care that you're okay. And I don't think you are making the right decision here. I get you're scared, and you don't want to remember the past. That's why I'm handling it. Let me handle it. You're not okay, Flynn. I know you don't see it, but you're not okay. Who decides if you're unfit to make a decision about your own health? There's no one else here but me, is there? The woman in the trenches, that's me. Well, I'm deciding. I won't let you suffer when I can do something about it."

He shook his head. "It's all about you, isn't it? You won't listen to me. I'm not okay because *you've* decided I'm not. How can I trust you, Ange? What's to stop you leading government officials to my door to register and imprison the potentially dangerous shapeshifter because you say that's what's best?"

"Come on, Flynn, I'm not gonna do that."

"Wouldn't you? What the fuck was your plan, then? If I hadn't found you reading that journal, what would you have done? Would you even have told me? Would you have just shared that with Dr Murphy and whoever else without my knowledge? All because you were able to cobble together some bullshit justification for why your judgement trumps mine over the matter of *my* life. You even told Kate without my knowledge."

"I didn't mean to tell Kate, but I'm glad I did. You can't honestly say our lives aren't better now she and Bridget know."

"But that wasn't my choice. You decided that, Ange. Whatever you say, goes … I can't trust you at all."

"Don't be silly, Flynn, of course you can trust me."

He shook his head. "I think you should go." He took the book from me and put it back on the bookshelf.

I didn't say anything.

"Ange, I want you to go. And leave your key."

I looked at him. I couldn't believe what he'd said, but his expression was serious. He meant it.

I took a breath. "Fine."

I made quick work of gathering up my things. I didn't keep much here anyway, just my laptop, some toiletries, and a few clothes. Most things I needed I just borrowed off Flynn.

Then I came back to the front room and set my key down on the coffee table. I looked at Flynn and said, "I just want you to be okay."

And then I left.

20 August

It was Tuesday afternoon, and I was back in my cosy little flat. I texted Flynn, but they didn't respond. Why would they? It was dawning on me now that maybe I'd made a bit of an error in judgment. Maybe a big error in judgment. Ugh, what the fuck is the matter with me?

I've been working and trying to keep myself busy, but my mind kept coming back to Flynn. I wondered about their father, whether he was still alive. Not that I planned to find him if he was; I think I've learned my lesson there. I was just curious. I ended up breaking and looking up Flynn's name. When I put "Flynn Jones Riley" into the search engine, something actually popped up:

"Flynn Jones Riley was the son of Doctors Mary and Johnathan Riley. He was born on 22 April 1931 and died in June of 1942 due to inconclusive causes. His father claims he ran away from home, desiring to go to Brighton to visit family; however, Brighton was at this time evacuated due to events taking place during the Second World War. The child's body was never recovered, and no military personnel reported seeing a small boy in the area. All the same, it is assumed that Flynn Jones Riley is deceased."

I looked up Johnathan Riley next:

"Johnathan Riley was a military scientist who served in World War I under the British Army ... he was found dead in March of 1951 due to an overdose of an unknown substance. It is believed this was a failed genetic experiment which Dr Riley tested on himself."

So Flynn's dad was dead. I wondered if he couldn't quite replicate what he did to Flynn on himself, and he accidentally killed himself in the process.

My phone rang. It was Kate.

"Hey," I answered.

"Hey, babes. How're you doing? Heard what happened."

"How?"

"Bridget told me. She and Flynn talk all the time."

"Oh. Well, you were right. I was being a control freak. Congratulations, you know me better than I know myself."

"Well, that's my job, kitten. Wouldn't kill you to listen to me every once in a while."

"I know," I sighed. "What am I gonna do, Kate? I really fucked up, and Flynn's not answering my texts."

"They'll come around eventually."

"How do you know?"

"Because Flynn loves you. They're just hurt at the moment."

"They asked for their key back," I countered.

"Same answer."

"Well, I'm glad you're so certain Flynn will come around. I kind of feel like they hate me."

"They don't hate you, Ange."

I roughed up my hair out of frustration. "Ugh! I just wanted to help. I was just trying to get the information Dr Murphy needs to have a better shot at curing Flynn's CMD. I didn't mean to betray Flynn's trust."

"But you did."

"Wow, Kate, very comforting. Thank you," I deadpanned sarcastically.

"What I mean is you know you messed up. You may have had good intentions, but you pushed things a bit too far, and you can admit that. You know what that means?"

"What?"

"One, you're not entirely a bitch, and two, when Flynn wants to talk to you again, and they will, you can apologise and put this behind you."

"*If* they talk to me again. They probably don't trust me anymore, anyway."

"Babes, if Flynn's still talking to Bridget, then they'll

talk to you, too, eventually. They haven't cut all ties. Flynn trusts Bridget, they trust me, and they trust you. No bridges have been broken here, just cracked a little. Easily fixed with time."

"You're sure?"

"I'm sure Flynn loves you, and you love them, so it will work out."

I smiled. "I hope so … Thanks for calling."

21 August

I still hadn't heard from Flynn.

I fell back into my usual, pre-Flynn routine pretty quickly. I read, worked, drank tea, worked, watched telly, worked some more, read again …

And I still hadn't heard from Flynn.

I decided to take a little walk and clear my head. Flynn just needed space; that's fine. I left my flat and closed the door, and then I saw Mandip coming out the lift. There was a man with her with neat hair and a short beard who I immediately recognised as her son Henry.

"All right, Mandip, Henry."

Mandip nodded at me and smiled.

"Hey. Angelina, is it?" said Henry.

"That's right. You doing all right, Mandip? You look a bit knackered."

"Long day," she said in a quiet and hoarse voice.

"Just got back from A&E," Henry explained. "Mum

dislocated her jaw and couldn't get it back in."

"Oh, shit, how'd you manage that?"

"Yawning," Mandip croaked.

"EDS acting up again?"

She nodded.

"Lucky I was here," said Henry. "Now just to get Mum seated and rest up her jaw a bit." They headed for Mandip's flat.

"All right, well, I hope you feel better soon."

She smiled at me. "Nice seeing you, my love. We'll catch up soon. I feel I've not seen you in ages. Spending lots of time with that boyfriend of yours, I reckon."

I smiled sadly. "Yeah, that's it."

"Talk soon, my love." Then she and Henry went into her flat.

And I still hadn't heard from Flynn.

I took the lift down to the ground floor and exited the building. It was an all-right day for a walk—not sunny but not miserable either—but after about ten minutes, it started spitting rain. Then, five minutes after that, it was proper raining. I got soaked, and my hair was clinging to my face, but I didn't mind. The rain put me in a weird, melancholy mood, and I just sort of wanted to feel sad and enjoy that. Is that weird? Do other people ever feel like that?

I just stood outside for a little bit, letting the rain shower over me, feeling each droplet dripping down my cheeks.

Then I went back home and got a towel to dry myself off. After that, I went back to work, translating a romance novel.

"*Ça fait si longtemps que je t'ai pas vu,*" went the protagonist. And I translated: "*It's been so long since I've seen you.*"

"*Pourquoi ? Pourquoi tu a gardé tes distances ?*" "*Why? Why have you kept your distance?*"

"*Parce que je t'aime, il a dit, et j'avais peur.*" "*Because I love you,*" he said, "*and I was afraid.*"

This was weirdly accurate to my actual life while at the same time being not at all accurate. That made me feel weird, like some deity above was watching over me, making a game out of hitting me over the head with my own mistakes.

When late evening came, I put on my pyjamas and went to bed.

And I still hadn't heard from Flynn.

22 August

I was sat at a table in the local café on Thursday morning, drinking a hot chocolate and writing in my diary. I still hadn't heard from Flynn, and I was starting to feel hollow because of it—like there was a hole going right through me, like I was missing a part of myself.

I drank my beverage quietly and watched the different people in the café. Some were tall. Some were short. Some had blond hair. Some had brown hair. Some had dark skin. Some had light skin. Some were old. Some were young. Any one of them could have been Flynn. None of them could have been Flynn.

Maybe that was the worst part about loving a shapeshifter. I couldn't pick Flynn out of a crowd. I couldn't be centred and grounded by their appearance alone. I had no clue what Flynn looked like now. They were lost to me until they wanted to be found.

I've been likening my experience with Flynn's shapeshifting to being at war. But the two aren't analogous, are they? I'm back home, back to my normal life. If this were war, then I shouldn't want to go back so badly. War doesn't involve this much love, but it does involve this much pain. Maybe that's why I've been confusing the two. Loving someone is hard, and it can be painful sometimes, but loving a shapeshifter, that's nearly impossible.

But I did. I did love them. I was in love with a shapeshifter. I was in love with Flynn. And so, it is possible to love a shapeshifter, because I'm making it possible.

Not easy. Never easy. But not impossible.

23 August

I was sat at a bench in Oak Corn Park, taking a short break from my weekly walk. It was spitting a little, but I had a raincoat on, and the rain was pitter-pattering all over it. I was people-watching again, wondering if any of them might have been Flynn.

I looked down at my phone, answering some work emails. And then the pitter-patter of the rain stopped. I looked up; it was still raining. Then I looked above my head; there was an umbrella over me. There was a woman sat next to me holding the umbrella over our heads. She had fair skin, short blonde hair that barely reached her earlobes, and sparkling green eyes.

I looked at her, and she smiled back at me. Then I stared more closely.

"Flynn?" I hoped.

She nodded quietly, and my heart leapt.

"Can we talk?" she asked.

"Yeah, of course." I put away my phone. "Flynn, I'm so sorry. I betrayed your trust. I went behind your back …"

Her hand on my thigh stopped me. "I know," she said. "I'm sorry, too."

"Why?"

"Well, firstly, for not answering your texts. But also because I know you meant well, and maybe I overreacted."

"But, I mean, you were justified in doing that."

"No, I wasn't. Ange, I trust you more than anyone. You need to know that. I know you were just trying to help." She sighed and watched the raindrops showering down. "I guess I get scared sometimes. It's been instilled in me since I was young: Keep your condition secret. And for the longest time, I was the only one who knew. I had full control over what I did with that information. But now you know, and Kate and Bridget know, and I can't control any of you. I can only trust you. And that's scary."

"You can trust us, Flynn," I assured her. "I promise."

"I know. And I do trust you. All of you. I don't want any of you to think I don't, especially you." She dipped her hand into her pocket and pulled out a key. "I want you to have this back; it's yours."

She took my hand and placed the key to her house in my palm. I took the umbrella from her so I could hug her and she could wrap her arms around me untethered.

We were silent for a bit. Flynn held me close, and I held up the umbrella for the both of us.

"Can I ask you something?" I said.

"Yeah?"

"Have you ever read your father's journal?"

There was a slight hesitation. "No. I try to every now and then, but I always change my mind."

"Do you want me to tell you what's in it?"

She hesitated again. "Tell you what, if I ever do want to know, you'll be the one I ask. But I think, for now at least, I don't think I want to know."

"Okay. And you still don't want to show it to Dr Murphy?"

"No. I don't think so."

"Okay. That's fine."

After a silence, Flynn said, "I know that my illness has been hard for you to deal with, Ange, and maybe I need to be more sensitive to that."

"It's fine. I mean, it is hard, but what's worse is seeing you unhappy. You weren't yourself when we tried Dr Murphy's treatments; I see that now, and I don't want to see you like that again. If ever you want to go back to him and try again, that's fine. We'll show him the journal and see what he can do. But if not, that's fine, too. I won't force you, Flynn. I'll follow your lead."

Flynn took a quiet breath. "You know, I've changed my mind. There actually is something I want to know."

"About your father?"

"Yes."

"Okay, if you're sure. Ask me."

She took a breath. "Was it him? Did he give me my illness?"

"Yes. He and your mother, they both experimented on you."

"Experimented? So it's not genetic?"

"They couldn't change like you, if that's what you mean. But I think it is genetic. They did something to you that mutated your genes."

She was quiet.

"You okay?"

"Why?" she asked. "Why did they do it to me?"

"Um … I think they wanted to make you immortal. They wanted to protect you from the world by making sure you couldn't die. It was wartime."

"What war? You know, never mind. I don't want to know anymore."

She was tense. I could feel how tight her muscles were.

"You okay?" I asked again.

"Yeah. I mean, I'll forget next time I change, anyway."

"That's true."

"But it is comforting that you know, actually. There's no one I trust more than you, and now there's no one who knows more about me than you. You even know more about me than I do."

I felt kind of bad about that, but she said it as if it was a good thing.

"Oh, that reminds me," said Flynn. "I got you something."

"You did?"

She reached into her pocket again and pulled out a little jewellery pouch. She opened it and presented me with a brilliant silver bracelet.

I read the inscription. "It says 'Flynn'?"

"Yeah. I suppose it's technically a gift for me. I'm gonna wear it every day. I've bought it in loads of different sizes. That way, no matter what, no matter how I look, you will always know who I am."

I stared at the bracelet.

"Though, now I'm saying this, maybe I should have gotten you a matching one as well. That would have been good."

I smiled. "I love it. Can I put it on you?"

"Yeah, go ahead."

I handed her the umbrella and clipped the bracelet onto her dainty wrist.

"I thought about what it must be like for you," she said, "to know me but not be able to recognise me. So this bracelet can be something you can recognise me by. You'll never lose me."

It was unorthodox, maybe, but Flynn had given me the greatest gift. It was the most meaningful thing she ever could have given me. It wasn't just a silver bracelet; it was Flynn surrendering her anonymity to me. She trusted me completely.

I took her hand in mine, and she kissed my cheek. And we sat there together for the rest of the afternoon.

Interlude

t was at this point that I felt I had truly become connected to Flynn, irrevocably tied to them. I had truly taken up my role as the shapeshifter's partner and keeper. Over the years, I became privy to more information about Flynn's past, things they remembered and then forgot again. But I won't record those things here. They'll stay with me, locked away in the back of my mind. If Flynn ever wants me to tell them, then I will, but if not, those secrets will die with me.

Ever since the day I put Flynn's bracelet on in the park, we'd just enjoyed our lives together, so much so that I didn't write much in this book at all. Sometimes I regret that—we had some really good memories that I haven't written here—but I was living my life, with Flynn and Kate and Bridget. My little family. My perfectly imperfect family.

But I did pick this book up every now and then to write in something new. Usually for significant moments in my life, like when Flynn and I adopted our son.

25 Years Old

It's been almost a year since I've written in this book. I feel like so much has happened, but at the same time, not too much has changed. I'm still enjoying my life with Flynn, and Kate and Bridget. Flynn and I still take our weekly walk in Oak Corn Park. We still have lots of dinner parties with Kate and Bridget. We live life.

Flynn did end up getting me a silver bracelet with my name engraved into it, and I wear it every day. The engraving says: *Angelina: The Keeper*. It was a bit of an inside joke between us. It was a reference to me being a keeper, as in, a good girlfriend, and also to my acting as Flynn's keeper and caring for them when their illness got bad.

And it did get bad. One time, Flynn was changing for three days straight, and I was so scared. But I was used to it, and I knew what to do, and I watched over them until they were better. Then there were other times when Flynn's illness was barely a factor in our lives. They would just change, and it would be like getting the hiccoughs. Well, not really; it was always violent and horrific. But for Flynn and me, who are used to it, it was just something that happened.

We never ended up going back to Dr Murphy. Flynn never wanted to, and eventually, due to the nature of their illness, they'd probably forget we ever went in the first place. That was fine. We just lived with Flynn's illness. That was how they wanted to live.

So I was The Keeper, officially. I kind of felt good about that. Sure, it was a lot of work, really stressful, and often scary, but I did it because I love them. And they love me enough to trust me with that role in their life.

I also officially moved in, like, moved out of my flat and all. Flynn and I now both lived in that beautiful old house. It was great, but it did mean that I didn't have my flat to retreat to anymore when I needed a break. And breaks were very important when it came to dealing with Flynn. I think I'd explode if I had to see Flynn explode for the millionth time without any sort of respite. So, I've started taking little trips on my own every now and then, whenever I needed some space. I've only been on two so far: Ireland to see Andrew and Saoirse, and France to brush up on my French (and also for the food). But I plan on going farther away in future. I'll go explore Germany, Spain, Italy; I'll visit Sydney in Canada (maybe order her a poutine in Montréal); I'll go to Japan and see where my grandparents grew up; maybe the US, I've always wanted to see New York. Of course, I have to keep an eye on the level of acceptance afforded to trans people in the countries I'm visiting, which puts a bit of a downer on things. But some countries really don't like the sort of person I am, so I have to be careful. (Not to mention when the airports have those body scanners that can't figure out why a woman has an "anomaly" in her pants, and I have to be patted down. Imagine trying to explain to someone that there's nothing dangerous in my pants; it's just my penis. Mortified.)

I never worried when I was away, though. Kate and Bridget were there if Flynn ever needed help, and I always made sure at least one of us was on standby if Flynn did need something. But as Flynn's said before, they survived this long without me, and although I make their life so much better, they don't need me. So I can live my life, and I know Flynn will be there when I get back. That's how I maintain my sanity in this insane life I live with a shapeshifter. And my life is all the better for it.

27 Years Old

Flynn and I decided to expand our circle a little bit by telling Margaret and my mum about Flynn's illness. We'd discussed it at length for months. Flynn was apprehensive at first, but it would benefit our little family if they knew. Margaret knowing meant Kate and I were able to be completely open with her, as we have been our whole lives. And my mum knowing would mean she'd stop wondering why Flynn was always "sick" during the annual Christmas gatherings, and it would protect us from an awkward situation should she decide to randomly stop by after deciding to take a road trip across England on a whim … again. I trusted the two of them, even Mum, as annoying as she could be. And Flynn trusted me. So the decision was made.

Kate and I told Margaret. We'd started making more of an effort to plan our visits with her together, so she could see us at the same time. It meant a lot to her to see us together, being sisters.

When we told her, it took a while for her to figure out what we *weren't* saying. We weren't saying Flynn was a cross-dresser, even though they kind of were. We weren't saying Flynn was gender-fluid, even though they absolutely were. We weren't saying Flynn had dissociative identity disorder, which was an understandable thought but not what we were saying. What we were saying was Flynn had cellular metamorphosis disorder, a genetic disorder that effectively made Flynn an immortal shapeshifter.

Once she understood what we were saying, she actually believed us. I guess she trusted me and Kate, and we didn't seem like we'd gone mad. Margaret agreed to keep Flynn's secret to herself, and we left it up to her to tell Kate's dad if she felt he could be trusted to keep the secret, too.

As for my mum, I decided to go up to Scotland and tell her in person, and I took Flynn with me. We planned to stay in Scotland for a week so Mum could see proof of the change. I didn't think she would take my word for it like Margaret did. Plus, we could go sightseeing and look at some old castles and stuff.

When we got to Mum's, Flynn was a little girl, and that made things quite a bit harder. I had to start by telling her that Flynn was my friend's kid, who I was taking care of while they were on holiday. That got her to stop questioning things long enough for Flynn and me to explain what was really happening. Of course, she didn't believe us at first, so we had to come back in a few days when Flynn was a middle-aged man. (Honestly, no luck with the changes. This would have been much easier if Flynn were a nice, appropriately aged man.) I had to ring Kate and get her to vouch for us, and I had to sneak Mum's phone away from her, just in case she decided she needed to ring the police or something.

Eventually, we got her to believe us, but it was a loose belief. She sort of just went with it. It would take a few years of seeing me with different versions of Flynn, chatting with Flynn over the phone, and us sticking to the same story for her to fully believe us. But she wouldn't tell anyone. I knew that about Mum; she could keep a secret if I needed her to, even if she didn't really get it.

We planned to tell Andrew and Saoirse, too, next time we saw them. I didn't think it would be too hard to convince them, not with Mum on board. And I knew they were trustworthy.

And so, everyone who needed to know knew. And that was how our little family gained an extended family.

29 Years Old

Bridget and Kate got married!

Bridget proposed, and then she announced on her

stream the following day that she was making Kate her actual bitch wife. Bridget's audience was super excited about it, and so was I. Flynn and I took them out to a nice dinner to congratulate them on the engagement.

At the wedding, Flynn and I met a lot of Bridget's family. They were nice for the most part. Some of them were a little homophobic, which I found funny as they were attending Bridget's marriage to a woman, but sometimes family trumps your opinions of said family, I guess. That doesn't happen often enough—I would know—but when it does happen, when all these people can put their prejudices and differences of opinion aside to be there for their family, that's beautiful. I wish it happened more often.

Margaret and Dave were there, obviously. Most of their time was spent by Dave handing Margaret tissues because she couldn't stop crying.

I gave a speech at the wedding, and I did my best to really let Kate have it, to make her blush just like she'd been making me blush all these years. I'd been practising my lewd jokes. Unfortunately, I couldn't quite get Kate to blush, but I embarrassed Bridget enough for her Tourette's to start acting up. It wasn't so bad that her tics interrupted the wedding, so I felt pretty good about that. At least I made someone blush. I did end up apologising to Bridget later on, though, but she said it wasn't me. She'd been trying to suppress her tics for the wedding, but it was getting too much and they all just sort of exploded out of her. She couldn't stop herself. That did sort of undermine my victory, but what can you do?

During the wedding, Flynn asked me if I ever thought about marriage. I said I wasn't opposed to it, but it didn't matter as much to me. We discussed that a few times after the wedding as well, and we decided that we probably wouldn't ever get married. It would be too much of a hassle with Flynn's condition. Not only would we have to hope that Flynn didn't change on the day of the wedding, but we'd also have to hope they were an appropriate age. Then there's the question of whether Flynn would be my husband or my wife. There's no option for a gender-neutral marriage in this country, so we'd have to pick one. And then, after marriage, we'd have to worry about the marriage certificate being wrong a lot of the time as Flynn changes. It was just too much to deal with, and neither of us thought it was all that worth it.

But we did start thinking of each other as spouses, even if we weren't legally married. Flynn didn't call me their bitch wife like Bridget did Kate, but I was Flynn's wife, for all intents and purposes. And Flynn was my spouse. And that was enough for us.

30 Years Old

Flynn and I have been talking about becoming parents recently. It's something I've always wanted for myself, but Flynn and I had to have a serious discussion about it. The biggest issue was Flynn themself. Flynn's condition was a lot to handle as it was. Bringing a child into that might be rough on everyone. But kids are pretty resilient. If we explained Flynn's condition to them properly, it might just turn out to be nothing special. They'll grow up with one of their parents being a shapeshifter, and that'll just be normal.

As for the task of raising a child while also taking care of Flynn, well, they do say it takes a village to raise a child. We don't have a village, but we do have Aunty Kate and Aunty Bridget. They had no plans to have kids of their own, so they were free to be good aunties to mine and Flynn's. What else are sisters for?

The next issue was how we were going to have a kid. Flynn and I couldn't just have sex and get pregnant. Firstly, I'm infertile, thanks to the fact that I had an orchidectomy years ago. But even if I didn't, I couldn't bring myself to have a child biologically. Usually, I'm quite neutral about being a trans woman. It's like being left- or right-handed to me. I'm just not bothered about it. I'm a woman; it doesn't really matter what sort most of the time. But this was a situation in which I was a little upset that I wasn't a cis woman. I would have loved to have been able to bring a child into this world by getting pregnant and birthing them myself. But that's not going to happen. There was only one way I could have a child naturally, but I would *never* bring a child into this world by impregnating someone else. I couldn't. I knew that from when I was a child, since before I knew I was trans. The thought of impregnating someone made me so uncomfortable, and in hindsight, dysphoric. I just couldn't. That was part of the reason I had an orchidectomy all those years ago in the first place. I knew I would never use them.

Then there was Flynn. We didn't know if Flynn was fertile or not. They weren't when they were a prepubescent child, but Flynn has menstruated, and they've produced semen. So it's possible that Flynn was fertile, at least sometimes. But with that came the possibility that Flynn could pass down their illness, and cursing a child with that wasn't something either of us could live with.

So the next option—and if we're honest, the first option I thought of—was adoption. Margaret adopted Kate, and it felt right for me to carry that forward and adopt my child, too.

And so, Flynn and I adopted our little baby boy— Benjamin. Kate was quick to remind me that I now owed her fifty pounds for adopting a child. I don't recall making that bet with her, but she wouldn't shut up about it, so I took her out for a nice fifty-pound meal.

I was also able to breastfeed little baby Benjamin, just like Margaret did for Kate when she was a baby. And it felt just like how Margaret described when I talked to her about it years ago. I was doing something I never imagined possible when I was young. There was a time when I thought I'd have to grow up and be a man, that the only way I could be a parent was to be a father. But here I was, being a mother to my child, nourishing him with milk I made in my own body. And it was wonderful.

Interestingly, the entire time Benjamin was a baby, Flynn was much more likely to be a woman more than anything else, and most times they could produce milk as well. It was as if Flynn's body knew there was a baby around and wanted to nourish him. We decided it was okay for Flynn to breastfeed Benjamin, too, when they could. We weren't worried that Flynn's condition would be passed down somehow. It was genetic; it couldn't be passed down from breastmilk. But we did have Flynn's milk tested, just in case.

And so, our family gained a new member. Flynn and I were parents.

I was a mum.

55 Years Old

God, it's been years since I've written in this book. I'm definitely falling out of the routine. I've had a lot of life to live, and ever since Benjamin, I've been pretty busy.

It feels like time has just flown by. Benjamin's all grown up now, and as of last week, he's moved out, off to live with his girlfriend in Hackney. It's been amazing raising him, and he's grown into a sweet and wonderful man. Though, there were some rough years in his childhood due to me and Flynn being his parents, and I felt bad about that.

In primary school, he mentioned that his dad—which

we agreed is what he would call Flynn—was a shapeshifter. Thankfully, no one really believed him, but his insistence that he was telling the truth made his teachers suspect there might be some mental health issues with him. On top of navigating that, Benjamin started to misbehave a lot because he didn't really understand why we would lie to anyone who asked why he thought Flynn was a shapeshifter. He felt we were gaslighting him—though he didn't use those words at the time. He was right, though; we were gaslighting him. We had to, to protect Flynn and the family. It took some time for Benjamin to understand that, and until he did, things were rough.

In secondary school, he mentioned that his mum was transgender, and he lost a lot of his so-called friends because of that. He became pretty depressed during that time. He felt like he'd lost everything because of something that was out of his control. And I felt really bad about that, that my son was being punished for who I was. It was nothing to do with him. He became angry with me, resentful, like I was the personification of everything bad in his life. So I talked to Kate and had her speak to him. Kate also grew up with a transgender mum, and she grew up in a time when transphobia was much worse than it is these days. I don't know what they talked about, and it wasn't really my place to know, but since then, Benjamin's had a really close relationship with his Aunty Kate, and things got better.

Now, Benjamin is a wonderful young man with so

much to offer this world, and I'm so proud to call him my son.

But after twenty-five long and wonderful years, it was just me and Flynn once again. Things have been quieter but never calmer with Flynn's condition. I've gotten older without even realising it. How the bloody hell did that happen? One minute, I'm a young twenty-four-year-old woman, next minute, I'm a mother in her fifties whose child has gone off to start his own life. I can feel my joints creaking. How did that happen? I picked up my diary today and realised I hadn't written in it for twenty-five years!

I'm beginning to feel my mortality, but Flynn never will. I guess we always knew it was coming. Flynn is immortal, so a day will come when they outlive me. Flynn will outlive Bridget and Kate. Flynn will outlive our son. In the end, Flynn will outlive all of us. And I do worry about that. What a lonely existence that must be. Eventually, we all must accept the gift of death, but Flynn is for ever cursed with life. And by the nature of Flynn's illness, I know that, years after I'm gone, they won't remember me. They won't remember this little family we've created, the life we have. I don't think I'm okay with that. I won't accept it. If I have to leave this world eventually, I'll leave it knowing that Flynn will be okay.

I finally know why I've been writing this little diary all these years. I may not be able to live for ever, but a story, once told, can last an eternity …

I don't think I'll write in this book again after this; I want to enjoy the rest of my time with Flynn. I'll just put it on the bookshelf next to their father's journal. And one day, when I'm gone, maybe Flynn will find it. Maybe they'll read it and remember the life we once lived. Maybe Flynn will remember how much I loved them.

This is what I can do for them. I can't live for ever, but this story will: The Story of How I Fell in Love with a Shapeshifter.

Postface

{{I}} don't remember this book. I've read it because Ange told me to; she told me where it was. And it's the story of how we met, how it all started. But it feels like it happened to someone else, because I don't remember any of it. But I guess we knew that would happen eventually.

Ange is gone now. And it hurts. And knowing that I'll just forget her one day hurts even more. She lived ninety-four years. Impressive, but it had to end eventually. Everything comes to an end … except me.

I sat with her when she passed. She was lying in bed, and somehow, she knew it was coming. She placed her old, wrinkled hand over my young, smooth hand and said to me: "Don't be afraid, Flynn. I'm not. I have lived such a good life, with you, and Kate, and Bridget, and of course Benjamin. I'm ready. This is the end, but the moment has been prepared for … I want you to promise me, Flynn, promise me that you'll find someone. You and I both know that you'll forget me eventually, and once Kate and Benjamin pass as well, there will be no one left to remind you. So promise me you won't be alone. Find someone new to spend your life with. Because I think you need someone. You do. It must be such a lonely life, the life of an immortal, and I don't want that for you. So, Flynn, I let you go, and I'll leave you a piece of me. Check the bookshelf, next to your father's journal. And promise me, promise me, don't be alone. Find someone."

I wonder if this book is what she meant by "the moment has been prepared for." I may forget the life we lived together, but thanks to Ange's diary, I can always remember. I'll even remember what she looked like thanks to the painting of her on the wall. The diary says I painted it, but I don't remember doing that. It's just a painting of a young woman working on a laptop, and whether I remember its significance or not, I always think that, out of all the paintings I have on the walls, it's the most beautiful one.

I'm not really sure why I'm writing in this diary now. Maybe it's a little therapeutic, a good way to say goodbye to her. Or maybe I don't want to forget this moment. Maybe I just wanted to complete it—Ange wrote the beginning, and so I should write the end. Maybe that's it.

I saw Benjamin the other day; he came by to discuss funeral arrangements for his mum. He looked older than I do, which is becoming more and more commonplace, I suppose. He'll only get older, but I don't age so linearly. He said something to me, though, that I've not been able to stop thinking about. He said, while staring at the painting of his mum, that I looked a little like her. He said I had his mother's nose, her eyes, her hair. And now, having gone through this book, I see that at some point we apparently saw a doctor about my illness, some Dr Murphy. And he theorised that my eyes had something to do with my changes, that maybe I change into the people I've seen before. I didn't think that was true at first, but now Benjamin's said that, I wonder if maybe it was partially true. What if the people I become are a combination of people I've lost in the past, people I've loved? What if I'm carrying a piece of them with me into eternity?

I don't know if that's what's really happening, but I think I'd like it to be. That would mean that Angelina isn't just The Keeper, she's my Eternal Keeper. Her influence in my life will for ever be felt. She'll always be with me.

And I promise you, Ange, I won't be alone. I will find someone new to spend my life with. But I'll always carry you with me. Eternally.

Afterword

This story began one day when I was watching Doctor Who. For anyone unfamiliar, the Doctor—the main character of the show—is an alien who travels through time and space. And they can also regenerate, changing their physical appearance and personality, among other things. I was watching the episode in which the Eleventh Doctor regenerated into the Twelfth Doctor, and, seeing the massive difference between those two versions of the character, it got me thinking: What would it be like to fall in love with the Doctor? But that wasn't my question, not really. I didn't care about the time travel and the alien side of things; I only cared about the regeneration, or the shapeshifting. My real question was: What would it be like to fall in love with a shapeshifter? That is the question upon which this entire story is based.

From there, different ideas popped into my head. I knew I had to set the book in England. I was born in England, and Doctor Who is a British programme; it just seemed right. But also because I needed a contemporary location for this sort of story. It wouldn't be the same if this book took place in some fantasy realm or ancient kingdom (although, the United *Kingdom* is close enough). I knew this had to be more grounded than some of the more fantastical stories I usually write. However, there was one problem: I hate writing in real-world settings. I always write in a fantasy world because I like to have complete control over the setting of my story. Writing in a real place means I'm bound by the real rules of that place. I'm bound by the geography and architecture; I'm bound by the culture and customs. That's not always a bad thing. Setting the story in the UK allowed me to have British characters, use British dialects and British locations, and write in British English (except for inverted commas. I may be English, but I reject that wholeheartedly. Double quotation marks all the way). So, the compromise I made with myself was to set the story mostly in the fictional town of Thivleton, where I could have everything be the way I wanted. Even if it's not all that different from any other real-world location, I had complete control. I didn't have full control over dates and times, but that is the sacrifice required to write in a contemporary setting.

After I had my setting sorted, some initial scenes popped into my head—scenes exploring various versions of Flynn and various ways to answer the question this book is based on. Some of the first scenes that popped into mind were Ange and Flynn meeting in the café, Ange talking to Flynn without knowing she was doing so while she sat on the kerb outside their house, Flynn changing into a man while in the women's toilets, and Flynn giving Ange the bracelet at the park in the rain. The task of writing this book was really the task of stringing those scenes together.

When I came up with the original idea, I was busy writing *Darphopia: The Second God War*, so I had time to work things out in the back of my mind. Mostly I was just working out the order of events, secondary and side characters, and things of that nature. But what really changed from the initial idea to the finished book was Angelina's character. She was originally meant to be a bit of a blank slate—someone who the reader could experience Flynn through. But I later decided that Ange needed something through which she could really relate to Flynn on a deep level. That was when I considered giving her Tourette's Syndrome. I was watching something on telly one day (don't remember what) and a character with Tourette's showed up. I also have Tourette's, and I must admit, I've seen very few good representations of it in media. So I thought it would be interesting for Ange to have Tourette's, and not just to have it but to develop it over the course of this story. I would showcase her struggles of living with tics and getting used to them—learning what triggers them, trying different medications. And through that struggle, she would come to understand Flynn better by their shared experience with disability. But obviously, I didn't end up doing that. I had a much better idea.

Angelina is transgender. I don't think there are very many people—if anyone at all—who can relate to a shapeshifter better than someone of trans experience. She knows what it's like to live in a male role. She knows what it's like to live in a female role. She knows what it's like to feel a little in-between. She knows what it's like to struggle to conform to gender norms. She knows what it's like to break those gender norms. She knows what it's like to not be recognised by people she's met before. And she knows what it's like to not be accepted.

Just like that, this little romance exploring what it would be like to love a shapeshifter also became a trans story, and it did so in the best possible way, I think. This isn't a trans story because it's about being transgender or transitioning. (There's nothing wrong with those stories; they're needed. But I feel they tend to have the effect of othering the people they are about.) No, this is a trans story because Angelina happens to be trans, and that means the story is told from the perspective of a trans person. In the same vein, this is also a women's story because it is told from the perspective of a woman (and also because ninety per cent of the characters here are women). Ange being trans allowed her to understand Flynn on a deeper level while remaining in a supportive role for them. I didn't want to say goodbye to the Tourette's representation, though, so that's why we have Bridget.

I got to do things with Ange in this story that I don't see much of when trans people are in media. I made sure that Ange started her transition a long time ago so that it wouldn't end up subsuming this story—this isn't a story about transitioning. Instead, I got to explore gender-affirming clothing, gender dysphoria, people's reactions to you as a trans person, decisions behind trans surgery, trans bodies, the effects of hormone replacement therapy for medical transition, the functions of a feminine penis and how it may differ from a masculine one, sex and sexuality, overt and minute transphobia, and found family. This story isn't meant to explain these things to someone unfamiliar. I'm sure there's a lot one could learn from it if they were previously unfamiliar, but it's not a guidebook. I explored these things in the book as if they were a normal aspect of life that everyone is familiar with, because they are a normal aspect of Angelina's life, and they are a normal aspect of a lot of people's lives.

There was one thing I was hesitant to explore, though: transphobia. Honestly, I think we see enough of it in the world already; I didn't want to write a book about it. This is a philosophy I tend to follow in my other works—both *Darphopia's* and *Tales of the Multiverse's* trans representation is without transphobia. But this story is more contemporary than my others, it's more grounded in reality, and that meant facing the reality that transphobia does exist. It comes from strangers, and it comes from the people you love. It would be a disservice to ignore that here. Ange faces transphobia from many places. Her father leaving her, comments from family members, "jokes" she stumbles upon online, or even her well-meaning mother who doesn't always say the right things. Some of these things are big, and some are small; some are unforgivable, and some can be tolerated. It can be an isolating thing to face this sort of prejudice not just from strangers but from people who mean well, from your own family. Often trans people aren't just a minority in society, they're a minority within their own family as well. There's no shared experience to be had there. Transphobia can come from anywhere. But I made sure not to go overboard with it. As I said, there's enough transphobia in the world. This is a happy story, or perhaps more accurately, a hopeful one.

In the end, this isn't just a story about falling in love with a shapeshifter; it's about hope. Hope is something you must believe in—you can't have proof of it, or else you wouldn't need it, and if you stop believing in it, you'll never ever find it. Angelina started writing her diary because of hope—hope that her life would be better than it is now, or if not, proof that her life was once good, and thus, hope that it will be better again. Angelina's life didn't begin terribly, but that doesn't mean she shouldn't have hope. She keeps it with her daily, and she uses it to make active choices that will better her own life. That's how she went from being a dysphoric little child to an old woman who lived a wonderful life and, when her time came, was ready to leave it. She surrounded herself with people who loved her and understood her completely. She found a family in Flynn, Kate, Bridget, Benjamin, and Margaret. She said this book was written to make Flynn remember the life they lived together, but I think it was also to give them the hope that she always held.

As always, thanks for reading, I hope you enjoyed, and I hope to see you next time.

–   R. J. F., February 2024

PS

As a nod to the fact that this idea all started with me watching Doctor Who, I actually made some references in some of the dialogue in this book to actual things the Doctor has said. Did you notice any of them?